ASAKUSA PARK

A COLLECTION OF SHORT STORIES

RYUNOSUKE AKUTAGAWA

Contribution by
KAN KIKUCHI

Translated by
SHELLEY MARSHALL

SHELLEY MARSHALL

CONTENTS

1

THE SAKE BUG

1

This heat had not been seen in recent years. Wherever you looked, the roof tiles of the houses fixed by mud dully reflected the sunlight like lead. In this situation, some thought the baby chicks and eggs would die from the steam in a swallow's nest beneath the tiles. And in the fields, whether hemp or millet, all heads drooped from the steam rising from the ground. There's nothing that had not withered, even the still green plants. Were the skies visible above the fields affected by the muggy heat at that time? The atmosphere near the Earth, although clear, was murky and overcast. What resembled peaks of clouds floated in scattered lumps, like rice cakes baked in an earthenware pan. This story of *The Sake Bug* begins with three men going out to a threshing floor under the scorching sun.

Mysteriously, one of these men was naked and lying face up on the ground. And for some reason, a thin rope wrapped around his hands and feet. The man himself didn't appear to be suffering from an illness. This man was short, had a good complexion, gave off the impression of clumsiness, and was fat like a pig. A handy unglazed bottle was placed near the man's head. However, he didn't know what was inside.

Another man wore a yellow priest's robe and small bronze rings in his ears. At a glance, he was a curious, old Buddhist monk shaped like an elephant. Judging from his extraordinarily dark skin tone, curly hair, and beard, he probably came from the exotic western regions of the Silk Road. He had been patiently swinging a *hossu* brush with a bright red handle to chase away the horseflies and other flies trying to swarm the naked man, but he looked a little worn out. He went over to the unglazed bottle and squatted with an air of importance, but his posture resembled that of a turkey.

The last man was a distance from these two. He stood under the eaves of the thatched hut in a corner of the threshing floor. This man grew a scraggly beard like a rat's tail at the tip of his chin. He arranged a tea-brown sash in a loose knot over a coarse black robe long enough to hide his heels. Sometimes, he manipulated a fan made from white bird feathers as if it were precious. Perhaps, he was truly a Confucianist.

As if all three had agreed, they kept their mouths shut. They didn't even move their bodies. Had all of them quieted their breathing because of great interest in what was about to happen?

The sun probably marked noon. Did dogs also take afternoon naps? Not one bark could be heard. The hemp or millet surrounding the threshing floor was quiet and peaceful. Sunlight illuminated their green leaves.

The sky visible in the distance was stifling hot in all directions. The blazing heat made one drunk. The cloud peaks may have labored to breathe in the drought. In a sweeping view, no one other than these three men breathed. These three maintained silence like the figurines of unfired clay installed at the Temple of Guan Yu.

Of course, this is not a story from Japan. This incident occurred one summer on the threshing floor of the Liu clan in a place called Chōzan in China.

2

The one lying naked under the blazing sun was the owner of the threshing floor. His family name was Liu, and his given name was Taisei. He was the preeminent wealthy landowner in Chōzan. This man's sole hobby was drinking sake. It could not be said that he was ever far from a sake cup from the morning on. He always said, "Every time I drink alone, I empty a whole sake-brewing pot," because the quantity he drank was far from ordinary. As I said earlier, half of the eight acres of fields near the castle walls were sown with millet. Thus, he never worried about the strain his drinking placed on the family finances.

Why was he lying naked under the blazing sun? There is misfortune in this.

That day, Liu and his usual drinking buddy, Son-sensei—the Confucianist holding the white fan—reclined on bamboo body pillows and waged a battle in a game of Go in a breezy room. A servant with an elaborate Y-shaped hairstyle entered.

"A priest who says he's from Hōdō-ji Temple has come. He insists on seeing the proprietor. What should I do?"

"What? Hōdō-ji Temple?"

Liu blinked his small eyes, as if they were dazzled. As his chubby body rose in the heat, he added, "Well, show him in." Then, he peeked at Son-sensei's face and said, "It's probably that priest."

The priest at Hōdō-ji Temple was a foreign priest who came from the western part of China. He also provided medical treatment, practiced the traditional bedroom arts, and was highly regarded in the area. For example, he reduced Zhang San's cataracts and instantly cured Li Si's impotence. Rumors abounded about near miracles.

Both men heard these rumors. Why did that foreign priest deliberately come out to Liu's estate? Of course, Liu had no recollection of ever going to see him.

As an aside, let me say Liu was not a man who enjoyed guests. If a new guest arrived while another guest was already there, he was usually pleased to see the new arrival. In front of the guest, he could be said to be proud of having a guest there because of his childish vanity. These days, this barbarian priest had become well-regarded all over. This was not a guest he would be too embarrassed to see. His motive was primarily to meet Liu.

"I wonder what he wants?"

"First of all, it's not begging. You should call it an act of charity and faith."

While the two were discussing this matter, they noticed the guest being escorted in by the servant with the Y-styled hair. He was a wandering priest, tall, with eyes like amethysts, and a slightly odd appearance. He wore a yellow robe. His curly hair annoyingly hung down to his shoulders. He carried a red-handled hossu and stood in the center of the quiet room. No greetings were exchanged, and no one said a word.

For a short time, Liu hesitated but as an uneasiness developed, he asked, "How may I help you?"

The barbarian priest said, "You enjoy sake, don't you?"

"I do," said Liu. As he shakily answered the unexpected question, he looked at Son-sensei, as if seeking help. Son-sensei pretended to be concentrating and lowered a stone onto the game board. He paid no attention.

"You are suffering from an unusual disease. Are you aware of that?" said the barbarian priest with emphasis. Liu heard disease and looked perplexed as he stroked his bamboo body pillow.

"A disease."

"Yes."

"No, since infancy—"

Liu was about to say something, but the barbarian priest interrupted.

"Even when you drink sake, you do not get drunk."

Liu was speechless. His mouth stayed shut as he looked at his companion's face. No matter how much this man drank, he never got drunk.

"That is proof of a disease."

Wearing a thin smile, the barbarian priest said, "You have a sake bug in your stomach. If you don't rid yourself of it, this illness will not be cured. This humble monk came to cure your disease."

"Cure it?" said Liu without thinking. He sounded doubtful and was embarrassed.

"I came because I've been cured."

Silent until now, Son-sensei heard the exchange and promptly interrupted.

"How? Do you use medicine?"

"No, I don't use any medicine," answered the barbarian priest curtly.

Naturally, Son-sensei held unjustified contempt mostly toward the teachings of Taoism and Buddhism. Therefore, even when with a Taoist or Buddhist monk, he rarely spoke. Now, however, he felt compelled to speak. He was intrigued by the words *sake bug*. When the sensei, who likes sake, heard this, he was a little worried that he may also harbor a sake bug in his stomach.

But when he heard the barbarian priest's restrained answer, he suddenly worried that he was being made a fool. He frowned slightly and, as before, gently started to lower a stone. At the same time, he remembered thinking the proprietor Liu was a fool for seeing this arrogant priest.

Of course, Liu was not concerned.

"Well, are needles used?"

"What? It's not so complicated."

"Then, it works by incantation."

"No, no incantations."

After this conversation was repeated, the barbarian priest briefly explained the treatment. You strip naked and bask in the sun. Liu thought that was an easy task. If that were the cure, then nothing surpassed being cured. Moreover, he was not consciously aware of this, but he was a little intrigued about being treated by the barbarian priest.

Finally, Liu lowered his head and said, "Well, I'll try one cure."

Liu was instructed to lie naked on the threshing floor under the blazing sun.

The barbarian priest said he must not move his body, so a hemp rope was wrapped around Liu. Then he called to a young manservant and had him bring an unglazed bottle of sake to his bedside. In this situation, Son-sensei, a good friend of sake dregs and, needless to say, struggled with this mysterious treatment.

What is this creature called a sake bug? If it is no longer in his stomach, what will happen to it? What did he intend to do with the bottle of sake at his pillow? No one knew except the barbarian priest.

Liu went out naked to bask under the blazing sun and seemed fairly thoughtless. This was similar to the way an ordinary person receives an education at school.

3

It was hot. Sweat resembling balls speckled his forehead and flowed in warm, smooth streams to his eyes. Unfortunately, with his hands tied by a rope, he couldn't wipe the sweat away. So he shook his head to change its path. He instantly got dizzy. He reconsidered this plan. Sweat freely wet his eyelids and flowed around the sides of his nose and mouth to beneath his chin. This was quite unsettling.

Until then, his eyes were open and gazed at the sky scorched white and a field of hemp with hanging leaves. The cascading sweat made him give up. Now, for the first time, Liu realized the sweat had penetrated his eyes and stung.

While his face resembled a slaughterhouse sheep, he meekly shut his eyes as the sun beat down on him. Not his face, not his body, but the skin in the areas on top gradually ached. Forces for moving in all directions worked over the entire surface of his skin, which had lost most of its flexibility. The best explanation was that he tingled all over. This was not the pain of sweating. Liu became irritated by the dearth of treatment given by the barbarian priest.

However, when he thought about this later, some areas did not ache. Meanwhile, his throat had dried up. Liu also knew that Cao Cao or someone else once said, "The plums in a plum orchard up the road will quench the soldiers' thirst." However, no matter how much their minds thought about the sweetness and bitterness of plums, their thirst remained unchanged. They moved their jaws and bit their tongues, but their mouths still held heat.

If the unglazed bottle hadn't been near his head, it definitely would have been a little easier to endure. However, the powerful aroma of sake from the bottle's mouth constantly assaulted Liu's nose. It might have been his imagination, but he felt the scent of sake intensified minute by minute. Liu thought, at least, he could try to see the bottle and opened his eyes.

He glanced up and saw only the bottle's mouth and half of his torso swelling rhythmically. At the same time, however, Liu imagined the usual state of golden sake filling the dark interior of the bottle. Without realizing it, he tried to lick his cracking lips with his dry tongue. Nothing triggered saliva to well up. Dried up by the sun, sweat no longer flowed.

The awful dizziness happened a couple of times. The earlier headache never stopped. Finally, Liu resented the barbarian priest in his heart. He wondered why he was fooled by that man's smooth talking and endured this foolish suffering. Meanwhile, his throat grew drier. His chest became strangely irritated. He couldn't endure even a little more. Then, Liu gathered the resolve to tell the barbarian priest beside him to stop the treatment. While wheezing, he opened his mouth.

At that moment, Liu felt a mysterious lump creeping bit by bit from his chest to his throat. It was like a worm. He wondered whether it was wriggling or crawling like a gecko. The supple object was softening, squirming, and climbing up to the top of his esophagus. Finally, he thought it had forced its way to below his Adam's apple, slipped out a warm, dark place like a loach, and flew out with force.

At that moment, he heard what sounded like a plop into the sake in the unglazed bottle. The barbarian priest quickly raised his buttocks that had settled down and began loosening the rope tied around Liu's body. He said, "Calm down. The sake bug is out."

"So it's gone," Liu groaned. While shaking his head, he was fascinated by the novelty and had forgotten about the dryness in his throat. Still naked, he crawled to the side of the bottle. Seeing this,

Son-sensei used his white feather fan to block the sun as he hurried over to the two men. The three men peered into the bottle. A small salamander-like creature with flesh resembling red clay was swimming in the sake. It was about three and a half inches long. It had a mouth and eyes. It seemed to be drinking while swimming. When Liu saw it, his chest was seized by a horrible feeling.

4

The impact of the barbarian priest's treatment was immediate. From that day on, Liu Taisei never drank sake again. He said its odor was repugnant. Since then, however, mysteriously, Liu's health slowly deteriorated. This year, three years since he vomited the sake bug, his chubby, round face of years gone by was nowhere to be seen. Dull, pale, and greasy skin wrapped his sharp facial bones. Little of the thick hair invaded by frost remained at his temples. He didn't know how many times he had been sick in bed over the years.

But since then, Liu's health was not the only thing that weakened. Liu's family fortune gradually worsened. Even now, most of the eight acres of millet fields had passed into the hands of others. Liu also spent miserable day after day plowing with hands unaccustomed to that task.

Since vomiting up the sake bug, why has Liu's health deteriorated? Why has his family fortune declined? Vomiting the sake bug and Liu's later downfall are in a cause-and-effect relationship. This suspicion easily arises in anyone. This suspicion was repeated by all the tradesmen living in Chōzan. Their mouths provided every variety of answers. The three answers presented here were selected as the most typical ones.

1. The sake bug was Liu's good luck and not an illness. By chance, he met the foolish barbarian priest and lost a Heaven-sent blessing.

2. The sake bug was Liu's illness and not his good luck. If you ask why, downing a bottle in one gulp would never be conceived by a normal man. Therefore, if the sake bug had not been eliminated, Liu would not have lasted much longer and surely died. Poverty and

illness affect each other. But for Liu, it should be called good fortune.

3. If the sake bug was not Liu's illness, it was also not Liu's good luck. For a long time, Liu only drank sake. After sake was removed from Liu's life, nothing was left. Liu was surely the sake bug, and the sake bug was surely Liu. Therefore, Liu getting rid of the sake bug was the same as killing himself. In other words, from the day he stopped drinking sake, Liu became Liu and was no longer Liu. When Liu himself suddenly disappeared, the health and family fortune of Liu in the old days were lost. This may be the most reasonable story.

Which of these answers is the best, the most correct? That I don't know. Following the *didacticism* of a Chinese novelist, I end this story with this list of moral judgments.

(April 1916)

2

EARLY SPRING

Nakamura, a college student, mulled over his body temperature under his light spring overcoat as he climbed the gloomy stone stairs to the second floor of the museum. At the top of the stairs on the left was the reptile specimen room. Before Nakamura entered, he glanced at his gold wristwatch. Fortunately, the watch hands did not yet point to two o'clock. Nakamura thought, I'm not late. That was a surprise, but he felt closer to being at a loss than relief.

The reptile specimen room was hushed. Not even a watchman patrolled today. Only the scent of insect repellent wafted through the chilly interior. After scanning the room, Nakamura stretched his body as if taking a deep breath. He stood in front of a large tropical snake coiled around a thick, withered tree in a large glass cabinet. Since the previous summer, they had settled on this reptile specimen room as the place for Mieko and him to meet.

They did not select this room because they had a fondness for the morbid. Rather, they felt the need to avoid people's eyes. Given their timidity, locations like parks, cafes, and stations would only embarrass them. Mieko, in particular, would only drop her shoulders and feel more than embarrassment. They felt the gazes of

10

numerous people focused on their backs. Actually, they felt their hearts were keenly reflected in the eyes of others. If they came to this specimen room, no one would see them other than the mounted snakes and lizards. Although they may encounter the occasional watchman or visitor, the stares at their faces lasted mere seconds.

The rendezvous time was two o'clock. The wristwatch hands showed exactly two. Today, his wait should not even be ten minutes. While he thought about this, Nakamura gazed at the reptile specimens. Unfortunately, his heart didn't leap with the slightest bit of joy. Rather, it was filled with something comparable to surrendering to some obligation.

Like all men, was he bored with Mieko? He had to face the same thing repeatedly to be bored. Today's Mieko, happy or unhappy, is not yesterday's Mieko. Yesterday's Mieko was a truly graceful coed who exchanged greetings with him with her eyes on the train on the Yamanote line. The Mieko who first went with him to Inokashira Park still harbored a tender loneliness.

Nakamura glanced at his watch again. It said five past two. He briefly hesitated and entered the adjacent room, the avian specimen room. He gazed through the glass at a variety of beautiful stuffed birds—canaries, golden pheasants, hummingbirds—both large and small. Like these birds, Mieko remained nothing more than a stuffed figure but had lost the beauty of her soul.

He clearly remembered. During their last meeting, Mieko only chewed gum and sang opera songs. What particularly surprised him was the Mieko he met a month ago. After a merciless teasing, she called a pillow a football and kicked it toward the ceiling.

His watch said quarter after two. A sigh escaped as Nakamura returned to the reptile specimen room. Mieko was nowhere to be seen. In a lighthearted mood, he said, "Excuse me," to the monitor lizard. This lizard had been eternally devouring a small snake since some year during the Meiji era.

Eternally … but he is not eternal. After the watch says two-thirty, he intends to rush out of the museum. The cherry blossoms had not yet bloomed. The trees in Ryōdaishimae framed the red buds on the branches cast against a cloudy sky. This walk through the park provided greater happiness than going off somewhere with Mieko.

Two-twenty! Maybe I've waited long enough. He wanted to go home but walked around the specimen room. The lizard and snake specimens, lost to the tropical forest, strangely radiated transience. This may be an abstraction. Maybe his abstraction of love lost passion over time. He was faithful to Mieko. But she was an unknown delinquent for half the year. His lost passion was entirely Mieko's responsibility. He ended up slightly disillusioned but never bored.

Two-thirty seemed to come quickly to Nakamura. He left the reptile specimen room. However, before he reached the door, he abruptly returned to the shoe locker. Mieko may have entered this room and just missed him. That would be pitiful for Mieko.

Pitiful? No, it's not pitiful. He was troubled more by his sense of obligation than by sympathy for Mieko. He had waited long enough to ease his sense of obligation but was sure Mieko wasn't coming. Whether he waited or not, he should enjoy a pleasant afternoon alone.

Of course, the reptile specimen room was quiet. The watchman still had not made his rounds. Only the faint, chilly scent of insecticide drifted in the room. Nakamura felt a creeping irritation. In the end, Mieko is just a delinquent girl.

However, his love may not have gone completely cold. If not, he would have left the museum long ago. Most of the passion was lost, but the desire remained. Desire? But there was no desire. Now, he is certain that he loves Mieko. She kicked a pillow. Her leg was pale, and her toes bent elegantly. Her laughter at that time was special. He recalled Mieko's laughter with her head tilted.

Two-forty. Two-forty-five. Three o'clock. Three-o-five. Three-ten.

While contemplating the biting cold that penetrated his springtime overcoat, Nakamura descended the stone stairs, always gloomy, like sunset, behind the deserted reptile specimen room.

～

WHEN THE ELECTRIC lights burned that day, Nakamura was talking to a friend in a corner of a cafe. His friend was a college student named Horikawa who hoped to become a novelist. Before cups of tea, they discussed the aesthetics of automobiles and debated the economic value of Cezanne. After they had tired of this, as he lit the golden tip of his cigarette, Nakamura brought up today's events as if talking about a stranger.

"I am a dummy," blandly added Nakamura when he finished.

"Uh-huh, the dumbest dummy."

Horikawa easily formed a sarcastic smile. He immediately said this as if it were a recitation.

"You already went home. The reptile specimen room is empty. How much time did you waste there? About three hours and fifteen minutes. The coed with the pale face entered alone. Of course, there is no watchman or anybody else. How long did the coed stand motionless among snakes and lizards? It probably got darker faster than you think. Meanwhile, the light fades. Closing time is approaching, but the coed still stands there motionless. Huh, that's a novel but not a clever novel. Forgetting about Mieko, on the day you're made the leading man…"

Nakamura grinned broadly.

"Unfortunately, Mieko is getting fat."

"More than you?"

"Shut up. I weigh 195 pounds. Mieko is probably around 140."

Ten years passed. Nakamura worked at Mitsui in Berlin doing something. He heard Mieko had married. By chance, the novelist Horikawa Yasukichi spotted Mieko in an illustration in the New Year's edition of a women's magazine. Mieko was behind a large piano in the photograph. She and three children were smiling happily. She looked like she hadn't changed much over the last ten years. Her weight, Yasukichi inwardly feared, may have slightly exceeded 165 pounds.

(January 1925)

3

THE TIGER STORIES

One December evening, a father hugged his son, who was about to turn five. They sat together at a *kotatsu* heating table.

Son. Daddy, tell me a story!

Father. What story?

Son. Any … uh, I like tiger stories.

Father. A story about a tiger? Well, a tiger story. That's a hard one.

Son. Tell me a tiger story.

Father. A tiger story … All right, I'll tell you a tiger story. Long ago, a military bugler in Korea was dead drunk and asleep on the side of a road. Because his face was wet, he woke up wondering what had happened. All of a sudden, a huge tiger stroked the bugle soldier's face with water on the tip of its tail.

Son. Why?

Father. Because the bugler was drunk, the tiger was getting rid of the smell of the sake before he ate the soldier.

Son. Then what happened?

Father. The soldier readied himself and, with all his might, shoved the bugle into the tiger's butt. That hurt. The tiger was surprised and sped toward the village.

Son. Did he die?

Father. When he reached the center of the village, the tiger finally collapsed because of its wounded butt and died. The bugle stuck in his butt blared doo-doo-dooo until the tiger died.

Son (laughing). What happened to the bugle soldier?

Father. Well, the bugler was highly praised and given a reward for killing the tiger. The End.

Son. Do you have another one?

Father. This time, the story won't be about a tiger.

Son. No, tell me another tiger story.

Father. There aren't only tiger stories. Let me see, what did I miss? Okay, I'll tell you one more. This one is about a Korean hunter who hiked deep into a mountain to hunt. Right below him, at the bottom of a valley, a lone tiger was walking around.

Son. Was the tiger big?

Father. Yeah, it was a big one. The hunter thought it would make a great trophy and quickly loaded the bullets into his gun.

Son. Did he shoot it?

Father. Well, when he tried to shoot it, the tiger suddenly scrunched its body and leaped up to a large boulder on the other side. But right after it leaped into the air, unfortunately, before it could land on the boulder, it fell onto the hard ground.

Son. Then what happened?

Father. Then the tiger went back to where it was and leaped onto the huge boulder.

Son. This time, he jumped better?

Father. This time, he fell down again. He hung his long tail, looking embarrassed, and left.

Son. So the hunter didn't shoot the tiger?

Father. Right. At that moment, the tiger seemed almost human. The hunter felt sorry for him and quit.

Son. That story is boring. Tell me another tiger story.

Father. Another one? This time, I'll tell you a cat story. A story about a cat who wears high boots.

Son. No, tell me another tiger story.

Father. If I must ... so long, long ago, there was a big tiger. It had three or four cubs. The tiger played with the cubs all day long. At night, it took the cubs to a cave where they all slept ... Hey, don't fall asleep.

Son (sleepy). Okay.

Father. One autumn day at sunset, the tiger was shot by a hunter's arrow. It didn't die but went home. The cubs who knew nothing started playing right away. The tiger played, jumping and leaping as always. Then they went into the cave as they did every night and slept. But when dawn came, the tiger lay down surrounded by the cubs and died. All the cubs were shocked ... Hey, are you awake?

Son (asleep and not answering). ...

Father. Hey, is somebody there? The little fellow is already fast asleep.

From a distance, he could hear the reply, "Yes, I'm back."

(December 1925)

4

THE MONKEY

My ocean voyage had ended. Finally, the apprentice period as a *hangyoku*, geisha-in-training, came to an end. *Ship A* I was serving on probably entered the port at Yokosuka around three in the afternoon of the third day. The usual bugle call for assembling the landing crew blared. I thought it was starboard's turn to go ashore, but everyone lined up on the upper deck. Suddenly, the bugle sounded to call all hands on deck. Of course, it wasn't a trivial matter. We had no idea what was going on and asked each other while they raised the hatch.

When the crew assembled, the commander spoke.

"Recently, on this ship, a few people have been robbed. In particular, when the town watch dealer visited yesterday, two silver pocket watches disappeared. Today, the entire crew will be body searched along with their belongings."

This was the gist of what he said. We were hearing about the watch dealer incident for the first time, but we were aware of the thefts. The rumor was that money was stolen from one petty officer and two sailors.

Of course, everyone was made to strip naked for the body search. Fortunately, at the beginning of October, we watched the sun beating down on the red buoys floating in the port. It still felt like summer, so this wasn't horrible. The trouble was the crew members had planned to soon go on shore for entertainment. When they were searched, the erotic art and condoms spilling from their pockets caused an uproar. Faces blushed red. The men fidgeted and fell behind. An officer slapped a few of the men.

The crew numbered six hundred men, so the searches were cursory but time-consuming. The sight might be called spectacular, but it was not. All six hundred men were naked and filled the upper deck in formation. Among them, deeply tanned faces and wrists belonged to the engineers. For a short time, this group was suspected of the thefts, so they stripped to their undershorts and also wore fierce expressions that said, "If you're gonna search, search everywhere."

While this commotion erupted on the upper deck, their belongings were being searched on the middle and lower decks. With a cadet stationed at every hatch, of course, no one on the upper deck could set foot below.

I was assigned the role of searching the lower decks. Together with other shipmates, we walked around and searched the sailors' duffle bags and small boxes. This was the first time I had been given this assignment since boarding the ship. I searched behind beams and rummaged deeply on the shelves holding the duffle bags. This job was more exhausting than I imagined.

Among them, a man named Makita, also a cadet like me, discovered stolen goods. Watches and money were put together in the hat box of a signal man named Narajima. A knife with an inlaid mother-of-pearl handle that a waiter said had disappeared was inside, too.

Right after "Dismissed!" came the order "Signalmen, fall in!"

The engineers, the previous suspects, looked amused. I scanned the signalmen and noticed Narajima was missing.

I was inexperienced and knew nothing about these matters. Even when items are stolen on the ship, sometimes a criminal never emerges. Of course, there were suicides. Eight or nine out of ten times, the man would hang himself in the coal bunker. They rarely jumped to their deaths. Once on my ship, however, a man cut open his guts with a knife. He was discovered before he died, and his life was saved.

Because things like this happen, when Narajima didn't appear, as expected, all the officers looked shocked. Particularly, even now, I vividly see the upset executive officer. During the previous war, his reputation for bravery spread. But he paled and sounded worried; he looked ridiculous.

We saw that and exchanged glances of contempt. Why did he panic given his spiritual discipline? He had an ulterior motive.

Immediately, by the commander's order, the search of the ship began. I was not the only man driven by a pleasant excitement. Our feelings mirrored those of a busybody going to gawk at a fire. When the police came to arrest the criminal, he was probably uneasy about possible resistance from the suspect. On a warship, incidents like that never happen. Especially among the sailors and us, the distinction between upper and lower exists. Unless a man tries to become a soldier, he has no idea how strict it is, but that strictness is an incredible strength. I eagerly ran down the hatch.

At that moment, Makita was in the group that went down with me. In a wildly fascinating atmosphere, he tapped my shoulder from behind and said, "Hey, this reminds me of the time that monkey was caught."

"Yeah, it's all right because today's monkey isn't that nimble."

"If you underestimate him, he'll get away."

"What? He's escaped. A monkey is a monkey."

While telling this joke, he went down.

On an ocean voyage to Australia, this monkey was given to the gunnery officer in Brisbane. During the voyage, two days earlier when entering Wilhelmshaven, a huge commotion erupted on the ship when the monkey disappeared holding the captain's watch.

On an eternal voyage, you suffer from boredom. This gunnery officer, naturally, and all of us mobilized and dressed in work uniforms, searched from the machine room below to the gun turret on top. The crowded passages weren't in their usual state. Many animals had been received or bought from outsiders. As we walked around briskly, dogs got tangled around our legs; a pelican squawked; and parakeets wildly flapped their wings in baskets hanging from loops. It looked like a fire had been started in a circus tent.

Where was that monkey in all this? It quickly left for the upper deck, still holding the watch. Suddenly, it scrambled up the mast. Since several sailors were working there, it couldn't escape. One sailor caught it with ease; his hand snatched it by the nape of its neck. The glass on the watch was broken, but the watch was mostly undamaged.

Later, the gunnery officer proposed the punishment of no food for the monkey for two days. But that made no sense. Before the sentence ended, the gunnery officer defied the punishment and fed ginseng and yams to the monkey. He said, "He looked so sad. He may be a monkey, but he looked so pitiful."

This is insignificant, but our feelings as we searched for Narajima closely resembled our feelings when we chased after that monkey.

At that time, I was the first man down to the lower deck. As you know, the lower deck is a gloomy place. Down there, polished metal and plated iron plates dimly shimmered here and there.

For some reason, I felt suffocated, but there was nothing I could do. I thought I heard a few footsteps walking toward the coal bunker. I was about to shout when the upper half of a man emerged from the loading dock of the coal bunker.

He was going inside the coal bunker through the narrow opening. He appeared to be trying to go in feet first. I couldn't see his face, blocked by a shoulder of his navy blue sailor uniform and the hat on his head. The light was so dim, I could only see his upper body silhouetted in black. Intuitively, I thought he was Narajima. If it were him, he probably was going into the coal bunker to kill himself.

I felt a strange excitement. This pleasant excitement made the blood in my body dance and left me speechless. I could say I resembled a hunter holding a gun and waiting for the prey to come. Like in a dream, I jumped at the man. Quicker than a hunting dog, both of my hands locked onto his shoulders and pressed from above.

"Narajima."

I spoke with no rebuke or abuse. My voice strangely rose and quivered. Actually, I couldn't say it was the criminal, Narajima.

"…"

Without shaking free of my grip, Narajima moved his upper body through the loading opening and calmly looked up at my face. However, *calmly* may not be the right word. He had to use every bit of his power to achieve this calm.

This unavoidable calm is inflexible and desperate; in other words, a sail arm snapped in half by the wind will try to return to its original position simply by relying on its remaining strength after the wind passes. Subconsciously, I expected no resistance but harbored a subtle dissatisfaction that grew into greater anger and frustration. I was silent and looked down only at the serene face lifted up.

I didn't see that face twice. Even the demon's face, at a glance, looked on the verge of tears. That said, if you've never seen it, you can't imagine it. I intended to tell you the story of those eyes filled with tears.

I could see the muscle spasms at the corners of his mouth, resembling rapid changes in involuntary muscles. Only his sweaty, pale face could be easily explained. The frightening expression emerging from all of that cannot be written by any novelist. Even the man before you, a man who writes novels, can speak with certainty about that incident with peace of mind. I felt that expression struck something in my heart like lightning. This signalman's face gave me a deep shock.

"What are you going to do?"

I asked this mechanically. Was it my imagination? The way I said "you" sounded like I was asking myself.

"What are you going to do?"

If asked this, how could I answer?

"I will make this man a criminal."

Who can calmly answer that way?

Who can look at this face and imitate it? Writing this takes a long time. In fact, at this moment, this self-reproach flashed in my heart. At that moment, I heard these words, quiet yet sharp.

"I'm not ashamed."

You would probably describe my heart as if it spoke to me. I felt as though these words echoed in my nerves, like needles pricking them. At the time I said, "I'm not ashamed," with Narajima, I felt I wanted to bow my head before something bigger than us. Eventually, I let go of Narajima's shoulders and idly stood in front of the coal bunker as if I were the captured criminal.

Later, you can probably guess without my saying anything. Narajima was confined to a detention cell the entire day and sent to the naval prison in Uraga. I don't want to say too much about that, but at that place, they make the prisoners do what they call *Carrying a Bullet*.

An iron ball weighing just four pounds is repeatedly placed on one stand and then on another one eight feet away. What is hard about that? That's probably not grueling to a prisoner.

In a borrowed copy of Dostoyevsky's *The House of the Dead*, this was written:

> But let him [the prisoner] be constrained to pour water from one vessel into another, or to transport a quantity of earth from one place to another, in order to perform the contrary operation immediately afterwards, then I am persuaded that at the end of a few days the prisoner would strangle himself or commit a thousand crimes, punishable with death, rather than live in such an abject condition and endure such torments.

The prisoners there do that; yet, no one commits suicide. That is rather mysterious. That signalman I restrained went there. This man had freckles and was short, timid, and mild-mannered.

That day, I, along with other cadets, leaned on the handrail and watched the port at sunset. Makita came to my side and mockingly said, "Capturing the monkey alive was impressive."

He probably thought I was feeling proud of myself.

"Narajima is a human being. He's not a monkey," I bluntly said and abruptly left the handrail. The others surely found that strange. Makita and I remained close friends since the military academy and never argued.

As I walked alone from the stern to the bow on the upper deck, I fondly remembered the commander's confused state of concern over the life and death of Narajima. Even when we made that signalman the monkey handler, only the commander had the same human-like compassion.

The stupidity of our contempt for that means nothing in this story. I was oddly embarrassed and lowered my head. Then, trying to walk as soundlessly as possible, I went back from the bow to the stern along the darkening deck. I felt I should apologize to Narajima, forced to listen to our loud footsteps in solitary confinement.

Narajima stole because of a woman. I don't know the length of the prison sentence. Anyway, it was probably at least several months in that dark place. Although a monkey is pardoned from punishment, a human is not.

(August 1916)

5

SHINO

Usually around this time, sunlight streamed through the stained-glass windows in the hall of the barbarian temple of the Christian missionaries. Today, however, the low light at sunset did not merely change with the cloudy skies of the rainy season. Gothic-style pillars inside softly brightened the wood surfaces. A tall lectorium was preserved in this space. A single flame from an oil lamp, continuously burning deep inside the hall, illuminated the images of saints standing in the alcove. Not a single worshipper was there.

One Western priest was inside the darkened hall; his head bowed in prayer. He looked to be forty-five or -six years old. The man had a narrow forehead, prominent cheekbones, and thick whiskers on his cheeks. His kimono, dragging on the floor, was a monk's robe called an *abito*. He had wrapped a string of *kontatsu* prayer beads around his wrist and gently dangled its blue beads.

Of course, the hall was silent. The priest didn't move a muscle.

One Japanese woman appeared and quietly entered the hall. The woman, who looked like a samurai's wife, tightened some sort of black band around her old ceremonial kimono with a dyed crest. She seemed to be in her thirties. After a glance, however, she looked much older than her age. Her complexion was strangely poor. Dark rings formed around her eyes, but most of her features could still be called beautiful. No, she seemed too proper, even stern.

The woman looked amazed at the holy water basin or prayer desk and strode fearlessly deeper into the hall. The priest was kneeling in front of the darkened altar. Surprised, the woman suddenly stopped there. She seemed to instantly grasp that he was praying. She stood in silence, her gaze locked on the priest.

The interior of the hall was quiet as usual. If the priest didn't move, the woman did not move an eyebrow. This situation lasted a fairly long time.

The priest finished praying and finally stood. If he looked, he saw the woman standing in front of him like she wished to say something. Visitors often came to the hall of the barbarian temple to see the unfamiliar crucified Buddha. This woman, however, seemed to have come out of curiosity. The priest smiled deliberately and spoke in broken Japanese.

"May I help you?"

"Yes, I have a small request."

The woman politely nodded. Despite her poor clothing, she lowered her head with her hair neatly bundled with a hairpin. The priest greeted her with smiling eyes. His hand twisted and untwisted his fingers in the kontatsu of blue beads.

"My name is Shino. I'm the widow of Ichibangase Hanbei. The truth is, my son Shinnojō is gravely ill," the woman said hesitantly. Then, she nimbly broached her reason for being there like a recitation. Shinnojō was turning fifteen that year. Since the spring, he has been afflicted by some illness. He also developed a cough, lost his appetite, and came down with a high fever.

Shino had done all she could. She had him examined by a doctor, bought medicine, and did everything possible to help him recuperate. However, she had not seen the slightest effect. He continued to weaken gradually.

Now, everything had gone awry; she couldn't cure him as she had hoped. She heard that medical treatment of the priest at the barbarian temple even cured vitiligo. She asked him to find a way to save Shinnojō's life.

"Would you please visit him? Is that possible?"

As she spoke, she stared at the priest. If the cast of pleading for compassion was missing from her eyes, she showed no sign of being crushed by anxiety. She radiated serenity, bordering on true stubbornness.

"Very well. I will see him."

While tugging his whiskers, the priest looked to be in deep thought as he nodded. The woman had not come to seek spiritual help. She sought help for the body. However, not scolding her for that was best. The body houses the soul. If the house is completely repaired, the person's illness is easily driven away. Actually, Fabian the Catechist and other evangelists bowed to the crucifixion cross for that reason. The woman may have been sent here by divine will.

"Can your son come here?"

"That would be a little difficult ..."

"Well then, please take me to him."

The woman's eyes brightened instantly with joy.

"Will you? I couldn't be happier."

The priest felt compassion. For an instant, he undoubtedly saw a mother in the woman's face that resembled a Noh mask. The woman standing before him was not the honest wife of a samurai. She wasn't a Japanese woman. She became the same woman as the extraordinarily loving and sympathetic, remarkably gentle, superior and sweet queen of Heaven, whose beautiful breasts nursed Christ in the manger long ago. The priest spoke lightheartedly to the woman as he puffed out his chest.

"Please, rest assured. I'm fairly familiar with illness. If I'm entrusted with your son's life, I'll do all that I can. If it's beyond human strength—"

The woman gently interrupted.

"No, if you visit just once, I'll have no regrets no matter what happens. I simply implore you to rely on the secret aid from the compassionate Kannon-san at Kiyomizu-dera Temple."

Kannon-san! These words immediately swelled the color of

anger in the priest's face. He stared at the sharp eyes of the ignorant woman. While shaking his head, he was about to admonish her.

"Be careful. The ones revered by you—Kannon, Shaka Hachiman, and Tenjin—are idols of wood and stone. There is only one true God, one true Lord of Heaven. Killing or saving your son is only God's will. An idol knows none of this. If your son is important, please stop praying to idols."

The woman lightly pressed her chin on the collar of her old summer kimono and looked with surprise at the priest. She didn't fully understand the priest's words laced with anger. He stuck out his bearded face to admonish and caution her with all his might.

"Please, believe in the true God. The true God is only Jesus Christ, born in the town of Bethlehem in the land of Judea. There is no other God. One who thinks so has an evil spirit. It is a fallen angel in another form. To save us, Jesus's body was nailed to the cross."

The priest solemnly reached out a hand and pointed to a stained glass window in the back. The window illuminated by faint sunlight projected the tormented Christ in the gloom cast over the temple compound. Mary and the disciples, in tears under the cross, were also projected. The woman pressed her hands together in prayer in the way of the Japanese and calmly looked up at the window.

"Is that the Buddha of the barbarians I've heard about in rumors? If he can save my son's life, I may serve that crucified Buddha for the rest of my life. Please, pray for divine protection."

The woman's calm voice harbored deep emotions. The priest slightly turned his head as though he triumphed at last and spoke more eloquently than before.

"Jesus was born on Earth to cleanse away our sins and to save our souls. Please listen to the trials and tribulations of his life."

The priest, full of holy inspiration, paced back and forth as he rapidly described the entire life of Christ. An angel came to announce his conception by the Virgin Mary, who possessed all virtues. Jesus was born in a stable. Wisemen from the East, informed of his birth by a star, brought offerings of frankincense and myrrh. Fearing the appearance of the Messiah, King Herod killed the firstborn sons. John baptized Jesus. Jesus gave a sermon on a mountaintop. He turned water into wine. He gave a blind man sight. He drove out the seven evil spirits possessing Mary Magdalene. He restored the dead Lazarus to life. He walked on water. He entered Jerusalem on the back of a donkey. He held the melancholy Last Supper. He prayed at the Mount of Olives ...

Like they were the words of God, the priest's voice echoed inside the dim hall. With brightened eyes, the woman silently listened to that voice.

"Please consider this. Jesus and two thieves were nailed to crucifixion crosses. Even thinking about it now, our flesh can't stop trembling over their sorrow and pain at that time. Especially forlorn feelings come from the final words spoken by Jesus on the cross. 'Eli, Eli, lama sabachthani?' that is to say, 'My God, my God, why hast thou forsaken me?'"

Instinctively, the priest closed his mouth. The woman, now pale, bit her lower lip and stared at the priest's face. The sparkle in her eyes was not a sacred emotion. It was simply cold contempt and hatred that seemed to penetrate to the bone. The priest was dazed and, for a short time, only blinked like he had been stunned silent.

"Is the true God, the Buddha of the barbarians?"

The woman no longer looked demure and spoke bluntly to deliver the final blow.

"My husband, Ichibangase Hanbei, was a ronin of the Sasake Clan. However, he never showed his back to the enemy.

"At the siege of the castle at the long-gone Chōkō-ji Temple, because of a gambling loss, my husband stole a horse, as well as armor and a helmet.

"But on the day of the battle, he wore on his naked body a *haori* jacket made of paper with *I bow to Amitābha Buddha* written in large characters. Instead of an offering of bamboo with branches, he unsheathed a three-and-a-half-foot-long sword with his right hand, and opened a fan made of red paper with his left.

"As he loudly chanted, 'Rather than steal another's young man, prepare to lose your head,' he slashed through and made yield the military strength of Shibata, the reputed demon among the relatives of Lord Oda.

"Even if he were God, although nailed to the cross, he's a despicable sort who whines with excuses. What are the merits of a faith that worships that coward?

"If you descend from that line of cowards, I can't show you my son's illness before the memorial tablet of my husband, no longer of this world.

"Shinnojō is also the son of my husband, known as Hanbei the Beheader. Rather than force him to take the medicine of a coward, I'd rather he cut open his belly. Had I known these things, I certainly would not have come here. I regret only that."

While swallowing tears, she abruptly turned her back to the priest and quickly left the compound like someone avoiding a toxic wind. The priest remained, eyes wide open in shock.

(March 1923)

6

A DAY IN THE LIFE OF ŌISHI KURANOSUKE

Bright sunlight shone through the closed *shōji* sliding door. The shadow of plums on an old, leaning tree vividly traced brightness over a dozen feet like a picture from the left edge to the right edge. At the time, a former retainer of Asano Takumi-no-kami, Ōishi Kuranosuke Yoshikatsu, held in the custody of the Hosokawa Clan, sat with knees properly aligned behind that shōji. For some time, he had been concentrating on reading. Perhaps, the document was a volume of *The Records of the Three Kingdoms* borrowed from a vassal of the Hosokawa Clan.

Of the nine people in the parlor, Kataoka Gengoemon had gone to the toilet moments earlier. Hayami Tōzaemon moved to join the conversation in the lower room and had not yet returned.

Later, six men, Yoshida Chūzaemon, Hara Sōemon, Mase Kyūdayū, Onodera Jūnai, Horibe Yahei, and Hazama Kihei, indulged in reading as if they had forgotten about the shadow cast on the shōji screen and wrote letters. Was the silence in the chilly parlor in early spring because all six of the gathered men were elders, older than fifty? Despite occasional coughs, no sounds caused the scent of ink to drift.

Kuranosuke's eyes suddenly left *The Records of the Three Kingdoms*.

30

As he seemed to look at some place off in the distance, he gently held his hands above the hibachi beside him. In the hibachi covered by a metal screen, the beautiful red glow of the live coals brightly lit up the ashes. When he felt the heat of the fire, quiet satisfaction filled his heart. Fortunately, on December 15 of last year, revenge was taken on the enemy of his deceased lord. When they withdrew to Sengaku-ji Temple, he recited to himself:

> *I give in to joy.*
> *I leave behind this world.*
> *My body is free.*
> *The moon in a fleeting world*
> *Not hidden by a lone cloud.*

The satisfaction of that time returned. Since leaving Akō Castle, he had spent close to two years somewhere between impatience and scheming.

He did not have ordinary troubles but only constrained the rash enthusiasm of men prone to following trends and patiently waited for the right opportunity. The spies unleashed by the enemy clan constantly scrutinized every facet of his life. He had pretended to be licentious to deceive the eyes of those spies. He also had to allay the doubts arising among his comrades also tricked by his dissolute behavior. If the old stories of conspiracies hatched in Yamashina and Maruyama are recalled, the anguish of those days was read again in his heart. However, everything had reached the destination.

If there were a loose end, it would be the government decree concerning the forty-seven men in the party. Despite the decree, it was surely not a distant matter in any way. That's it. Every goal had been achieved. More simply, not only was that revenge fulfilled, every last moral demand was attained in a way close to perfection. He was able to simultaneously experience the satisfaction of completing a task and the satisfaction that embodied morality. Even while pondering the objective of the revenge or the method, that satisfaction did not cloud over the qualms of conscience. Could he have found greater satisfaction? While thinking about this, Kuranosuke looked at ease. Had he lost interest in reading? From beside the hibachi, he spoke to Yoshida Chūzaemon, engaged in writing practice using a finger above the reading material face down on his knees.

"Today, it's too warm."

"You're right. Even though I'm here, it's so warm I can't fight this drowsiness."

Kuranosuke smiled. On this New Year's Day, Tominomori Suke'emon, drunk on three cups of the spicy *toso* sake, chanted:

> *Today, too, is spring.*
> *Living without any shame.*
> *A samurai sleeps.*

That verse popped into his mind. The verse's meaning did not change the satisfaction Kuranosuke Yoshikatsu now felt.

"Perhaps, the achievement of the true objective may be a lapse in vigilance."

"That's true. That may be it."

Chūzaemon raised the *kiseru* pipe near his hand and tasted a gentle plume of smoke. Light blue smoke disappeared in a luminous quiet while the early spring afternoon smoldered slightly.

"Neither of us expected to pass time in tranquil days like these."

"That is true. I also don't have the dream of meeting again in the spring."

"We seem to be very lucky."

The two men's smiling eyes met; both had looks of satisfaction. This time, a silhouette was projected on the shōji screen behind Kuranosuke. The silhouette put a hand on the shōji's handle and disappeared. In its place, the burly figure of Hayami Tōzaemon appeared but did not enter the parlor. Until the end, Kuranosuke could experience the warmth of the pleasant spring sun with proud satisfaction. In reality, a broad smile floated on and didn't hesitate to get between Tōzaemon's cheeks. Of course, they didn't notice him.

"The lower room sounds rather lively," said Chūzaemon, then took a puff on the pipe.

"Den'emon is on duty today, so the conversations are probably extra lively. Kataoka just joined them and sat down."

"I thought the logic was slow."

Chūzaemon choked on the smoke and forced a smile. Onodera Jūnai, who effortlessly wrote with his brush, slightly raised his face in contemplation. His eyes immediately dropped again to the paper; he diligently wrote the rest. Perhaps, he was writing a letter to his wife in Kyoto. Kuranosuke smiled, deepening the wrinkles at the corners of his eyes, and said, "Was there a funny story?"

"No. Just the usual idle talk. A short time ago, when Chikamatsu told the story of Jinzaburō, Den'emon listened as he held back tears. In other words, the story was funny. Since we exacted revenge on Lord Kira, acts resembling vengeance are gaining popularity throughout Edo."

"Ah, ha, ha, I never thought of that."

Chūzaemon looked doubtfully at Tōzaemon. For some reason, his companion seemed extremely proud of having told this story.

"I just heard two or three similar stories. The funniest one happened near Mina-chō in Minami Hatchōbori. It started with an argument in the public bathhouse between the proprietor of the neighborhood rice shop and a worker at the dyer next door, looks like the spark was a minor thing. 'Why did you splash hot water on me?' In the end, the worker severely beat the rice shop proprietor in the tub. An apprentice at the rice shop thought it was a grudge. Did he lie in wait where the worker would come out at night and hook onto the other guy's shoulder? As he did this, he seemed to be saying, 'My boss's enemy! I'll show you!'"

While gesturing, the laughing Tōzaemon said, "That turned into extreme violence."

"The worker was seriously injured. The neighborhood was confused because the apprentice was a good kid. Another one happened at Tōri-chō, 3-chōme; another at Shinkōji-machi, 2-chōme; and another somewhere else. Anyway, they were everywhere. They were probably copying us. Isn't that funny?"

Tōzaemon and Chūzaemon looked at each other and laughed. Even over trivial matters, they were pleased when they heard about the effect of their act of revenge on the human spirit in Edo. Only one man, Kuranosuke, gently touching his forehead, looked disinterested and said nothing.

Tōzaemon's story dropped a strange, misty cloud onto his heart's satisfaction. Of course, he didn't necessarily feel responsible for all the effects of his deeds. Since the success of their revenge, followed by the rise in popularity of revenge in Edo, his conscience and indifference from the beginning were natural. Unrelated to this, however, the warmth of spring he felt in his heart until now had diminished slightly.

At that time, he was a bit amazed by this effect of their action that burst out in unexpected places. Ordinarily, he would be laughing with Tōzaemon and Chūzaemon, but seeds of discontent were sown in his currently satisfied heart. Maybe, this was caused by the logical contradiction to his satisfaction inside the darkness and his selfish nature that upholds all of his actions and their effects. Of course, none of the finely dissected thoughts entered his heart. He simply felt a chilly vein of the spring breeze and became somewhat uncomfortable.

Kuranosuke's lack of laughter did not especially attract the other men's attention. No, like the easygoing Tōzaemon, he was probably convinced of and didn't doubt Kuranosuke's interest resembled his interest in this story. If not, he would go to the lower room again. This time, however, he would intentionally bring back Horiuchi Den'emon, the retainer of the Hosogawa Clan on duty that day.

Tōzaemon paid close attention to everything. Looking back at Chūzaemon, he said something like "Let's invite Den'emon," then swept open the sliding partition and casually stepped down to the lower room. Before long, wearing his usual smile, he triumphantly returned with Den'emon, who, at a glance, looked uncouth.

"Ah, I thank you for your extraordinary efforts," said the smiling Chūzaemon, instead of Kuranosuke Yoshikatsu, when he spotted Den'emon. Since being put in charge, Den'emon's lack of sophistication and honest nature connected him to the others with the kindness of an acquaintance from long ago.

"Hayami-san insisted I come. I appeared despite thinking it would be an intrusion."

As Den'emon sat, he moved the muscles in his sunburned cheeks in an attempt to smile while his thick eyebrows twitched. He surveyed the room and then greeted everyone present, the readers and the writers. Of course, Kuranosuke courteously nodded. In front, the modest comic, Horibe Yahei, had set down the *Taiheiki* historical chronicles he had begun, nodding off still wearing his eyeglasses. He jerked awake, took off his glasses in a fluster, and politely bowed his head. The surprised Hazama Kihei looked delighted but turned away toward the partition beside him to fight off laughter.

"Den'emon seems to dislike the older men. Anyway, he never comes up here."

Out of character, Kuranosuke spoke in a smooth tone. Although somewhat flustered, the earlier feelings of satisfaction probably flowed warmly in the depths of his heart.

"No, that's not the reason, but somehow I'm stopped by those men and get drawn into conversation."

"From what I hear, a hilarious story was told."

Chūzaemon injected a few words from the side.

"Did you say a funny story?"

"That story about the popularity of imitating revenge throughout Edo," said Tōzaemon, while smiling at Den'emon and Kuranosuke, impartially compared the two.

"Ah, that story? Human emotions are strange things. When I feel the loyalty of your group, you should want to see imitations among the townspeople and the farmers. I don't know whether the depraved customs of the upper and lower classes will improve. That's fine because we're in times where only the things you don't want to see become popular in dramatic *jōruri* recitations or kabuki.

The conversation progressed in a direction Kuranosuke found uninteresting. He consciously spoke in a more solemn tone and deftly changed the direction with an explanation spoken in self-deprecating words.

"We are grateful for your praise of our loyalty. In my opinion, shame comes first."

Then, while staring at the group, he said, "If you ask, why, the men you see here are like many in the Akō clan? Everyone had a low wage. At the very beginning, a head clerk and third-rank officer named Okuno consulted with me on various matters. Midway, however, he changed his mind and left the alliance. That was regrettable. Shindō Genshirō, Kawamura Denbyōe, and Koyama Gengozaemon sat at higher seats than Hara Sōemon and had higher status than Sasa Kozaemon and Yoshida Chūzaemon. As we approached the moment of action, minds changed. Also, among them were family members. Looking at it, feelings of shame are reasonable."

Accompanying Kuranosuke's words, the tone of the group lost its previous cheerfulness and quickly turned serious. In this sense, the conversation was fine even though it changed course as he intended. How pleased Kuranosuke was with the new direction was another problem.

As he listened to the recollections, Hayami Tōzaemon clenched both fists on his knees several times.

"All those guys were only beasts in human disguises. As men, they are a disgrace to warriors."

Chūzaemon raised his eyebrows in agreement and seeking approval, looked at Horibe Yahei. The passionate Yahei wasn't silent as before.

"When we met them on the morning of the withdrawal, even spitting at them would have been unsatisfying. They shamelessly showed their faces to us after our long-desired ambition was accomplished and great joy achieved."

"Takada, well, Takada is a complete fool like Oyamada Shōzaemon," said Mase Kyūdayū to no one in particular. Hara Sōemon and Onodera Jūnai spoke in one voice and began cursing the followers who broke the pact. Even the taciturn Hazama Kihei said nothing but nodded his white hair again and again to endorse the group's opinion.

"I can't believe those scoundrels were in the same clan as the vassals in your party. From the start, samurai, as well as townsmen and farmers, have badmouthed the cowardly samurai dogs not worth their stipends.

"Okabayashi Mokunosuke committed seppuku last year. One rumor said his relatives made the decision and forced him to kill himself. Even if that hadn't happened, in a situation like this, they would be dishonored.

"It's certainly more so with other people. They talk about Edo, where people are easily roused to justice, will imitate the revenge and the righteous anger of your party. Someone who will kill those guys may come out."

Den'emon spoke bluntly and with pride about this situation, as if he thought of it as his and that of other men. More than anyone else, he might have felt the urge to kill them.

The agitated Yoshida, Hara, Hayami, and Horibe were so provoked that their emotions surged, and they verbally eviscerated the traitors and rebels. However, only one of them, only Ōishi Kuranosuke, kept both hands on his knees, looked bored, and lazily gazed at the hibachi, gradually speaking less.

As a result of the conversation shifting in the direction he desired, the newly discovered fact was their loyalty was gaining more praise at the expense of comrades who changed their minds. That and the spring breeze that blew at the bottom of his heart reduced the warmth somewhat again.

Naturally, he mentioned regret over the oath breakers simply because he wanted to change the conversation's direction. He thought with discomfort and regret about their change of mind. However, he pitied these disloyal samurai, but his thoughts didn't reach hating them.

If the state of human emotions and the changes in the world are seen from his experienced eyes, the change of mind by most of them was perfectly natural. If honest words were allowed, it was a miserable honesty. Consequently, he did not alter his constant tolerance toward them. If the revenge is looked at now, the only thing left to give to them is a smile of pity.

This world seemed to believe they were not satisfied despite the killing. Why to become loyal warriors, we must turn into human beasts? The difference between us and them is not unexpectedly large. Without the prior pleasure, Kuranosuke pondered the strange effect on Edo's townspeople and reflected in public opinion, represented by Den'emon. The influence of the alliance of deserters slightly altered the current meaning. His pained face was not a coincidence.

However, Kuranosuke's displeasure still had the fate of receiving the final blow.

Den'emon noticed his silence and likely assumed it revealed his characteristic humility. Ultimately, he held deep respect for his character. To express that deep respect, when this honest samurai from Higo forced the topic change, he immediately began heaping words of lavish praise about Kuranosuke's loyalty.

"A few days ago, I was told this by a well-informed man. Warrior So-and-so in China shadowed the rival of his lord and even swallowed coal to lose his voice. However, wasn't that easier than the insincere, fake debauchery displayed by Kuranosuke?"

Den'emon talked for a long time about anecdotes from a year ago when Kuranosuke acted wildly. How difficult was autumn-leaf viewing in Takao or Atago for him, a man faking madness? A flower-viewing party in Shimabara or Gion was surely painful to him who indulged in a strategy of self-sacrifice.

"I've heard that recently, a poem that says a large rock* lightened to a papier-mâché rock has become popular in Kyoto. Until then, deceiving the whole world was impossible without a compelling reason. The praise of Amano Yazaemon the other day for his quiet courage is perfectly reasonable."

"No, it's not that important," reluctantly answered Kuranosuke.

To Den'emon, the humble attitude of that man was both unsatisfactory and seemed to produce a more elegant sensibility. Until now, he had faced Kuranosuke but then turned toward Onodera Jūnai, who has been on duty in Kyoto for many years. With enthusiasm, he began to confess his admiration. His childlike enthusiasm

---

* Ōishi literally means big rock.

might be amusing and, at the same time, enchanting to Jūnai, known among the group as a sophisticated man. Kuranosuke meekly welcomed Den'emon's wish and recounted in detail the story of the time he wore a priest's robe and often visited Yūgiri in Masuya in order to deceive the enemy clan's spies.

"The serious-looking Kuranosuke also wrote a poem entitled *A Scene from the Pleasure Quarters** at that time. This poem was highly regarded. Its song could be heard everywhere in the red-light districts. The public morals of Kuranosuke at that time were to dress in priestly robes dyed black and walk around drunk while floating among the falling cherry blossoms in Gion. The popularity of that poem and Kuranosuke's well-known reckless behavior were not the least bit unreasonable. Even Yūgiri, Ukihashi, and famous courtesans in Shimahara and Shumoku-machi always extended every courtesy to Kuranosuke. "

Kuranosuke listened with difficulty and felt mostly contempt for Jūnai's story. At the same time, he remembered without remembering the memory of his past debauchery. To him, that memory was unbelievably colorful. In this memory, he looked at the light of a tall candle, smelled the aroma of aloe oil, and heard the sounds of a *Kagabushi* shamisen.

No, even in the verse of *A Scene from the Pleasure Quarters* mentioned by Jūnai, which says *On a sleeve scattered with tears/More tears spill onto the sleeve/Tears as fleeting as dew*, distinctly floated to mind together with the graceful figures of Yūgiri and Ukihashi slipping out of the Spring Palace. Somehow, he boldly accepted the entirety of a dissolute life that often appeared in this memory. Somehow, he experienced peaceful moments in which he completely forgot about the revenge.

When he deceived himself and denied this fact, he was too honest a man. Of course, this fact is immoral. A man with insight into humanity couldn't dream of this. Thus, all of his debauchery was lavishly praised as a way to demonstrate his loyalty.

As these thoughts crossed his mind, Kuranosuke was praised for

---

* Sato-geshiki (里景色)

the plan of feigned madness and self-sacrifice. His pained face was no mystery. He received another blow and became aware of the quickening of the gentle spring breeze remaining in his heart.

What remained was opposition to all misunderstandings and opposition to his foolishness that didn't anticipate misunderstandings, which only spread a cold, faint shadow. Perhaps, his revenge, his comradeship, and finally the man himself can be communicated to later generations with voices of self-serving praise.

While he faced this unpleasant fact, he held his hands above the hibachi, its warmth dying. Avoiding Den'emon's eyes, he sighed pathetically.

SEVERAL MINUTES LATER, Ōishi Kuranosuke left his seat with the pretext of going to the toilet and leaned against a pillar on the veranda. He gazed at the flowers on an old plum tree in the cold between the moss and rocks in the old garden.

The color of the sun faded away. From the shadows of the bamboo thicket, twilight quickly spread. Behind the shōji screen, the usual amused storytelling voices continued. While listening, he was conscious of the natural hint of sorrow gradually enveloping him.

Accompanying the slight scent of plums, from somewhere came an indescribable loneliness, one that penetrated to the depths of his bright heart. Kuranosuke remained standing as he gazed up at the hard, cold flowers as if they were inlaid into the blue sky.

(August 15, 1917)

7

UNREQUITED LOVE

I heard this story one summer afternoon on a Keihin train where I bumped into a close friend from college.

This story is from the time I went to Y for a company affair. They were holding a banquet and invited me. Because it was Y, the alcove had a hanging scroll with a lithographic print of General Nogi on the wall and fake peonies arranged in front.

Rain had been falling since the evening. Not too many people were present, and the event was more pleasant than I had imagined. The banquet of another party seemed to be taking place on the second floor. Fortunately, that party wasn't noisy like a local affair. However, among the servers pouring drinks for others—you probably know her—was Toku, who had been a maid at U where we often went drinking long ago. She had a flat nose, narrow forehead, and a sense of humor. She asked, "Would you like a drink?" Wearing the formal kimono for the parlor, she held a sake flask with an air of elegance but was aloof like her colleagues.

At first, I mistook her for someone else, but when she came to my side and I looked at her, I recognized Toku. Just like the old days, whenever she spoke, she had the habit of jerking her chin

41

upward. I sensed the impermanence of reality. Nonetheless, I asked, "Weren't you Shimura's secret crush?"

Back then, Shimura was the boss and a stern fellow. He went to the Aokidō shop and returned with a small jar of peppermint. He said, "It's sweet. Have a drink." The sake seemed sweet, but Shimura was sweet, too.

Now, Toku is working in this sort of place. If Shimura in Chicago heard about this, how would he feel? I had this thought and was about to say something but held back. Did I mention that I was living in Nihon-bashi? Then she spoke.

"It's been a while, hasn't it? The last time I saw you I was at U. You haven't changed a bit."

She was already drunk when she came over.

No matter how drunk she was, the Shimura episode so long ago guaranteed a lively conversation.

"You look like you understand that the duty of the other party is to keep things lively and be boisterous."

Anyway, the hostess took the lead. The entire situation was awful because no one was allowed to leave his seat until she confessed every detail.

Then, I brought up Shimura's peppermint.

"He rejected a close friend of mine."

It's ridiculous, but she said that.

The hostess was already old. From the beginning, I was brought along by my uncle who had the status to enter the teahouse.

When that rejection was mentioned, they all rushed in. All together, the geisha teased Toku, but Toku, also known as Fukuryū, was clueless. Fukuryū was a fine name. Somewhere in a lecture about a dragon in *Hakkenden*, this is written.

The one who was joyful and free-spirited was called Fukuryū.

However, this Fukuryū was amusing because she lacked joy and a free spirit. Naturally, this is a digression.

Her lack of awareness was quite logical.

"Shimura had fallen in love with me, but I wasn't obligated to fall in love."

There's more.

"If that weren't so, I would have had better days years ago."

That seemed to be the sorrow of so-called unrequited love. And in the end, she probably wanted to give an example. Toku began telling a strange love story and wanted me to hear it. It's not interesting because it is a love story.

That's a mystery, isn't it? There's nothing more boring than listening to the stories of dreams and love affairs.

Then I said, "Except to the man himself, that's uninteresting."

"Well, even when writing a novel, dreams and romance are difficult."

"At least, dreams are like that only when intuitive. In dreams that appear in novels, not one resembles a real dream."

"But, are there many romance novels that are masterpieces?"

"I worry about the number of worthless works that were not handed down to future generations."

If this story is understood, that is very reassuring. Somehow, this is also a foolish work among foolish works. For some reason, I mimicked Toku's way of speaking and said, "Well, I'm the type who has experienced unrequited love."

Do your best to listen while keeping that in mind.

The man Toku fell in love with was an actor. She was still living in her parents' home in Tawara-machi in Asakusa when she fell in love with him at first sight in the park.

You probably think he was an extra or supporting actor at the Miyato-za or Tokiwa-za theaters. That wasn't the case. Originally, I mistakenly thought he was Japanese, but that actor was a Westerner. Anyway, it's so half-baked, it'll make you laugh.

If Toku didn't know the man's name, she didn't know his address, either. She didn't even know his nationality. Or, whether he was married or single?

Of course, these facts were just questions and tactless, but it's funny. Even if it's unrequited love, it's too absurd. When we used to go to Wakatake, even if we did not understand the story, we knew the other person was Japanese and that Shogiku was a stage name. After I said this and teased her, Toku became serious.

"Well, I wanted to know. Because I didn't know, was there anything I could do? Anyway, we only saw each other on the curtain."

To say "on the curtain" was strange. I'd understand if she said "behind the curtain." I peppered her with questions. She said her lover was a member of a Western family similar to the Sogas she saw in a silent film. This surprised me. Of course, that's definitely on the curtain. Others seemed to think it had a bad ending. Some said, "The performances were over the top."

Because it's a port area, the place was rowdy. But from what I saw, Toku didn't seem to be lying. Her eyes were quite bleary.

"I wanted to go every day but didn't have the pocket money. So I tried to go once a week."

That was fine, but she later abandoned that.

"Once, I begged my mother to take me. She did, but the theater was packed, and we could only get in at a corner on the side.

"After going to all that trouble, although that man's face was projected, I could only see it as strangely flat. That made me sad."

Holding her apron to her face, she could be said to be crying. If the face of her lover became a curtain and was flattened, she became unhappy. I sympathized with that.

"Twelve or thirteen times, whatever, I saw him play other roles. He had a long face, was thin, and had a beard. Like you, he mostly wore black clothes."

I was wearing a morning suit. Because I learned a painful lesson earlier, I seized the initiative.

"Do we look alike?" acting unconcerned, I said, "He's a better-looking man."

Was *a better-looking man* too harsh?

"What could you do? You only meet him on the curtain. If the other person were flesh and blood, you could exchange a few words or show resolve in your eyes. But doing something like that ... well, it's just a picture."

More than that, it's a moving picture. She stopped going because she couldn't get close to him.

"They say love and be loved. If no one loves you, you can prod someone into loving you. Even Shimura often brought me a blue liquor. He was unable to nudge me into falling in love. Isn't that ironic?"

All of this is reasonable, but the humor didn't move her.

"And after I became a geisha, I often took patrons out to see movies. The reason was that the man suddenly disappeared from the movies.

"Whenever I went to see one, why were they only showing movies I didn't want to see, like *The Broken Coin* from America or *Zigomar* from France? In the end, I felt no connection and gave up. And you ..."

Because the others wouldn't associate with her, Toku singled me out to continue her chattering. Her voice was half crying.

"But you know, on the evening the first time I came to this area and went to see a movie. He hadn't appeared in a movie for many years. It was set in some Western town. It had pavement and trees that looked like parasol trees in the center. Both sides were lined with Western buildings. Was that because the movie was old? On the whole, it was dimly lit and yellowish like the evening. All the houses and trees strangely quivered. The atmosphere was sad.

"He appeared with a small dog while smoking one of those cigarettes you like. Of course, he was wearing black, leaned on a cane, and had not changed a bit since I was a child."

After ten years, she saw her lover again. He had not changed from the pictures, but she had become Fukuryū. These thoughts saddened her.

"At the location of the tree, he stopped, turned to me as he took off his hat, and smiled. Did it look like he was about to greet me? If he knew my name, would he have called out to me?"

Call out, and people would have thought she was crazy. Despite it being Y, probably no geisha had fallen in love because of a motion picture.

"A small, foreign woman walked toward us and clung to him. In the lines of a silent movie narrator, I'm his mistress. Perhaps, it's my age, but her hat, decorated with large bird feathers, looked awful."

Toku was jealous. Was that in a movie, too?

At this point, the train arrived at Shinagawa. I was going to get off at Shinbashi. My friend knew this and continued talking in a rushed tone while glancing out the window from time to time as if he were afraid of not finishing the story.

After that, various things happened in the motion picture. He ended up getting arrested at this place. What did he do to get arrested? Toku told me the story in detail, but unfortunately, I can't remember it now.

"A large crowd ganged up and arrested him. No, that time was not the street seen earlier. It was probably a Western liquor store. Many liquor bottles were lined up. A large parrot cage hung in a corner. It seemed to be nighttime. Everywhere in the scene was blue. Within that blue, I saw his face on the verge of crying. If you saw it, you would have become sad. Tears filled his eyes, and his mouth was half open ..."

Then a whistle blew, and the image vanished. Only a white curtain remained. Toku's words were lovely.

"Everything disappeared. Does everything vanish and become fleeting? Isn't everything that way?"

When I asked only this, she seemed profoundly enlightened. As Toku cried, in a tone tinged with malice toward me, she said, "You know, if things get any worse, I'll become hysterical."

Even if it was hysteria, it had a serious side. Perhaps falling in love from a movie is a lie. The truth might be that someone experienced unrequited love with someone in our group.

The train the two were riding arrived at Shinbashi Station at twilight.

(September 17, 1917)

8

THE HELL OF LONELINESS

I heard this story from my mother. She said she heard it from her great-uncle. I have no idea whether the story is true or not. But judging from the great-uncle's character, I can only think that this sort of thing happens often.

The great-uncle was a so-called Daitsū, a networker, and had many acquaintances among entertainers and literary figures in the last years of the Edo period.

They included Kawatake Mokuami, Ryūkatei Tanekazu, Zenzai Aneiki, Zenzai Tōei, Kudaime Danjūrō, Uji Shibun, Miyako Senchū, and Kenkonbō Ryōsai.

Of them, Mokuami wrote about Kinokuniya Bunzaemon in the play *Edo Zakura Kiyomizu Seigen* and drew this great-uncle in a sketch book. Fifty years have already passed since his death. At some time during his life, he gained the nickname Imakibun. Even today, some people may know of him by that name alone. This man's surname was Saiki; first name, Tojirō; pseudonym as a poet, Kōi; and nickname, Yamashirogashi Tsutō.

That Tsutō got close to a monk at Tamaya in the pleasure district of Yoshiwara. He was the head priest of a Zen temple in the Hongō neighborhood. It appears his name was Zencho. Of course, he was a client and became intimate with a courtesan called Nishikigi of Tamaya. Because a priest was forbidden to marry and be sexually active, he was never officially ordained.

By chance, one evening when the lanterns were lit, Tsutō blithely passed down the hall on the way back from the toilet. A man leaning on the railing was looking at the moon. The man had a shaven head and was short and gaunt. In the moonlight, Tsutō thought he was Chikunai, a quack doctor who frequented this place. As he passed by, he extended his hand and lightly tugged the man's ear. He expected surprise and laughter from the man.

When he saw the turned face, he was the one taken by surprise. Except for being a head priest, he bore no resemblance to Chikunai. This other man had a broad forehead, and the space between his eyebrows was steep and narrow. His eyes appeared bigger because the flesh hung down. Even at that time, he saw a large mole on his left cheek. Also, he had high cheekbones. Just this much of his features chaotically entered Tsutō's eyes.

"How can I help you?" the head priest said in an angry-sounding voice. His breath seemed to have a touch of alcohol.

I forgot to write this earlier. A geisha and a male entertainer had accompanied Tsutō. These companions apologized for Tsutō and couldn't just watch in silence. Then, instead of Tsutō, the entertainer apologized for the thoughtlessness toward the guest. Meanwhile, Tsutō and the geisha hastened back to his sitting room. Even the Daitsū looked rather uncomfortable. When the head priest heard the details from the entertainer, his mood changed instantly, and he burst out laughing.

Later, Tsutō offered him cake and apologized. The other side pitied him and took the trouble to bow. From then on, the two were joined in friendship. Although they could be said to become connected by merely meeting on the second floor of Tamaya, they were strangers on public streets. Tsutō didn't drink a drop of sake, but Zencho was a heavy drinker.

Also, Zencho's possessions were luxurious. Ultimately, Zencho indulged in womanly charms. Tsutō remarked to himself that he couldn't tell which one became a monk. Tsutō, obese and ugly, wore a shaven forelock hairstyle, a protective amulet hanging from a silver chain, and his preferred striped kimono closed with a pale brown, short obi belt.

When Tsutō saw Zencho one day, Zencho was wearing a haori jacket decorated with a burning bush pattern and was playing a shamisen. His complexion was always sallow, but he looked worse than usual that day. His eyes were full of blood. The stiff skin near his mouth twitched. Tsutō immediately thought something was worrying him.

"If you need someone to talk to, I'd like to help," he seemed to let slip, but nothing was divulged. However, Zencho spoke less than usual and often lost the thread of the conversation. Tsutō explained it as the boredom that afflicts frequent clients.

This boredom afflicting people who indulge freely in drink and sex is not cured by sex and drink. The two conversed more solemnly than usual. Then, Zencho looked like he just thought of something and said, "According to Buddhist teachings, there are various hells. First, they can be divided into three: the Lowest Hell, the Peripheral Hell, and the Hell of Loneliness. An old Buddhist verse claims they've been underground since ancient times.

Of them, only the Hell of Loneliness suddenly appeared somewhere in the mountains, in wild fields, under the trees, and in the air. The border before one's eyes immediately confronts the suffering hardships of hell.

A few years ago, I fell into this hell and have no lasting interest in anything. Therefore, at any time, I live by pursuing one boundary to the next.

Of course, I can't escape hell. I wonder if the boundaries don't change, I'll suffer. Therefore, I live life so that I forget the suffering day after day. However, if it becomes unbearable in the end, I'll do the only thing left. I'll die. Although the past is painful, I hate death. Even now ..."

Tsutō did not hear his final words. While Zencho tuned the shamisen, he spoke softly.

"After that, Zencho never came back to Tamaya. No one knew what became of this dissolute Zen priest. One day, Zencho forgot his notebook about the Diamond Cutter Sutra at the base of a burning bush tree.

In his later years, when Tsutō fell into ruin and lived in seclusion in Samukawa in Shimōsa Province. This book was always on his desk. On the back of the front cover, Tsutō had written this verse:

> *At forty years old*
> *I see fields of violets*
> *And the morning dew, at last.*

That book is gone now. No one alive recalls that verse.

This story took place around year 4 of Ansei (1857). Mother was greatly interested in stories about hell and remembered this one.

As someone who spends most of the day in a study, I am a man who lives totally apart from the world of my great-uncle and this Zen priest. Speaking of interests, I'm not a man who has a special interest in the frivolous entertainment or ukiyo-e of the Tokugawa era. Moreover, certain feelings are easily provoked in me by the words *Hell of Loneliness*, so I try to pour my sympathies into their lives. I don't think that's a contradiction. Why? Perhaps it means I am a man who suffers the torments of the *Hell of Loneliness*.

(February 1916)

9

FROGS

I'm now lying beside an ancient lake. Many frogs are there.

Reeds and cattails grow thickly all around the lake. Beyond the reeds and cattails, tall poplar trees growing in a row sway gracefully in the wind. Beyond them lies the quiet summer sky with clouds like fine glass shards always glistening. Everything there is far more beautiful than reality when reflected in the lake.

The frogs never tired of croaking during long days in the lake. If you listen for a moment, those croaks are the only sounds you'll hear. They are engaged in vigorous, heated debates. Talking frogs are not confined to the time of Aesop.

Of them, the frogs on the reed flowers spoke like university professors.

"What is the purpose of water? It exists so that frogs can swim. What is the purpose of insects? They exist so frogs can eat."

In the lake, the frogs croaked, "Ribbit. Ribbit." With the frogs mostly submerged beneath the watery surface of the lake, reflecting the sky, grasses, and trees, naturally, the chorus of their voices was impressive. At that precise moment, a snake asleep at the root of a white poplar was jolted awake by the racket of croaks. As he raised his crooked neck, he looked toward the lake and licked his lips as if still drowsy.

"What is the purpose of the Earth? To grow the grasses and trees. And the grasses and trees, what is their purpose? To provide shade for frogs. Thus, isn't the vast Earth for the frogs?"

The snake listened a second time to the voices in unison and snapped his body like a whip. As he slithered into the reeds, his black eyes gleamed and watched the events on the lake with great caution.

"What is the purpose of the sky? It's there to hang the sun. What is the purpose of the sun? To dry the backs of frogs.

"Consequently, isn't the vast sky for frogs? Water, grass, trees, insects, Earth, air, and the sun exist for all frogs. There's no room for doubting the fact that every last thing in the universe is for frogs.

"I've explained these facts before all of you and would like to offer my heartfelt thanks to the god who created the entire universe for us. The name of God shall be praised."

The frog looked up at the sky, swiveled one eyeball around, and spoke with mouth wide open.

"The name of God shall be praised—"

Before the frog finished his words, the snake's head seemed to stretch as if readying to strike. In a flash, the eloquent frog was in his mouth.

"Ribbit. Ribbit. That's awful."

"Croak. Croak. Oh no, that's terrible."

"Oh no! Ribbit. Croak."

While the frogs in the lake shouted in surprise, still holding the frog in its mouth, the snake took cover in the reeds. The ensuing uproar was unprecedented, perhaps not since the lake was created. While wailing, a young frog among them asked, "Everything exists for us: the water, grass, trees, insects, Earth, sky, and sun. So, what about snakes? Are snakes here for us?"

"Um, snakes also exist for frogs like us. If snakes don't eat us, the number of frogs will only increase. If that happens, the lake ... the world will become cramped. Therefore, snakes come to eat frogs.

The eaten frogs can be thought of as sacrifices for the happiness of the many. That's it. Snakes benefit frogs. Every single thing in this world is for all frogs. The name of God shall be praised."

This was the answer I heard from an elderly-looking frog.

(September 1917)

10

SAN'EMON'S CRIME

It was the end of year 4 of Bunsei (1821). A samurai named Hosoi San'emon worked as a mounted guard on the 120-acre estate owned by a retainer, Harunaga, Prime Minister of Kaga. This samurai had killed a young man named Kazuma, the second son of Kinugasa Tae, but not in a duel. One night around the Hour of the Dog, eight at night, it appears that below the southern riding ground under the cover of darkness, Kazuma tried to kill San'emon on his way home from a Noh recitation meeting. Instead, he was killed by San'emon.

Harunaga heard about this incident and ordered San'emon to attend an audience. The order was not unexpected at all. First, Harunaga was an intelligent lord. As expected, he was an astute lord in all things and did not leave matters to his underlings. He felt uneasy if he did not personally hand down the judgment and order its execution. One time, Harunaga gave rewards and punishments to two falconers. This story illustrates a facet of Harunaga's honor in dealing with issues. Below, I'll outline the main points.

The Falconry Inspector sent an official report to the Falconry Office that stated a herd of red-crowned cranes had descended on unharvested rice fields in Ichikawa village in Ishikawa District. A junior elder directly informed the Lord, who seemed greatly satisfied. Around seven the next morning, the lord went to Ichikawa village with his retinue.

Starting with the exceptional falcon specimen, Fujitsukasa, graciously bestowed by an official decree, he brought two great falcons and two peregrines with him.

The name of the falconer of Fujitsukasa was Aimoto Kizaemon. On that day, the lord intended to see Fujitsukasa. After the rain, the paths between the rice fields became unstable for walking. Falcons soared through the sky, and the red-crowned cranes abruptly flew away.

Watching this situation, Kizaemon forgot himself in a moment of anger and cursed, "What did that bastard do?"

He was suddenly aware he was in the lord's presence. Cold sweat moistened his back. He squatted and waited for the blow.

"I've made his lordship laugh heartily. It's my error, may the lord pardon me."

The lord was moved by Kizaemon's loyalty. After returning to the castle, the lord granted him new land worth one hundred *koku*, issued an imperial decree for the unaffiliated, and graciously appointed him the official in charge of the Falconry Office.

Later, the official falcon Fujitsukasa became the responsibility of Yanase Seihachi and was a sick bird for a short time. One day, the lord summoned Seihachi and was informed about the illness of Fujitsukasa, who had already fully recovered. Seihachi humbly told the lord he had been unable to catch anyone because of the bird's recent recovery. The lord hated Seihachi's cleverness and ordered him to capture people.

Since then, Seihachi had to place the mashed feed and bait of small white rice grains in a feeding tray worn on the head of his son Seitarō. Then, he released Fujitsukasa in the morning and the evening. The falcon gradually learned to swoop down to the feeding tray worn by someone. For now, Seihachi reported the method for catching people to the assistant falconer. That sounds amusing. By an imperial order, tomorrow, he will go to the southern riding ground and try to catch the tea attendant Ōba Jūgen.

If he goes out to the riding ground around seven in the morning, Ōba Jūgen will be made to stand in the center. By the lord's will, Seihachi cared for the falcons.

When Seihachi released Fujitsukasa, the falcon immediately went straight to and grabbed the feeding tray worn on Jūgen's head.

Seihachi succeeded but remained agitated. He pulled out a small blade for raising the tidbit treat with one hand and leaped at Jūgen to stab him. The lord said, "What are you doing, Yanase?"

Seihachi did not fear the lord's words. The falcon caught the prey, and the tidbit had to be raised. When about to stab Jūgen, the lord flew into a rage and may have ordered a weapon to be brought. He shot his usual training pistol, instantly killing Seihachi.

In the second story, Harunaga usually paid special attention to San'emon. Once, while capturing a crazed man, the foreheads of San'emon and another samurai were injured.

The other man was bruised purple between his eyebrows, and San'emon, near his left temple. Harunaga summoned the two and rewarded them for their highly commendable conduct. Then he asked, "Well, does it hurt?"

The other man answered, "It's the happiness of gratitude. A fortunate wound doesn't hurt."

Sounding distressed, San'emon said, "If the wound does not hurt, I can't say I'm alive."

Since then, Harunaga thought San'emon was a man of integrity. At any rate, he believed that man was not glib but was reliable.

This time, too, Harunaga believed there was no shortcut other than asking San'emon for the details.

San'emon, who received the command, timidly served his superior. However, he showed no signs of embarrassment. A shadow of resolve was suggested on his slightly moody, taut, muscular, and tanned face. First, Harunaga asked, "San'emon, did Kazuma launch a sneak attack on you in the dark? It seems he held a grudge against you. What was the grudge?"

"What grudge? I have no idea."

Harunaga thought for a moment, then again asked, "Don't you remember anything about him?"

"I would not say remember. But I think something did lead to the grudge."

"What is that?"

"It happened four days ago. It was the year-end tournament at the dōjō of Instructor Yamamoto Kozaemon. At that time, I refereed instead of Kozaemon. I witnessed only the matches of those listed in the catalog. When we reached Kazuma's match, I was the referee."

"Who was Kazuma's opponent?"

"He was Tamon, the heir to Hirata Kidayū, a personal attendant to the lord."

"Did Kazuma lose that match?"

"Yes, he did. Tamon scored one strike to the forearm and two strikes to the face. Kazuma didn't even have one strike. It was an embarrassing defeat in a best-of-three match. I don't know, but he may have resented me as the referee."

"So Kazuma thought you showed favoritism as the referee?"

"I believe so. I favored no one. I had no reason to be biased. But I think Kazuma suspected favoritism."

"How is it, ordinarily? Do you recall quarreling with Kazuma?"

"We've never argued, but ..."

San'emon hesitated for a moment but showed no sign of further delaying his words. His expression seemed to be wondering in what order to speak now. Harunaga's expression softened as he quietly waited for San'emon to speak. San'emon soon said, "It was simply this. The day before the match, out of nowhere, Kazuma apologized for his rudeness earlier. However, I had no idea what this earlier rudeness was. I even asked. Kazuma gave a strained smile but didn't answer.

"I told Kazuma that if I couldn't recall the rude act, I also don't remember any reason for an apology. Kazuma seemed to understand, but I may have misunderstood and honestly said not to worry about it. I remember him forcing a smile again and chuckling."

"Did Kazuma misunderstand again?"

"I don't know, but it was a trivial matter not worth bothering with. There's nothing other than that."

Another short silence emerged.

"What was Kazuma's character? Did he seem deeply suspicious?"

"I don't think he was deeply suspicious. I'd say he seemed young and not ashamed to show his feelings. Instead, he was a bit temperamental."

San'emon paused for a moment. Rather than speaking, he sighed.

"Additionally, the match with Tamon was important."

"What do you mean by an important match?"

"Kazuma was an intricate paper cut-out. However, if he had won that match, he should have been added to the catalog. To be fair, Tamon was in the same predicament. Being in the same class, Kazuma and Tamon were students evenly matched in skill."

Harunaga was silent for a moment, perhaps in thought. He had a sudden change of heart and now moved the questioning to the night San'emon killed Kazuma.

"Are you sure Kazuma was waiting for you at the riding ground?"

"That may be so. It began to snow early that evening, so while holding an umbrella, I passed below the riding ground. I went unaccompanied and was not wearing rain gear. The winds strengthened and quickened, and snow blew in from the left. I instantly tilted my half-open umbrella around to the left. Kazuma struck at that moment and slashed only the umbrella and not my hands."

"Did he try to stab you without yelling anything?"

"I think there was nothing."

"At the time, who did you think it was?"

"I had no time to think. The moment the umbrella was slashed, I automatically jumped to the right. My clogs had already come off by that time. The second strike came. It cut a six-inch slash in the sleeve of my haori. As I jumped again, I quickly drew my sword. I think I cut Kazuma's abdomen at that moment. My rival said something."

"What?"

"I didn't understand what he said. But he sounded ferocious. That's when I thought, Oh, it's Kazuma."

"Did the voice sound familiar?"

"No, it didn't."

"So what made you think it was Kazuma?

Harunaga stared at San'emon, who said nothing, and attempted to prod him by repeating the same words. This time, San'emon's eyes dropped to his *hakama* trousers, and he didn't readily open his mouth.

"San'emon, why?"

Harunaga assumed a solemn demeanor, like a different man. The quick change of behavior was a customary technique employed by Harunaga. With eyes cast down, San'emon finally opened his sealed mouth. However, the words that slipped out did not answer "Why?" His sudden words of apology for a crime were unexpectedly disheartened.

"Unfortunately, a samurai who would serve commendably was killed, turned into rust on a sword, in a crime committed by me."

Harunaga frowned slightly, but his usually stern eyes scanned San'emon's face. San'emon continued speaking.

"Kazuma's grudge was reasonable. When I refereed, I played favorites."

Harunaga's frown deepened.

"A little while ago, you said you had no reason to show favoritism."

"That hasn't changed."

San'emon continued to speak like he was confessing as he considered each word.

"I favored no one. As I said, but I didn't want Kazuma to lose or help Tamon to win. But with just that, I can't say there was no favoritism. I placed more hope on Kazuma than Tamon.

"Tamon's talent was his attention to detail. This unorthodox skill deemed that winning was all that mattered, no matter how cowardly the act, and focused solely on winning and losing.

"Kazuma's talent was not so lowly. To the very end, his righteous talent truly approached that of his rival. Even after several more years, I don't think Tamon would have progressed to Kazuma's level."

"Why did Kazuma lose?"

"That's the point. I thought I wanted Kazuma to win more than Tamon. However, whenever I refereed, I had to cast off all biases.

"When I stood holding a fan between the bamboo swords of two men, I had to follow the path of divine justice. Because I thought this, I made the effort to only be fair in the face-off between Tamon and Kazuma.

"However, as I said earlier, I wanted Kazuma to win. The balance of my heart leaned toward him. Because my heart wanted to level the balance, naturally, I added a weight to Tamon's tray. Thinking about it later, I added too much. Instead of being lenient on Tamon, I was too severe on Kazuma."

San'emon paused again. Harunaga listened in silence.

"With both men in the *seigan* sword stance equally ready to attack or defend, neither one made the first move. Did Tamon see an opening during that time and strike Kazuma's face? Kazuma yelled a battle cry as he deftly countered. Simultaneously, he hit Tamon's forearm. My favoritism began at this moment.

"I was certain Kazuma won that point. Whether he won or not, I believed his strike with the bamboo sword was timid. This second thought dulled my decisions.

"I failed to raise the fan over Kazuma as I should have. For a short time, the two men continued to stare at each other in the seigan stance. This time, Kazuma initiated a hit on Tamon's forearm. Tamon swept away the bamboo sword and hit Kazuma's forearm.

"The hit on Tamon's forearm seemed weaker than the one on Kazuma's. At least, it can't be said it was more spectacular than Kazuma's hit. But at that moment, I raised the fan for Tamon. That is, I gave the first winning point to Tamon. I thought I made a mistake. Behind these thoughts was the idea that a referee doesn't make mistakes. Those who believed a mistake had been made whispered that Kazuma had been favored."

"Then what happened?"

Harunaga looked disgusted as he urged the closed-mouth San'emon to speak.

"The two men rubbed the tips of their bamboo swords as before. This time, I remember the back and forth in the longest exchange of blows. However, Kazuma seemed to quickly touch his bamboo sword to his opponent's and make a sudden thrust. The thrust was strong. At the same time, Tamon's bamboo sword hit Kazuma's face.

"I raised the fan straight up to declare a simultaneous strike. However, that time might not have been a simultaneous strike.

"Or I may have been confused about who struck first. No, the thrust came before the bamboo sword struck his face. But the two who struck simultaneously entered their fourth face-off. The initiator this time was Kazuma. He thrust once more.

"Then Kazuma slightly raised the tip of his bamboo sword. Tamon tried to hit Kazuma's trunk under the bamboo sword. Then, in just ten rounds, the sides of their swords scraped each other. However, Tamon finally entered his opponent's space and hit Kazuma's face."

"His face?"

"That hit was splendid. It was a win by Tamon without a doubt in anyone's eyes. After being struck in the face, Kazuma slowly grew impatient. Although I saw his impatience, I wanted to raise the fan for Kazuma. As much as I thought that, the fact is I hesitated to raise the fan.

"A short time later, the two men exchanged blows for just seven or eight bouts. What was Kazuma thinking during that time? He tried to body slam Tamon. I wondered what he was thinking because Kazuma never attempted body slams. I was jarred by that thought, which was natural. When I thought Tamon opened his body, surprisingly, he was struck again in the face.

"Until the final match, nothing astonishing happened. Finally, I raised the fan for Tamon for the third time. This could be called my favoritism. If viewed from the balance of the heart, a slight loss of balance was added. However, Kazuma failed the important match because of this favoritism. I was the source of Kazuma's rage. Now, I think this was a natural, unsurprising course of events."

"Well, when you were slashed, you realized it was Kazuma?"

"That's not clear to me. But thinking about it now, I may have felt I needed to apologize to Kazuma somewhere deep in my heart. Because of that, I immediately knew the thug had to be Kazuma."

"You felt sorry about the final moments of Kazuma?"

"Yes, that's true. As I mentioned earlier, I believe it is inexcusable to needlessly take the life of a samurai poised to distinguish himself in the important service to the lord."

San'emon stopped speaking and lowered his head. In the December cold, sweat lightly glistened on his forehead. Harunaga, whose mood had changed, gave several dignified nods.

"Good. Good. I understand your heart. What you did may be wrong. Moreover, it was senseless. But from now on ..."

Before Harunaga stopped speaking, he glimpsed San'emon's face.

"When the sword struck, you knew it was Kazuma. Well, why didn't you refrain from delivering the fatal blow?"

When Harunaga asked San'emon this, his proud, tanned face rose. The defiant glint previously in his eyes remained.

"I had to strike him down. I, San'emon, am a retainer. That said, I'm also a samurai. Although I pity Kazuma, I feel no pity for a lawless scoundrel."

(December 1923)

11

THE DREAM

I was exhausted. Of course, my shoulders and neck were stiff, and the insomnia was horrible. Occasionally, when I was drowsy, I was prone to dreaming. Someone once said, "Colorful dreams are proof of poor health." Perhaps aided by my work as a painter, the dreams I see weren't without color.

A friend and I entered through the glass door of a cafe in a run-down part of town. Outside the dusty glass door was the railroad crossing of the train that blew the new buds on the willow tree. We sat at a corner table and ate food from a bowl. What remained at the bottom of our wooden bowls after eating were snake heads, a little over an inch long. The colors in that dream were vivid.

My boarding house was in a freezing suburb of Tokyo. When I became depressed, I climbed the embankment behind the boarding house and watched the tracks of the prefecture-run train line. Several tracks shone on the gravel stained by oil and rust. On the embankment on the other side, a branch reached out at an angle from what looked like a chinquapin evergreen. That scene could accurately be described as melancholy. It perfectly fit my mood more than Ginza or Asakusa. As they say, *Fight poison with poison.* I squatted alone on the embankment and sometimes had that thought while smoking a cigarette.

It's not that I didn't have any friends. One was a Western-style painter, the young son of a rich man. He saw I was in low spirits and suggested I go on a trip. He kindly said to me, "I'll raise the money somehow."

Even if I took a trip, I had no doubt it would not cure my melancholy. I fell into this depression three or four years ago. I decided to distract myself for a short time with a trip to far-off Nagasaki, but once there, none of the inns interested me.

In the inn where I settled in at night, many large moths attracted to light fluttered and danced around. In the end, I suffered terribly and returned to Tokyo in less than a week.

In the afternoon with lingering frost needles, I felt the urge to create on the way home from picking up a postal money order. With money, I could use a model. My fitful urges to create grew stronger, too. But first, instead of going back to the boarding house, I went to the M House and hired a model to finish a human figure on a size 10 canvas. This decision invigorated me after a long period of depression. "If I can finish this painting, I'll be fine with dying." That feeling was practical.

The model hired from M House had a fairly plain face. However, her body, especially her breasts, was, without a doubt, splendid. Her hair was pulled back and hung down in thick locks. I was satisfied with this model. After I had her sit on a wicker chair, I set to work immediately.

The naked woman held a rolled-up English-language newspaper instead of a flower bouquet and posed with her head tilted and legs crossed. I faced the easel and suddenly felt tired. My north-facing room had only one hibachi.

I started a charcoal fire in the hibachi, but the room still hadn't warmed up. Seated in the wicker chair, the muscles in her thighs sometimes twitched reflexively. As I moved the brush, I was irritated each time that happened. More than being exasperated with her, I was mad at me, a man who can't buy one heater. At the same time, I couldn't help feeling tense and irritated with myself.

"Where do you live?"

"Where I live? In Sansaki-chō in Yanaka."

"Do you live alone?"

"No, I rent with two friends."

As we chatted, I gradually added color to an old canvas painted with a still life. Her head tilted, but she showed no expression at all. In addition to her words, her voice was monotone. I only thought that was her inborn nature. She was comfortable with me and sometimes continued posing beyond the scheduled time. However, I had a reason to feel oddly pressured by her figure that didn't move, even her eyes, at unexpected moments.

My work did not go well. When I finished the day's work, I rolled around on the rug, massaged my neck muscles and head, and lazily gazed around the room. Other than the easel, my room only had a wicker chair.

Occasionally, the wicker chair creaked despite no one sitting on it, perhaps the cause was the humidity. Those times spooked me, and I'd rush out and go for a walk. I call it a walk, but I only followed the embankment behind the boarding house to Inaka-machi, home to many temples.

However, I faced the easel day after day with no break. The model came to work every day. Meanwhile, I felt more oppressed by her body. Without a doubt, I envied her health. She was always expressionless, stared at a corner of the room, and lay on the pale red rug. As I moved the brush over the easel, I sometimes thought, This woman resembles an animal more than a human being.

On one slightly warm afternoon, I faced the easel and diligently moved the brush. Today, the model seemed more sullen than usual. I finally felt savage power toward the woman's body. An aroma emerged from under her arms or somewhere. That aroma was close to the stench of the skin of the black race.

"Where were you born?"

"XX town in Gunma Prefecture?"

"XX town? That town has many weavers."

"Yeah."

"Do you weave at a loom?"

"I wove when I was a child."

I noticed her nipples were getting bigger as we talked. They were close to coming apart like cabbage sprouts. I continued moving the brush as single-mindedly as always. I couldn't help fixating on the unsettling beauty of her nipples.

The wind kept blowing that evening. I woke with a start and went to the bathroom of the boarding house. When I was fully awake, I slid open the shōji door and walked all around my room. I stopped my legs without realizing it, and my eyes drifted down to the pale red rug, particularly where my feet stood in the room. The toe tips of my bare feet repeatedly stroked the rug. Surprisingly, the rug felt like thick fur.

"What color is the underside of this rug?"

This sort of thing worried me. Strangely, I was afraid to lift it and look at the underside. After I went to the toilet, I immediately got back into bed.

When I finished working the next day, I was more depressed than usual. Oddly, staying in my room didn't put me at ease, and I went out to the embankment behind the boarding house. The area was already beginning to get dark. Mysteriously, however, the upright trees and telephone poles were visible despite the dim light. As I walked along the embankment, I was tempted to scream but suppressed the temptation. While I felt like only my head was walking, I walked down to the shabby Inaka-machi by the embankment.

As usual, almost no foot traffic was seen in Inaka-machi. A single Korean cow was tied to a telephone pole on the roadside. As the Korean cow stretched her neck, it stared at me with strangely teary eyes like a woman's. Its expression looked like she had been waiting for me to come. I saw a quiet challenge to war in the cow's expression. *I'm sure that cow will have that look when it faces the butcher.* This feeling made me uncomfortable. I became increasingly depressed and turned down an alley to avoid passing by there.

One afternoon a few days later, I again faced the easel and brandished the brush with all my might. Naturally, the model who lay on the pale red rug didn't even move her eyebrows. For half a month, I continued to fail to create with the model in front of me. However, we did not reveal an iota of our feelings to each other.

My feelings of being coerced by her only strengthened slowly. She didn't even wear a shirt during her break. Also, she responded listlessly to my words. Today, however, her back was turned to me when she stretched her legs on the rug. I discovered a mole on her right shoulder, and then, she began to speak.

"Sensei, many slender stones are laid out in the road to this boarding house."

"Yeah …"

"That's a placenta burial mound."

"A placenta burial mound?"

"Yes, it's a rock placed as a sign of a buried placenta."

"How did you know?"

"I read the writing," she said and looked at me over her shoulder. The expression on her face was close to a brief sneer.

"Is everyone born covered by a placenta?"

"You're talking nonsense."

"I think people are covered by a placenta when born."

"?..."

"You know, it feels like a puppy."

I started to move the brush that didn't move forward in front of her. Not move forward? However, the reason was not a lack of willingness. I felt like I was searching for a wild expression always in her.

It's beyond my ability to express. I felt an irresistible urge to avoid this expression. Perhaps, I wanted to avoid this expression by using the tools and brushes for oil painting. In other words, what will I use? While I moved the brush, I remembered stone clubs or swords in a museum somewhere.

After she went home, I opened a large art book of Gauguin's work under a dim electric light and gazed at each of the Tahiti paintings. Suddenly, I noticed I was repeating these words several times in my mouth.

"I think it should be this way."

I had no idea why I repeated those words. However, I felt uneasy and had the maid lay out the bedding, took a sleeping medication, and fell asleep.

When I opened my eyes, it was close to ten. I was on the rug, perhaps, because of the evening warmth. More than that, I was troubled by a dream I saw before waking. I stood in the middle of the room and was trying to strangle her to death with one hand.

I knew it was a dream. Her face was tilted and, of course, had no expression. She slowly shut her eyes. At the same time, her breasts swelled, round and beautiful.

Veins faintly appeared in her dimly glowing breasts. I felt no concern over strangling her. No, I sensed something akin to the pleasure of finishing as expected. Her eyes finally stayed shut, and she quietly died.

After I woke from this dream, I washed my face and drank two or three cups of strong tea. But my mood only became more depressed. I didn't think I wanted to kill her at the bottom of my heart. Beyond my awareness as I smoked a cigarette, I stifled my odd excitement and waited for the model to come.

She hadn't arrived at my room by one o'clock. I was greatly distressed as I waited. I thought about going out for a walk instead of waiting for her but was too scared to go out. I stepped outside of the shōji door of my room. My nerves couldn't stand even that meaningless thing.

Sunset gradually closed in. I walked around my room and waited for the model who wasn't going to come. Meanwhile, I recalled an incident from twelve or thirteen years ago.

I was still a kid. I was lighting sparklers at sunset. Of course, I wasn't in Tokyo but on the veranda of the country home where my parents lived.

Someone shouted, "Hey! Stop that!" Not only that, someone shook my shoulders. I meant to sit on the veranda. Faintly aware, I glanced back. I squatted in front of the onion field behind the house and methodically set the onions on fire. In no time, my matchbox was empty.

While smoking, I couldn't help thinking about times I knew very little about myself in my life. This thought felt more eerie than unsettling to me. In last night's dream, I strangled her with one hand. But if I wasn't dreaming …

The model didn't come the next day either. Finally, I went to M House to check on her well-being. But M's proprietor didn't know what happened to her. I became more uneasy and got her address. According to what she said, she should have been in Sansaki-chō in Yanaka.

M's proprietor said she lived in Higashikata-machi in Hongō. I made my way to her lodging in Higashikata-machi around the time the lights turned on. It was a Western-style laundry painted pale red on a backstreet.

Two workers were busy ironing shirts in the laundry with a front sliding glass door. I leisurely slid open the door. Somehow, I hit my head on the door. The sound startled the workers and surprised me.

I timidly entered the shop and called to a worker.

"Is Miss So-and-so here?"

"She hasn't come home since the day before yesterday."

These words distressed me. I thought about asking more. I was careful not to provoke their suspicions if something had happened.

"Sometimes, she leaves and doesn't come back for a week," said one worker with a pale complexion who stopped ironing. I keenly felt feelings close to scorn in his words. I got angry and quickly left the shop. But that was still okay.

As I walked the streets of Higashikata-machi with many dilapidated houses, I suddenly remembered seeing this in a dream. The pale red Western-style laundry, the worker with the pale complexion, the iron glowing from the fire, going to ask about her was exactly what I saw in a dream several months—or years ago.

After I left the laundry in that dream, I walked these lonely streets alone. Nothing else remained about the memory of the earlier dream. However, if something were to happen now, I felt that it might instantly turn into an incident from that dream.

(1927)

12

THE FOUNDLING

"Shingyō Temple stands in Nagasumi-chō in Asakusa. It's not a large temple, but it houses a wooden statue of Saint Nichirō and has a suitably distinguished lineage. In the fall of Meiji year 22 (1889), a baby boy was abandoned in front of the gate of this temple. Of course, that was also the year of his birth, but no name was written on the paper.

"The baby was swaddled in an old, checkered, yellow silk baby garment. A woman's zōri sandal with a broken strap was discarded near its pillow.

"At this time, the head priest of Shingyō Temple was an elderly man called Tamura Nissō. While he was conducting the morning service, the gate guard, also advanced in age, came with news of the abandoned baby. The priest facing the Buddhist altar barely turned toward the gate guard and casually said, 'Is that so? You'd best cradle the child and bring it here.'

"The gate guard nervously brought the child. The priest immediately took it and soothed it.

"'Oh, what a cutie. Don't cry. Don't cry. From this day on, I will care for you.'

"After this time, the gate guard, who was favored by the priest and had the side job selling sacred anise and incense at the temple, often told this story to visitors.

"As you probably know, the priest named Nissō was originally a plasterer from Fukagawa. He was a deformed man with pock-marked skin. When he was nineteen, he fell off of scaffolding. After a short loss of consciousness, he aspired to Buddhahood.

"The priest named the abandoned baby Yūnosuke and began to raise him as his son. Because women had no influence in the temple since the Meiji Restoration, this was not an easy place to raise a child.

"From protecting him to giving him milk, the priest looked after him during breaks from chanting sutras. Once, when Yūnosuke had caught a cold or some other illness, Priest Nissō held the feverish child to the chest of his Buddhist robe and draped crystal prayer beads over one arm until he finished chanting the sutras for the memorial service for Nishitatsu of the Riverside, a major benefactor of the temple.

"But if possible during that time, Priest Nissō deep down wanted the child to meet his birth mother. Despite being a bold man, he was sensitive. The priest stepped up to the sermon seat. If you go there, even today, an old card stating *Monthly sermon on the 16th* hangs on a front column of Shingyō Temple.

"Occasionally quoting from Japanese and Chinese legends, he told stories that stressed never forgetting the kindness and affection between parent and child to show gratitude for Buddha's benevolence.

"Although the sermon days were routine, no one came forward to say, 'I am the orphan's mother.'

"Well, that's not so. When Yūnosuke was three, a woman wearing white face powder visited and said she was his mother. However, that was probably a scheme for a misdeed using the orphan as a pretext. When pressed for answers, only suspicions arose. The hot-tempered Priest Nissō seldom resorted to brute force, but after uttering biting remarks, he immediately drove her off.

"Then, in the winter of year 27 of Meiji (1894), rumors of war between Japan and China surfaced again across the world. Of course, when the priest returned from the temple kitchen on the 16th, sermon day, a refined woman of thirty-four or -five gracefully followed. Beside the hearth where a kettle hung in the temple kitchen, Yūnosuke was peeling a mandarin orange.

"As soon as she spotted the boy's figure, the woman somehow found it hard to approach him and prostrated herself before the priest. In a quivering but determined voice, she said, 'I am this child's mother.'

"Surprised by this, Priest Nissō was dumbfounded for a moment and unable to greet her. While the woman was indifferent to the priest and stared at the tatami, as if she were memorizing something, her emotional turmoil was evident throughout her body. She meticulously expressed her gratitude for his raising the child until today.

"After that went on for a short while, the priest raised a reddish-orange ceremonial folding fan to interrupt the woman's words and urged her to tell why she had abandoned the child. The woman dropped her eyes to the tatami and told this story.

"Exactly five years ago, her husband opened a rice store in Tawara-machi in Asakusa. He tried his hand at stocks but squandered the household wealth. Like absconding in the night, they went down to Yokohama.

"The burden was the baby boy, who had recently been born. To make matters worse, she had little milk. On the night they would finally leave Tokyo, the couple abandoned the crying baby in front of the gate at Shingyō Temple.

"They knew little when they went to Yokohama without boarding a train. The husband got a job at a delivery business. The wife became a maid at a yarn shop.

"For two years, the couple worked hard. During that time, their luck turned. In the summer of the third year, the owner of the delivery business noticed her husband's honest work and helped him open a small branch on the main street in the Honmoku district that was finally being developed. At the same time, needless to say, the wife quit her job and went with her husband.

"The branch shop did fairly well. The next year, a healthy baby boy was born to the couple. Of course, memories of the pitiful abandoned baby lingered at the bottoms of their hearts. The wife, especially, always vividly remembered the night they left Tokyo each time she poured scant milk into the baby's mouth.

"The shop was busy. The child grew bigger each day. Some savings were deposited in the bank. For a while, they lived their lives in a happy home.

"But that good fortune didn't last long. When they seemed ready to smile, especially in the spring of Meiji year 27 (1894), the husband came down with typhus and died before a week passed. If that wasn't enough, the woman might have given up, but she couldn't let go.

"Even the child born with such difficulty suddenly died of dysentery before the hundredth day anniversary of his father's death. The woman cried day and night as if she had gone insane. No, not just then, but for the next six months, she lived every day mostly in a daze.

"When her sorrow faded, her spirit was lifted by thoughts of seeing the abandoned baby.

"'If that child is healthy, no matter how hard it is, I'd like to take him back and raise him.'

"This thought made her restless. She immediately boarded a train. As soon as she arrived at her old home, Tokyo, she went to the front of the gate of Shingyō Temple. Again, it was the morning of the sixteenth, the sermon day.

"The woman thought she'd rush to the kitchen and ask someone about the boy. Of course, she couldn't see the priest until the sermon ended. She was frustrated by having to wait but mixed in among the many virtuous men and women filling the main temple and half-listened to Priest Nissō's sermon.

"That day again, the priest returned to the story when Lady Renge met five hundred children and kindly explained the preciousness of the love and gratitude between parents and children. Lady

Renge laid five hundred eggs. Those eggs floated down the river to be raised by the king of the neighboring country. The five hundred sumo wrestlers born from those eggs attacked the castle of Lady Renge, their mother they didn't know. When Lady Renge heard this, she climbed to the turret on the castle and said, 'I am the mother of all five hundred of you. The proof is here.'

"While producing milk, she squeezed with her beautiful hands. Milk poured from the breast of the lady on the high turret, like a spring with five hundred streams, to the mouths of the five hundred wrestlers without missing one. That parable from India stirred unusual emotions in the heart of the unfortunate woman who heard the sermon without truly listening. Thus, when the sermon ended, the woman holding back tears hurried from the main temple down the corridor to the kitchen.

"Priest Nissō listened to her entire story and introduced Yūnosuke, who was beside the sunken hearth, to his mother, now a stranger, after five years. Naturally, the priest understood the truth in her words. When she embraced Yūnosuke and held back her sobs for a time, the tears accompanying a smile in the eyes of the open-hearted and free-spirited priest glistened under his eyelashes.

"Without saying what happened later, you can probably guess. Yūnosuke returned with his mother to their home in Yokohama. After the deaths of her husband and child, she followed the suggestions of the owner of the delivery business and his wife and began to teach expert needlework. She was able to make a humble but adequate living."

When the visitor finished his long story, he picked up the teacup set before his knees but didn't bring it to his lips. He looked at my face and quietly added, "I am that abandoned child."

As I NODDED WITHOUT A WORD, I poured the cooled-down hot water into the teapot. I guessed at our first meeting that the story of this adorable child was the personal story of the early years of my guest, Mappara Yūnosuke.

After a brief silence, I spoke to the guest.

"Is your mother doing well now?"

His answer was surprising.

"No, she died last year, but the woman I described was not my mother."

The guest noticed my surprise, and a smile flitted over his eyes.

"Her husband working as a rice dealer in Tawara-machi in Asakusa, the move to Yokohama, and the hardships were not lies. However, I later found out that she lied when she said I was the baby abandoned by her. Last year, when my mother died, I was responsible for the shop's business affairs, and, as you know, the shop sold yarn, so I made rounds of the Niigata neighborhood. I rode the same train as the owner of the purse and handbag shop next to my mother's house in Tawara-machi.

He spoke without being asked. My mother had given birth to a daughter. The baby died before the shop closed. After returning to Yokohama, I immediately went to look at the family register without my mother's knowledge. Of course, as the handbag maker said, a girl was born during the Tawara-machi days, and she died after three months. What was my mother's intention? She fabricated the lie of the abandoned child to raise me, who wasn't her child.

"What was she thinking? Until today, I don't know how many times I have wondered that. Not knowing the truth, the most reasonable reason was Priest Nissō's sermon that stirred a queer emotion in my mother who was left behind in this world by her husband and child. Did my mother feel like playing the role of mother to me, who never knew her? She might have learned of my abandonment at the temple by a worshipper who came to hear a sermon. Perhaps the temple gate guard told her."

When the guest paused, he sipped his tea as if remembering, while his eyes looked lost in thought.

"Then, you are not that child. Did you talk to your mother about knowing you were not her child?"

"No, I said nothing. My saying that would have been too cruel to her. I did not say a word until the day she died. I think speaking about it would have been cruel to me, too. My feelings toward my mother underwent a complete change after I realized I was not her child."

"What does that mean?" I asked, staring at the guest.

"I am more nostalgic than before. Since learning of that secret, to me, a foundling, my mother became a better human being than my mother."

The guest gave a deeply touching response, as if he did not know he was a human being more than a child.

(July 1920)

13

ASAKUSA PARK

SCENARIOS

1

A large, unlit paper lantern hangs in the Niōmon temple gate in Asakusa. The lantern is slowly raised as if surveying the crowded stalls lining the road. However, only the lower part of the large lantern does not disappear. Scores of pigeons fly back and forth before the gate.

2

The shops in the temple compound are seen vertically from the Kaminarimon temple gate. The Niōmon gate can be seen in the distance. All the trees are withered.

3

At the shops on one side, a man wearing a raincoat strolls by with a twelve- or thirteen-year-old youth. Once in a while, the boy lets go of his father's hand and stops in front of a toy store. From time to time, of course, the father scolds the boy. As if he forgot about the boy, however, he occasionally gazes at the display window of a hat shop.

4

The upper half of the father's body looks like that of a man from the countryside. His face is unshaven. The boy's face is more sweet-looking than cute. Crowded shops are behind them. They walk over to them.

5

They see a toy shop at an angle. The boy stops in front of this shop and watches a toy monkey climbing up and down a rope. No one can be seen inside the toy shop. The boy's figure is visible to just above his knees.

6

As the monkey climbs up and down the rope, the tail of a tail-coat dangles down, and a silk hat tilts back on its head. Behind the rope and the monkey is deep darkness.

7

While the boy is looking at the monkey, he suddenly realizes that his father is gone from this side of the street. He nervously looks around. He spots something further ahead and dashes in that direction at top speed.

8

A man looks like his father from behind—but only to above the knees. The boy desperately chases after this man and grabs the sleeve of his raincoat. The surprised man's face turns back but, unfortunately, it isn't his father's. He is a cosmopolitan gentleman with a neatly trimmed mustache. An expression filled with disappointment and confusion crosses the boy's face. The gentleman briskly walks away from the boy. The dazed boy stands alone with the Kaminarimon gate far behind.

9

Once again, he sees a man who resembles his father from behind. This time, however, it is the upper half of his body. The boy follows this man and glances up fearfully at his face. Niōmon is far ahead of them.

10

The man is facing forward. A mask covers his mouth. His face looks closer to that of an animal than a man. His smile has a hint of malice.

11

Standing as if completely bewildered near one row of shops, the boy watches this man pass by. Unfortunately, no matter where he looks, he never sees his father's figure. After a moment's thought, the boy begins to walk without direction. Two girls dressed in Western clothes pretend to not glance back at him.

12

In the display window of an eyeglasses shop, amid the line-up of eyeglasses for nearsightedness, eyeglasses for farsightedness, binoculars, magnifying glasses, microscopes, and protective glasses, the head of a Western-style doll wears a pair of eyeglasses and a smile. Behind the boy standing in front of the window, the upper half of his body is seen at an angle. Then, the doll's head changes into a human head and speaks to the boy.

13

"Please, buy and wear eyeglasses. You must wear eyeglasses to find your father."

"There's nothing wrong with my eyes."

14

He sees the display window of an artificial flower shop at a slant. All the artificial flowers have bloomed in bamboo baskets and ceramic pots. The largest ones are the tiger lilies on the left. The plate glass of the display window reflects the upper half of the boy's body in a hazy image, like a spirit.

15

The plate glass of the display window separates the boy's upper body from the artificial flowers. The boy touches the plate glass. Perhaps, only his face is cloudy, fogged by his breath.

16

The tiger lilies are in the display window. It is dark behind them. At some point, the buds hanging beneath the tiger lily flowers are gently beginning to open.

17

"Please, look at my beauty."
"But aren't you an artificial flower?"

18

He sees the display window of a tobacco shop from the corner. Among a line-up of cans of cigarettes, boxes of cigars, and pipes, a card hangs at an incline. The writing on the card is *Smoke from ciga-rettes is the gate to Heaven.* Smoke slowly rises from a pipe.

19

The boy stands to the right in front of the display window filled with smoke. But this is also just above his knees. Three castles float lazily in the smoke. The castles look like a three-dimensional model of the Three Castles trademark.

20

One of these castles has a gate where a soldier armed with a gun stands. Many hemp palms sway beyond the iron lattice gate.

21

Above this castle gate, this phrase floats up nearly unnoticed on the side.

Those who enter this gate will become great.

22

The figure of the boy walks here. The display window of this tobacco shop stands at an angle behind the boy. The boy turns slightly, looks, and then quickly walks off again.

23

Inside the bell tower, with only a hanging bell visible, a hand pulls a rope to tap the bell with a wooden bell hammer. One, two, three times. Only pine trees are outside the bell tower.

24

He sees a target-shooting shop at an angle. The targets are cigar boxes stacked in the back and Hakata dolls in the front row. In front of them is a line of air rifles. One doll is a Western woman wearing a dress and holding a fan. The boy timidly enters this store, picks up an air rifle, and carelessly aims at a target. No one is in the target-shooting shop. The boy's figure is visible to just above his knees.

25

The doll of the Western woman gently spreads her fan to hide her entire face. Then a cork ball hits this doll. Of course, the doll falls backward and lands face up. Behind the doll is only darkness.

26

In this target-shooting shop, the boy picks up the air rifle again. This time, he enthusiastically aims at the target. Three shots, four shots, five shots, but the target does not fall once. The boy reluctantly takes out a silver coin and leaves the shop.

27

First, only a square object is visible in the dim light. This square object seems to suddenly turn on like an electric light, making characters float up on the side. On the top *Park, District 6* is written. On the bottom, *Night Watchman Station* is written. The top is white on black. The bottom is red on black.

28

In the upper part in the back of the theater, one window lit by firelight is visible. The remains of various peeling posters are on the wall with a rain gutter that runs straight down.

29

With the boy standing in the lower part in the back of the theater, for a short time, he doesn't go in either direction but looks up at a tall window. He's unable to see anyone in the window. A sturdy bull terrier passes by the boy's feet while sniffing his scent.

30

In the upper part in the back of this theater, a dancer appears in the lit window and indifferently gazes at the street below her eyes. Of course, her figure, especially her face, is unfocused because of the backlight. But her pretty face, resembling the boy for a moment, appears. The dancer gently opens the window and tosses down a small bouquet of flowers.

31

As the boy's legs stand in the street, the small flower bouquet drops down. His hand picks it up. The bouquet quickly leaves the road and changes into a bouquet of thorns.

32

A blackboard has *North winds. Clear.* written in chalk. That blurs and then becomes *Strong south winds. Chance of rain.*

33

At a nameplate stall seen at an angle, samples arranged under a tent display well-known names like Tokugawa Ieyasu, Ninomiya Sontoku, Watanabe Kazan, Kondō Isami, and Chikamatsu Monza-emon. In an instant, these names change into ordinary names. Also, a pumpkin patch faintly floats beyond the nameplates.

34

Several movie theaters are on the opposite side of the lake. Of course, numerous electric lights are reflected by it. The upper half of the boy's body stands to the left of the lake. Wind sweeps the boy's cap onto the water. After panicking, the boy starts walking this way. He wears a look of mostly despair.

35

In a cafe window, several human shadows move beyond a tower of sugar, unbaked sweets, and a cup of soda water with a barley straw. The boy walks past this window and stops on its left. The boy's figure is visible to just above his knees.

36

Outside of this cafe, a middle-aged man and woman, perhaps husband and wife, enter side-by-side through the glass door. The woman holds a child wearing a cloak. Meanwhile, the cafe revolves to reveal the back of the kitchen where a single chimney stands. Back there, two laborers are busy shoveling. One portable oil lantern is lit.

37

The child's upper body is seen on a child's seat in front of the table. While the child happily smiles, he shakes his head and raises his hands. Nothing can be seen behind the child. At some time, each rose quietly starts to drop off one by one.

38

An automatic calculator is seen at an angle. Two hands constantly move in front of the calculator. Of course, they are a woman's hands. The opening of a drawer never stops. Only coins are inside.

39

The front cafe window does not change the boy's figure. A short time later, the boy suddenly turns around and briskly walks this way. When only his face becomes visible, he stops to look at something. His expression is close to surprise.

40

In a crowd, an auctioneer stands among spread-out fabrics. As he waves an obi sash, he fervently calls out to the crowd.

41

As he waves the obi sash held in his hand back and forth, one end appears to be two- or three-feet long. The obi pattern is an enlarged snowflake. The snowflake falls to the outside of the twirling obi, slowly circling.

42

Beneath shirts and pants hanging in an embroiderer's stall, an elderly woman sits alone by a foot warmer. Embroidered items are also set in front of the old woman. Several knitted wool articles are mixed in. A black cat at the base of the foot warmer licks his front legs from time to time.

43

The black cat sits at the base of the foot warmer. On the left, the lower half of the boy's body is visible. The black cat, unchanged from the beginning, now wears a fez with a long tassel on its head.

44

"Young Master, please buy a sweater."
"I can't even buy a hat."

45

The top half of the tired boy's body leaves the embroiderer's stall. The boy starts crying. Eventually, he composes himself, looks up at the sky, and begins walking this way once again.

46

Stars dimly flicker in the evening sky. A huge face hazily floats toward him. The face looks like the boy's father. Although it is filled with love, his sorrowful expression is somehow infinite. A little later, however, the face disappears like mist to some unknown place.

47

The street is seen lengthwise. When the boy is seen behind this place, he is walking away down this street. Few passersby are around. A man walks past the boy from behind. This man turns slightly to reveal the mask he's wearing. The boy does not look back even once.

48

Outside of a house built with a lattice door seen at an angle, three rickshaws facing backward are stopped in front of the house. There aren't many passersby. A bride wearing a bride's headdress and some other people come out through the lattice door and quietly enter the first rickshaw. When all three rickshaws have passengers, they run off, the bride's rickshaw in front. The back figure of the boy follows. Naturally, the people standing in front of the house with the lattice door don't even glance at the boy.

49

A long board has the writing: *A special production by XYZ Corp. The Lost Child. An Artistic Movie.* It changes into a sandwich-board man with this board on the front and back. Although the sandwich man is older, he walks down the road of shops. He resembles the cosmopolitan gentleman. Behind him, the street lined with various shops has many more people than before. The boy passes there and receives an advertisement being handed out by the sandwich-board man.

50

The same street is seen lengthwise. A lone disabled soldier using a crutch slowly walks away. At some point, the soldier changes into an ostrich. However, after it walks a little longer, it becomes the disabled soldier again. One mailbox stands on the corner of a backstreet.

51

"Hurry! Hurry! Death may come at any moment."

52

The mailbox standing on the street corner becomes transparent. A pile of countless letters is visible inside the cylinder. Then, the mailbox changes before his eyes. Behind the mailbox is only darkness.

53

In a town of geisha houses seen from an angle, two geishas come to a formal tatami room, leave through the lattice door lit by a votive lantern, and quietly walk this way. Neither one's expression can be seen. After the two geishas pass by, the boy's figure is walking away. He turns slightly and looks. He appears to be lonelier than before. The boy gradually gets smaller as he goes. A short mimic standing in the distance walks this way alone. As he gets closer, the area around his eyes can be seen, he vaguely resembles the boy.

54

A number of hair pieces dangle down around a large metal ring. A board reading *Bang Hair Pieces* hangs alongside the hair pieces. At some time, these hair pieces transform into a barber pole. Only darkness is behind the pole.

55

Outside of the barbershop, some men and women are moving on the other side of the large glass window. The boy peeks inside as he passes by.

56

After he looks at the profile of a man getting his hair cut for a short time, the man turns into many hair pieces dangling from the large metal ring. A sign hangs alongside the hair pieces. Now, the sign reads *Toupees*.

57

A hospital is built in the Vienna Secession style. The boy approaches from this direction and climbs the stone steps. When he enters through the door, he immediately descends the stairs again. After the boy goes to the left, the hospital quietly approaches and eventually becomes only the entrance. He pushes open the glass door, and a nurse comes out. The nurse stops at the entrance and fixes her gaze on something in the distance.

58 ·

The nurse's hands are interlocked on her knees. Her left hand held in front wears an engagement ring. However, the ring quickly falls off.

59

A concrete wall leaves only a sliver of sky. The wall becomes transparent, revealing four or so monkeys crowded inside iron bars. Again, the entire wall changes into a stage of marionettes. The stage is the interior of a Western-style room. The dolls of Westerners peek timidly around them. They see someone wearing a mask who looks like a robber hiding in this room. A safe is in a corner of the room.

60

A Western doll is prying open the safe, but the many fine strings attached to the doll's hands and legs are visible.

61

The concrete wall is seen at an angle. The wall no longer appears. The boy's shadow passes over there. After that, it is the shadow of a hunchbacked man.

62

The street is seen at a slant from the front. A fallen leaf on the street is blown around. A smaller fallen leaf dances down there. Finally, a piece of paper that looks like an ad from a magazine flies over. Unfortunately, the paper looks torn. He sees *Life, January Edition* in the largest Shogō type size.

63

A bench is under a large evergreen tree. Visible beyond the trees is a part of the lake seen earlier. The boy walks over there and sits dejected. He starts to wipe away his tears. Then the hunchbacked man from earlier comes over to the bench and sits. Occasionally, the wind shakes the evergreen behind them. The man takes a baked sweet potato from his pocket and gobbles it down.

64

The face of the hunchbacked man eating the baked sweet potato.

65

The bench is in the shadow in front of the evergreen. The man is eating the baked sweet potato. The boy stands, bows his head, and walks off somewhere.

66

The bench is viewed from above at an angle. A coin purse was left on the bench with transparent slats. Someone's hand gently picks up the coin purse.

67

The bench is in the shadow of the evergreen. Now, however, it is inclined. The hunchbacked man on the bench examines the contents of the coin purse. At some point, some number of hunch-backed men appear to the left and right of the hunchbacked man. Eventually, only hunchbacked men are on the bench. Like the first, they fervently search the contents of a coin purse. They converse about something.

68

Framed photographs of men and women hang in the display window of a photography shop. At some time, however, the men's and women's faces change into elderly faces. But only half of an elderly man with a goatee and a medal decorating his frock coat does not change. At some point, his face becomes the face of the first hunchbacked man.

69

Kannon-dō temple is seen from the side. The boy walks beneath it. A crescent moon hovers above the Kannon-dō.

70

The door is closed in a part of the front of Kannon-dō. Many people are worshipping before it. The boy, showing his back, walks there and glances up at Kannon-dō. Suddenly, he quickly walks up a slope past them.

71

Looking down from above at an angle, a handwashing basin is large and long. The flame flickers on the water where a few ladles float. The boy's illuminated face is emaciated.

72

The boy sits on the base of a large stone lantern and hides his face behind his hands.

73

A man stands behind the lower part of the stone lantern and says something in his ear.

74

Reasonably, only the face of the upper half of the man's body does not face this way. When he slowly turns, it is the man wearing a mask. A little later, his face transforms into that of the boy's father.

75

The top part of the stone lantern in front turns into a flame and burns up, leaving behind the pillar. After the flame burns out, a single chrysanthemum starts to bloom. This chrysanthemum flower is bigger than the conical roof of the stone lantern.

76

As before, the boy does not move from the lower part of the stone lantern. A policeman with his hat lowered over his eyes walks over and places his hand on the boy's shoulder. The boy is surprised, stands, and says something to the policeman. Pulled by the police-man's hand, he quietly walks away.

77

Now, no one is behind the lower part of the stone lantern.

78

The large lantern at the Niōmon gate is slowly raised. As before, it watches over the passageway of shops. Only the lower part of the large lantern never disappears.

(March 14, 1926)

14

TEN NEEDLES

1. Some People

I know things about the people in this world. Those people will intuit and analyze anything. In other words, one rose is beautiful to those people and, in the end, is seen among the Rosaceae family in a botany textbook, even when the rose is picked.

People with simple intuition are happier than those people. One virtue called seriousness cannot be given to those people who are intuitive and analytical. Those people waste their entire lives in a terrifying game. Every kind of happiness is reduced to nothing because it is analyzed by them. At the same time, happiness grows because all pain is analyzed. The words "if I had never been born" precisely apply to those people.

2. Us

We are not necessarily us. Our ancestors live on entirely inside of us. Unless we obey our ancestors in us, we will fall into unhappiness. The phrase *past karma* is used to metaphorically explain this unhappiness. In other words, *the discovery of ourselves* is the discovery of our ancestors who are inside of us and, at the same time, the discovery of the gods in Heaven who rule over us.

3. Crows and Peacocks

The most terrifying truth about us is that we cannot surpass ourselves. If all the optimistic blinders are taken off, a crow can never become a peacock. A one-line poem written by some poet is always the entirety of his poetry.

4. A Flower Bouquet in the Air

Science explains everything. The future also explains all. However, what we respect is science or art. That is to say, it is only a flower bouquet caught in midair in our spiritual leap. Don't say *L'homme est rien* (Man is nothing). We are not remarkably different *as human beings*. Baudelaire *as a human being* fills the mental hospitals. Simply, *Les Fleurs du mal* (The Flowers of Evil) and *Petits poèmes en prose* (Paris Spleen) will never be created by their hands.

5. 2 + 2 = 4

2 + 2 = 4 is true. In reality, however, countless factors must be acknowledged between the plus sign. In other words, every problem is included in this plus sign.

6. Heaven

If Heaven could be created, it would only be on Earth. This heaven may be a heaven that blooms roses in thorn bushes. In addition to the people who have resigned themselves to despair, in a word, have given up, only many dogs walk there. However, becoming a dog is not a bad thing.

7. Confessions

All confessions should touch our spirits. However, all confessions will not take the form of "Do not do what I did. Do what I say."

8. And Certain People

I know certain people, too. Those people know nothing about being easily bored by anything. They will get another woman, idea, China pink flower, or slice of bread. Thus, no one lives a life as luxurious as those people. At the same time, no one leads a life as miserable as those people.

Those people become slaves in various ways in no time. Even if Heaven is given to others, or the road to Heaven is given, in the end, Heaven can never become theirs.

The words *lose oneself in excessive desires* may be applied to those people. A fan of peacock feathers or a meal of a piglet fed only human milk would never bring satisfaction to those people. Inevitably, they must seek sadness and suffering. There is also the natural sadness and suffering given but not sought. A ditch is dug that severs those people from other people. Those people are not fools but are fools beyond fools. Saving those people would simply be to change them into people other than those people. For them, there is no road to salvation.

9. A Voice

Amid the shouts of many people, the voice of one speaker can never be heard. However, it can always be heard as long as a line of flames remains in our hearts. Sometimes, this voice may wait for the microphone of future generations.

10. Words

We have difficulty conveying our emotions to others. That depends on how others communicate them. The olden days of *The*

Flower Sermon cannot be understood when it does not resonate with the feelings of others, even in a newspaper article over one hundred or so lines.

The understanding of the word *he* is always *a second he*. However, *he* always grows like a plant. Thus, the word *he* in some era cannot be understood as *he* in some second era. Fortunately, *the second he* believes he understood the word *he*.

(July 1927, Posthumous manuscript)

15

TANEKO'S MELANCHOLY

Taneko received an announcement for the wedding ceremony of a businessman, her husband's superior. She anxiously brought this up to her husband as he got ready for work.

"Would it be terrible if I didn't go?"

"That would be bad."

While tying his tie, her husband answered Taneko in the mirror. That response directed more to Taneko's eyebrows rather than Taneko herself was reflected in the mirror on the dresser.

"Will it be held at the Imperial Hotel?"

"The Imperial Hotel?"

"Oh, did you know that?"

"Yeah, … hey, my vest!"

Taneko quickly picked up the vest and mentioned the ceremony again.

"Does The Imperial Hotel serve Western food?"

"That's obvious."

"That's what bothers me."

"Why?"

"Why? I have never once learned how to eat Western-style food."

"Can't anyone learn anything?"

Her husband threw on his jacket and carelessly donned his spring fedora. He glanced at the wedding notice on the dresser and said, "What? Isn't it April 16?

"It's the sixteenth and the seventeenth."

"It's still three days away. In the meantime, practice."

"Well, tomorrow is Sunday. Please, take me somewhere."

However, her husband quickly left for work without a word. As Taneko saw him off, she was touched by a faint melancholy. That was certainly affected by her physical condition. When she, a woman with no children, was alone, she picked up a newspaper in front of the long brazier and scanned each column, wondering if there was a relevant article.

Even *Today's Menu* did not touch on how to eat Western food. Was there an article on how one eats Western food? She suddenly felt that would be written in textbooks for girls' schools and promptly retrieved two old home economics textbooks from a drawer of a portable chest.

In no time, these books had become worn and smudged. They emitted the undisputed scent of the past. Taneko opened the books on her slender knees and more closely scanned the index than when reading a novel.

Washing cotton and linen fabrics: handkerchiefs, aprons, socks, tablecloths, napkins, lace, …
Floor coverings: tatami mats, rugs, linoleum, cork-backed carpets, …
Kitchen utensils: ceramic and porcelain ware, glassware, gold and silver utensils, …

Taneko lost hope in one book and examined the other.

How to bandage: rolled bandages, bandage wrapping, …

Childbirth: newborn baby clothes, maternity room, childbirth instruments, …
Income and expenditures: workers' credit unions, interest, business income, …
Household management: family traditions, housewife's tips, diligence and frugality, relationships, hobbies, …

Taneko lost hope and abandoned the books. She tied back her hair in front of the large fir-wood vanity and left. She agonized only about how to eat Western food.

The following afternoon, concerned about Taneko, her husband deliberately took her to a restaurant on a backstreet in Ginza. Taneko faced the table and was relieved no one else was there. As she wondered whether this restaurant was unpopular, she couldn't help but fret over the effect the poor business climate had on her husband's bonus.

"This is pitiful. There are no customers here."

"Don't be silly. I chose a time when there would be no customers."

Then, her husband picked up his knife and fork and began her lesson on how to eat Western food. His way was not necessarily correct. He plunged the knife into the asparagus again and again and poured all his knowledge into teaching Taneko. Of course, she was diligent. However, when oranges and bananas were finally brought out, she couldn't help thinking about the prices of these fruits.

After they left the restaurant, they walked the backstreets of Ginza. Her husband seemed satisfied after fulfilling his obligation. Again and again, Taneko reflected on how to use a fork or drink coffee in her heart. If by chance she erred, she felt a pathological anxiety. The backstreets of Ginza were quiet. The sunlight falling on the asphalt hinted at the coming spring. Taneko tended to hesitate and answered her husband without much thought.

This was the first time she entered the Imperial Hotel. As Taneko climbed the narrow steps behind her husband, who wore a formal kimono, she felt uneasy within the space of Ōya volcanic rock and tile. She sensed a large mouse running over the wall. Sensed? That was sensed. She tugged on her husband's sleeve and said, "Oh, Honey, a mouse ..."

Her husband turned, and a slightly bewildered look rose on his face. He only answered, "Where? ... It's your imagination."

Before she could speak to him, Taneko recognized her illusion. This awareness made it impossible for her not to fixate on her nerves.

They sat at a corner table and manipulated the knives and forks. Taneko's eyes sometimes surveyed the bride, wearing a *tsunokakushi* bridal headpiece. More troubling than that was the food on the plate. She felt the trembling of the nerves throughout her body when the bread entered her mouth. Especially when she dropped her knife, helplessness was her only option.

Fortunately, the banquet was slowly coming to an end. When Taneko saw salad on the plate, she recalled her husband's words.

"I think when the salad comes, the meal is over."

But when she thought she could finally take a breath of relief, she had to stand with the champagne glass for the toast. This was the most trying moment of the banquet. She timidly rose from her seat, raised her glass, but felt a tremor cascade down her back.

They turned down a narrow alley from the last train stop. Her husband was fairly drunk. While Taneko watched her husband's footing, she excitedly said something to him. Meanwhile, they passed in front of the word DINER in bright electric lights. As a man wearing no jacket joked with a waitress at the diner, he snacked on octopus while drinking sake.

Her eyes only glimpsed that scene, but she couldn't help but have disdain for the man with an unshaven beard. At the same time, she unconsciously envied the man's freedom. After they passed the diner, the remaining buildings were only houses that had been converted from shops.

The area grew darker. Taneko sensed the aroma of leaf buds that night and reminisced deeply about the countryside where she was born. Her mother took pride in having bought several fifty-yen bonds.

"You know, real estate has grown!"

The following morning, Taneko looked strangely unhealthy and spoke to her husband. He was in front of the mirror, tying his tie.

"Honey, have you read the morning paper?"

"Yeah."

"Did you read the article about the daughter of the owner of a bentō shop somewhere in Honjo going mad?"

"She went mad? What happened?"

As her husband passed his arms through the vest, his eyes shifted to Taneko in the mirror—to Taneko's eyebrows more than to her.

"Was she kissed by a worker or something?"

"Would something like that drive her mad?"

"That will do it. I thought so. I had a frightening dream last night."

"What kind of dream? This tie has expired for this year."

"I'm making some horrendous mistake. I don't know what I did. In the dream, I made some horrible mistake and jumped onto the train tracks because the train passed by there."

"When you thought you got hit, you woke up."

Her husband put on his jacket and his spring fedora. Still facing the mirror, he fussed over tying his tie.

"No, even after being hit, I stayed alive in the dream. This body became a complete mess. Only my eyebrows remained on the tracks. … After all, I was concerned only about how to eat Western food for the past few days."

"That may be so."

When Taneko saw off her husband, she kept talking, as if half speaking to herself.

"Last night, I made a huge mistake, even I don't know what I did."

Without a word, her husband quickly left for work. When Taneko was finally alone, on that day, she sat in front of the long brazier, poured tea from the teapot into a handleless teacup, and drank the tepid tea. Her spirit somehow lost its composure.

The newspaper in front of her published a photograph of Ueno in full bloom. She lazily looked at the photo and was about to take another sip of green tea. Suddenly, sparkling oil resembling mica floated on the tea's surface. It may have been a trick of her mind, but it looked exactly like her eyebrows.

"…"

Taneko rested her cheek on her hand, blankly staring at the tea, unable to muster the energy to tie back her hair.

(March 28, 1927)

16

DOUBTS

In spring one year over ten years ago, I was asked to give a lecture on practical ethics. For just one week, I stayed in Ōgaki-machi in Gifu Prefecture. Originally, I was weary of the bothersome nuisance of a hearty welcome and gratitude from local supporters. Earlier, I sent a letter of refusal to the teachers' organization that invited me. I had hoped to avoid the entirely unnecessary time wasters associated with the lecture, such as the send-off and welcome, a reception banquet, sightseeing at famous places, and other activities.

Fortunately, gossip dubbing me an eccentric seemed to have spread throughout this region a short time earlier. I eventually went there through the mediation of the mayor of Ōgaki and the president of the teachers' organization. Arrangements were made for every last one of my selfish wishes. I avoided inns, particularly ordinary hotels, and arranged for a tranquil house, the vacation home of Mr. N, a wealthy resident of the town. I intend to recount the full story of a tragic event I happened to hear about during my stay at that vacation home.

The place where I stayed was on a plot furthest away from the vulgar world of a walled compound reminiscent of Julu Fortress. In particular, the eight-tatami-mat study where I spent my days had poor sun exposure but was a calming sitting room with shōji doors and partitions imbued with quiet grace. The caretakers of the home—a married couple who looked after me—showed up whenever they pleased, unless on a special errand. They were not fond of this dark, mostly quiet eight-tatami room.

It was so quiet that I heard the white flowers dropping occasionally from the lily magnolia tree branches stretching above the hand-washing basin at the Buddha statue. I only went out to give a lecture every morning. In the afternoon and evening, I could live in peace in the sitting room. At the same time, I brought nothing more than a suitcase with reference books and a change of clothes, and often felt the spring chill.

Most afternoons, visitors distracted me, and I never felt lonely. But when I lit the fire in an old-fashioned lamp with a bamboo cylinder base, a world where human-like breaths flow instantly shrunk to only the area around me illuminated by a faint light. And even the area around me never felt comfortable.

In the alcove behind me, a bronze vase with no flowers was arranged to be imposing. Above that hung a scroll of a suspicious-looking Kannon goddess holding a willow branch. Black ink was vaguely discernible in the mounting of a sooty brocaded fabric. When I occasionally looked up from my reading and turned to look at this old Buddhist painting, I sensed the aroma of an unburned incense stick somewhere.

I felt enveloped by a temple-like serenity in this tatami sitting room. I often went to bed early but didn't easily fall asleep.

Outside the rain shutters, the voices of night birds, unknown distances away, startled me. Those voices stirred me spiritually to envision in my heart a castle keep above this home. While the castle keep, always visible during the day, overlapped three tiers of white plaster walls between the lush pines, countless crows scattered into the sky above the warped roof.

While sinking into a cold, shallow sleep, I was still conscious of a spring chill drifting in like water settling in the pit of my stomach.

Then one night, an incident occurred around the time the many days of lectures was scheduled to end. As I sat cross-legged as always in front of the lamp and casually indulged in reading, the door with the adjacent room suddenly slid open with an eerie silence.

The moment I realized the door was open, I automatically expected to see the caretaker. I was thinking about asking him to mail a few postcards and inadvertently glanced over.

In the gloomy darkness beside the sliding door, a man around forty, absolutely unknown to me, sat properly there. At that moment, more than amazed, the threat I felt was close to superstitious terror. That man flooded faint lamp light. Its glow cast an eerie ghostly form worthy of the shock.

When he faced me, as he spread out his elbows in the old-fashioned way and respectfully bowed his head, in a voice younger than I expected but strangely mechanical, the man greeted me.

"Please, excuse my intrusion during your especially busy time at night. Sensei, I'd like to ask you a special favor. I have come for your advice."

In time, I recovered from my initial shock. I calmed down while the man was speaking and inspected my companion. He had a broad forehead, sunken cheeks, refined gray hair, and moved in ways unexpected for his age.

He wore a shabby haori jacket not bearing a crest and hakama trousers. His hand held a fan near his knees. My nerves were jarred at that instant by a missing finger on his left hand. I was suddenly aware of that and instinctively couldn't look away from that hand.

Closing the book I had just begun, I bluntly asked, "What is your problem?"

Needless to say, his abrupt visit surprised and angered me. At the same time, I was suspicious because the caretaker hadn't announced this visitor.

However, the man was not discouraged by my cold words and bowed, bringing his forehead to the tatami again. In the usual tone of reading aloud, he said, "I apologize for being late to say this, but I am Nakamura Gendō. Of course, I've been attending your lectures every day, but with so many attendees, you probably don't remember me. Let this be the beginning of a relationship. In the future, I humbly ask for you to find the time to guide me in many ways."

At this point, I finally felt I understood the man's intention. However, the destruction of my enjoyable pastime of nighttime reading was nothing short of unpleasant.

"Are you saying you have questions about my lecture?" I asked.

I said quietly to myself and prepared words to drive him away, "If you have a question, you should ask during tomorrow's lecture."

However, my rival did not move one muscle in his face and dropped his staring eyes to the knees of his hakama trousers.

"No, I have no questions. None. The truth is, I want to hear your opinion, good or bad, about my behavior.

"You see, twenty years ago, I experienced an unimaginable incident. As a result, I no longer understand myself.

"Sensei, I ask the opinion of an expert in the field of ethics, such as you, because I thought you would have an innate understanding. What do you think? It may be boring, but will you listen to the story I came to tell you?"

I hesitated to answer. Naturally, I was surely an ethicist, but as much as I engaged my knowledge in this field to provide vital solutions to current, real-world problems, regrettably, I couldn't be conceited about being the owner of an effective, versatile brain. He appeared to immediately sense my uncertainty and raised his eyes from his knees covered by hakama trousers. As if half in appeal, he nervously peeked at my expression and kept speaking courteously in a slightly more natural voice than before.

"No, it's not that I must ask for your opinion on the relative merits. However, until this year, an unrelenting problem has plagued my mind. If a sensei like you, at least, hears about that pain, I'll feel some relief."

Hearing this, I had no reason, even out of obligation, not to listen to this stranger's story. At the same time, I felt an ominous premonition and a broad sense of responsibility weighing heavily on my spirit. I wholeheartedly wanted to sweep away these uneasy feelings and deliberately assume a cheerful bearing. I invited my companion on the other side of the hazy lamp to come closer.

"Well, I'll listen to your story. I'll listen, but I don't know whether my words will be helpful."

When the man called Nakamura Gendō picked up the fan from the tatami using his hand missing a finger, he gently raised his eyes while stealing glances at the willow-branch Kannon in the alcove. Then, instead of me, he began to tell this story, often pausing and speaking in a melancholy tone with weak inflection.

"THE INCIDENT OCCURRED in year 24 of Meiji (1891). As you know, that was the year of the Great Nōbi Earthquake. Since then, the city of Ōgaki had transformed completely, but at that time, there were two elementary schools. They were unrelated. One was built by the feudal lord and the other by the townspeople.

"I taught at K Elementary School built by the feudal lord. Two or three years earlier, I had graduated from the prefectural teachers' college, gained the confidence of the principal, and received a lavish monthly salary of fifteen yen as a senior teacher. Lately, the fifteen yen monthly wage has become a meager existence. Twenty years ago, it was not enough, but my life was free of hardships. Even among my colleagues, I became a target of envy.

"My family in both Heaven and Earth was one person, my wife. We had been married for only two years. My wife was a distant relative of my principal. Both her parents died when she was young, so until we married, the principal and his wife took care of her like a daughter.

"Her name was Sayo. Although it's strange for me to say, she was honest to a fault and easily embarrassed. On the other hand, she was too quiet and, by nature, lonely, barely noticeable like a shadow. To me, a married couple like us is not meant to be spectacularly happy but can pass the days in peace.

"That great earthquake happened on October 28, a day I'll never forget—maybe around seven in the morning. As I stood beside the well, picking my teeth with a toothpick, my wife was carrying the rice pot in the kitchen.

"The house collapsed on top of her. For one or two minutes, the terrifying rumbling ground roared like a great wind. The house crumbled instantly. Later, I only saw flying roof tiles. Without warning, I was covered by the falling eaves. For a short time during my confusion, the wave of an approaching huge tremor shook me.

"I was probably in shock. Should it be called confusion? Distraught as before, I sank into my seat. I glanced above the houses with caved-in roofs to the left and right like stormy seas. I lazily listened to the seething chaos of the rumbling earth, falling roof beams, splintering trees, crumbling walls, thousands of people running around in a bid to escape, and indistinct echoes of voices and other sounds.

"However, the instant I discovered something moving under the eaves across the way, I leaped up and raced there while shouting nonsense as if I just awakened from a bad dream. Under the eaves, my wife Sayo writhed in agony with the lower half of her body trapped under a beam pressing on her.

"I grasped my wife's hand and pulled, attempting to push her shoulders to help her sit up. The pressing beam did not move enough for a bug to crawl out. I was alarmed but pulled out the planks of the eaves one by one. As I pulled, I kept screaming, 'Hold on,' to my wife. Was I encouraging my wife or myself?

"Sayo said, 'It hurts. Please help me.'

"While not encouraging to me, my expression looked like that of a stranger as I tried to raise the beam with all my might. Both of my wife's hands were covered in so much blood her fingernails were no longer visible. Her trembling hands never stopped groping for the beam. Even now, this remains a vivid, painful memory.

"This happened long, long ago. When I suddenly realized something during this time, dense, black smoke from somewhere slid over the roof and blasted my face. Suddenly, I heard a deafening explosion beyond the smoke. Sparks like gold dust fluttered up into the sky. I tightly clutched my wife like I was crazy.

"Once more, I single-mindedly tried to pull my wife out from under the beam. But I could not budge her lower body at all. Again, I was showered by the smoke blowing in. While kneeling on one knee, I spoke to my wife out of frustration.

"'You may be wondering what's happening? No, I'm sure you are.'

"But I asked something but recall nothing. Then, I remember my wife clamping her bloody hands onto my arm and saying, 'Darling.' I stared at her face. It had lost all expression. Only her eyes were wide open; this gave her face an eerie appearance. Then only smoke or a burst of flame stirred by sparks assaulted me and blinded my eyes. I thought there was no hope.

"My wife, while alive, thought she would be burned to death by fire. While alive? Still holding her bloody hands, I screamed again. Once more, my wife said, 'Darling.' Inside the word 'Darling' this time, I sensed an infinity of meanings and feelings. While alive? I shouted something three times. I remember saying something like 'Die.' I remember saying, 'I'll die, too.' While I don't know what I said, I haphazardly picked up a fallen roof tile and hit my wife in the head over and over.

"What comes next may be nothing more than your understanding, Sensei. I alone survived. While I chased the fire and smoke burning down the town, I passed between the roofs of the houses blocking the roads like small mountains, and eventually saved a life in peril.

"Fortunately or unfortunately, I didn't understand anything. That night, while wishing for the light of fires in the dark sky with a few companions in a shed outside of a thoroughly crushed school, I still couldn't forget the flowing tears with no end in sight when I picked up the emergency food of a rice ball."

～

NAKAMURA GENDŌ PAUSED for a moment and dropped his cowardly-looking eyes to the tatami. Without warning, I had listened to this story and felt as though the spring chill in the broad sitting room pushed closer to my collar and couldn't muster the spirit to say "Of course."

The only audible sound in the room was the suction of the oil lamp. My pocket watch, resting on the desk, clicked to mark the exact time. When I thought the willow-branch Kannon in the alcove seemed to move, there were the sounds of faint exhales.

I raised my fearful eyes and stared at my companion, who sat there looking dejected. Was he making those breathing sounds? Was it me? Before I could resolve my doubts, Nakamura Gendō slowly began speaking in a soft voice.

"Needless to say, I grieved the death of my wife. Was that all? At that time, I received kind words of sympathy from my colleagues, starting with the principal, and cried in front of others without embarrassment. Strangely, however, the only thing I could never speak about was killing my wife during that earthquake.

"I thought that killing her by my hand was better than her being burned alive by fire.

"Because I disclosed only this, I wasn't sent to prison. Rather, the public had sympathy for me. Why was that? My throat closed up immediately when I tried to speak, and my tongue no longer moved.

"At that time, I believe the cause was rooted entirely in my cowardice. But the truth was more than simple cowardice; the cause lurked in a deeper place. However, that made me consider marrying again. Eventually, up to the point of saying I will enter a new life, even I didn't understand. When I understood that, I was unqualified to lead an ordinary life once again and was nothing more than a spiritually defeated man who deserved pity.

"The principal who became Sayo's parent raised the subject of remarriage with me. I well understood this was purely the result of a plan for my benefit. Around that time, a little over a year after the great earthquake, even before the principal broached this issue, he never once opened up a similar discussion to try to determine my true intentions.

"But when I listened to the principal, surprisingly, the marriage prospect was the second daughter of this N family, in whose home you are staying, Sensei. At that time, wasn't she the older sister of an eldest son, an ordinary fourth-grade student I sometimes helped with extracurricular studies? Of course, I declined.

"There's a dramatic difference in status between me, a senior teacher, and the wealthy N family. Beyond the relationship as a private tutor, I thought about the path to marriage and the unpleasantness of being cross-examined for no reason. Also, behind the reason I didn't move forward, I have no memory as sorrowful as the one who died, no matter how much time passed. Sayo's face, beaten to death by me, surely lingered like a comet's tail.

"The principal adequately considered my feelings. He patiently explained a myriad of reasons. They included: a man close to my age continuing a single life will have problems in the future; this marriage proposal is the wish of the other party; he would willingly act as the matchmaker, so there'd be no reason for bad rumors to arise; and once married, my hope to go to Tokyo to study would be possible.

"When told this, I had no reason to refuse outright. The daughter was a well-known beauty and shy, but attracted to the wealth of the N family, the principal repeatedly recommended her. He began to gently urge me with words like, 'Carefully think it over,' or 'You're getting older each year.' The year changed. Summer in Meiji year 26 (1893) started. When fall finally came, the arrangements for the ceremony were finished.

"From the time this matter was settled, I was oddly depressed. As strange as I thought that, no matter what I did, my old energy disappeared. For instance, even though I went to school, while leaning against my desk in the teachers' room and lost in cloudy thoughts, I often failed to hear the woodblock clapper signaling the start of class.

"Because of that, if asked what was bothering me, I couldn't explain why to myself. As if the gears in my head don't fit precisely in places, I have an eerie feeling, as though a secret transcending my self-awareness lurked beyond that disharmony.

"This situation continued for about two months. During vacation at the height of summer heat, one evening while on a walk, I peeked at the storefront of a bookshop behind a branch temple of Hongan-ji. At that time, five or six issues of *Fūzoku Gahō*, an illustrated popular magazine; together with *Yasō Kidan*, a ghost story collection; and *Gekō Manga*, the ukiyo-e works of Gekō, were lined up with covers printed using lithography.

"As I stood in front of the store, I mindlessly picked up a copy of *Fūzoku Gahō*. On the cover was a picture of collapsed houses and fires. Two lines were printed in large characters.

NOVEMBER 20 MEIJI 24 ISSUE
OCTOBER 20 EARTHQUAKE REPORT

"My heart leaped at that sight.

"While someone happily sneered in my ear, he seemed to whisper, 'That's it. That's it.' In the dim light of the storefront with no fire lit, I hurriedly opened the magazine. First came a picture of the old and young members of one family who had been battered by a fallen beam and ended in tragic deaths. The next picture showed the Earth split in two, swallowing a woman and a child as they passed by.

"Although each one does not have to be enumerated, *Fūzoku Gahō* unfolded the scene of the great earthquake two years earlier before my eyes. One by one, ghastly images of the collapse of the iron Nagaragawa Bridge, the destruction of the Owari Spinning Company, the exhumation of human remains by Third Division soldiers, and first aid being administered to the injured at Aichi Hospital. I was pulled into memories of those damned days.

"My eyes blurred. My body trembled. "Feelings of perhaps anguish or great joy completely swayed my spirit. When the final image was opened before my eyes, even now, my astonishment at that time vividly remains in my mind. It was a picture of a woman being hit in the waist by a fallen beam and tragically writhing in pain.

"Was that black smoke thickly swirling, with bright red sparks flying around, beyond a beam on its side? This woman was not my wife. Who was she? If it wasn't the end of my wife's life, what was it? I nearly shouted.

"The instant my surroundings suddenly got redder and brighter, my fear intensified. The smell of smoke that suggested fire smacked my nose.

"As I forced my spirit to calm down, I put down *Fūzoku Gahō* and looked around the storefront. A shop boy had just lit the fire in the hanging lamp and thrown a matchstick, now drifting in the twilight, into the street.

"Since then, I've become a gloomier man than before. Even now, what frightened me was an undefinable feeling of unease. Later, doubt rooted itself in my head and tormented me day and night. Saying that, was killing my wife unavoidable at the time of the great earthquake?

"I had doubts. To say it more bluntly, had I killed my wife with the spirit, from the beginning, of wanting to kill her? Did the great earthquake give me my only chance? Of course, before these doubts, several times I answered with resolve, 'No. No.'

"The something that whispered in my ear, 'That's it. That's it,' in front of this bookshop, and asked me with a sneer, 'Well, why couldn't you tell anyone that you killed your wife?' When I recalled these facts, I was shocked. Ah, if I killed my wife, why couldn't I declare that I had killed her? Why, even now, do I desperately hide that terrifying experience?

"Also, the vivid memory that returned to my memory was the disturbing truth that my heart harbored hatred of my wife, Sayo, at that time. If I must say this, even if I risk embarrassment, you may not understand, but my wife was a woman who, unfortunately, had a physical defect.

(The next 82 lines are missing.)

"Until that time, I was uncertain but believed that my moral convictions managed to triumph. When a calamity like that great earthquake occurred and all social restrictions disappeared from the Earth, did a crack also develop in my moral sentiments?

"Did my selfishness start a fire? I could only acknowledge my suspicion that I reached the point where I killed my wife because I intended to kill her. This means I admit my doubts. My eventual depression should be called inevitable.

"However, a streak of the bloody road was still in me.

"In that case, even if I hadn't killed my wife, she definitely would have been burned to death in the fire. So killing my wife should not especially be called my crime.

"One day, however, the season had already turned from the height of summer to late summer, and school began. All the instructors were seated around a table in the teachers' room. While drinking crude tea, we exchanged small talk about current events. The great earthquake of two years ago was brought up.

"I alone held my tongue and passively listened to my colleagues' conversation. The conversation jumped from topic to topic: the collapse of the roof of the branch temple of Hongan-ji, the breach of the embankment at Funa-machi, and the fissures opened in the streets of Tawara-machi. Before long, one teacher recounted the story of the wife of the proprietor of a sake shop called Bingo-ya in Naka-machi. She was trapped under a beam and could barely move. During that time, a fire started. Fortunately, the beam burned and broke. She barely escaped with her life.

"When I heard that, the field before my eyes instantly darkened. My breath seemed to stop for a short time. I felt like I would faint. At last, my colleagues turned to look at me and were shocked by my pale complexion and seeing me leaning against a chair. They gathered around and fussed over me, made me drink water, and gave me medicine. But I didn't have the time to thank those colleagues. Those horrifying doubts clumped together and filled my head.

"Did I kill my wife because I intended to kill her? Although the beam pressed on her, did I beat my wife to death despite the slimmest chance of saving her life? If I hadn't killed her in that situation, as in the story about Bingo-ya proprietor's wife, my wife might have had a chance of narrowing averting death and still be alive.

"With no compassion, I killed her with blows from a tile. I'm asking for your opinion, Sensei, about my pain created by that thought. In my pain, I intended to break off marriage talks with the N family and was determined to purify my body at least a little.

"When I finally reached that conclusion, my single-minded determination dulled my lingering regret. On the verge of holding a wedding ceremony, I suddenly said I wanted to break off the engagement. Therefore, I had to confess the course of events from the beginning of killing my wife at the time of the great earthquake and the pain I've felt until now.

"When the cowardly me reached the critical point, despite my internal urging, I could not summon the courage to act. I chided myself multiple times for my spinelessness. But this chiding was in vain, and I failed to take any action. The late summer heat transitioned to chilly mornings. Wasn't the day of the wedding ceremony fast approaching?

"Around that time, as I spoke less and less to anyone, I became utterly depressed. More than one or two of my colleagues warned me to postpone the wedding. The principal advised me three times to see a doctor.

"But then, out of consideration of the kind words like those said to me, I didn't even have the energy to appear to others to be concerned about my health. At the same time, based on the group's concern, I delayed the wedding with the pretext of illness. To me, that was an underhanded and cowardly act.

"The head of the N family probably misconstrued the source of my depression as an effect of being single. He frequently urged me to marry as soon as possible. It was October, the time of the great earthquake two years earlier, but a different day. Finally, the wedding ceremony was held on the N family's estate.

"Emaciated by daily anxiety, I wore a bridegroom's crested kimono. When I was escorted to the sitting room surrounded by imposing golden folding screens, I felt I had shamed myself that day. I hid away from others and worried like a villain who commits serious crimes. No, it's not a good feeling. I am a fiend who conceals the crime of murder and is plotting to steal the daughter and wealth of the N family.

"My face heated up, and my chest ached. If possible, in this case, I want to give a detailed confession about killing my wife. That feeling started to race violently around my head.

"Then, like a dream, fine white silk tabi socks appeared before me on the tatami. Next, I could see the hazy hem pattern of auspicious pine trees and cranes in a faintly wavy sky.

"My eyes were drawn to an ornate *kinran* obi sash with golden threads, then to a small ornamental *hakoseko* box purse and a white collar, and stopped at the Takashimada hairstyle adorned with glittering tortoiseshell pins and combs. I felt trapped with no escape, as if I were suffocating, and spontaneously placed both hands on the tatami.

"In a desperate voice, I said, 'I killed a person. I am a monstrous, evil criminal.'"

NAKAMURA GENDŌ FINISHED his story like this and stared at my face for a short time. After the lull, he forced a smile and said, "I won't tell you what happened next, but one thing I want you to know is that I was called a madman only on that day. I must live the rest of my pitiful life. Am I indeed a madman? Sensei, I'll leave that to your judgment.

"But even if I'm a madman, is my becoming a madman the fault of a monster that had sunk to the bottom of our human spirit? As long as that monster lives, even the people who ridicule me today as a madman, tomorrow may become madmen like me. That's what I thought, but what will happen?"

The lamp moved the chilly spring flame as usual between me and this queer guest. With the willow-branch Kannon behind me, I lacked the energy to ask even about the missing finger of my companion and only sat in silence.

(June 1919)

17

THE QUALITY OF A HERO

"Did the man named Xiang Yu truly have the quality of a hero?"

The Han general Lu Matong spoke these words as he stroked his sparse beard, lengthening his already long face. The faces of the ten men surrounding him, lit by a lamp placed in the center, floated up in the reddening camp night. The joy of today's victory, when the head of the Hegemon-King of Western Chu (Xiang Yu) was raised, still had not been erased from those faces smiling more than usual.

"I guess so," said one proud face with sharp eyes, who forced a wry smile onto his lips and stared at the space between Lu Matong's eyebrows. Why did Lu Matong seem a little upset? He continued, "He was powerful. They say he could bend the three-legged kettle made of stone at Yu Wang Temple. His strength was present in today's battle. For a moment, I thought my life was over. Li Zuo was killed. Ō Kō was killed. There was none of that strength. In reality, his strength was immense."

"Uh-huh."

While the other men kept smiling, they nodded, unconcerned. Beyond the camp was silence. Other than several blasts from a distant horn, neither the neighs of horses nor voices were heard. Amid this, the scents of withered tree leaves intermingled.

"But ..." said Lu Matong and scanned the group of faces but blinked once to emphasize his doubt.

"But that is not the quality of a hero. The proof is today's battle. The Chu army was only twenty-eight horsemen cornered at the Wu River. Against a huge army of innumerable allies, the battlefield provided no way out. The local administrator of the Wu River deliberately went out to greet them and said to cross by boat to the east of the Yangtze River. If the quality of a hero were in Xiang Yu, he'd cross the Wu River, even if it were filthy. Then, he'd return from defeat with a vengeance, unconcerned about his reputation."

"By doing so, the quality of a hero is being good with numbers."

Accompanying these words, quiet laughter rose from the group. Surprisingly, Lu Matong didn't flinch. When he let go of his beard, his body bent slightly. While he glanced occasionally at the proud face with sharp eyes, he gestured energetically as he spoke.

"It's not my intention to disparage him. But Xiang Yu ... well ... in front of his twenty-eight subordinates before the battle started today, he said, 'Heaven will destroy Xiang Yu. There is no shortage of manpower. The proof will be my destruction of the Han army three times with only that military force.' Three times? In reality, they fought and won nine times.

"If you ask my opinion, I thought it was cowardice. He blames Heaven for his failure. Heaven is troubled. If after crossing the Wu River, he rallies the brave men to the east of the Yangtze River and again fights to dominate the central plains, there will be nothing left to do.

"But that is not so. Being able to live honorably is to die. My saying that Xiang Yu lacks the quality of a hero is not because I'm bad at numbers. Trying to gloss over everything by saying it is Heaven cannot endure. I don't find that heroic. I don't know what scholars like Prime Minister Xiao say."

Lu Matong paused for a short time and looked to the left and right. His argument seemed valid. The group gave their silent assent while exchanging brief nods. Among them, only one proud face unexpectedly revealed a shade of emotion in his eyes. Seemingly charged with heat, his black pupils sparkled.

"Really? Xiang Yu said that sort of thing."

"He did."

Lu Matong shook his head up and down for emphasis.

"Is he weak? No, at least, wasn't he unmanly? I believe a hero should fight Heaven."

"That's true."

"Despite knowing Heaven's will, I believe one should fight."

"Yes."

"So Xiang Yu—"

Liu Bang* raised an intense look in his eyes and saw the light from a lamp shimmering autumn. Half speaking to himself, he slowly answered, "So, he had the quality of a hero."

---

* Liu Bang and Xiang Yu were rivals for control of China after the fall of the Qin Dynasty. Liu Bang won and unified China under the Han Dynasty, which lasted nearly four hundred years.

18

FATHER

This story took place during my fourth year in middle school.

In the autumn of that year, I went on a school trip, lasting three nights, from Nikko to Ashio. The instructions, *Gather at Ueno Station by 6:30 AM. Train departs at 6:50 AM,* were printed on the mimeographed handout given to us at school.

On that day, I rushed out of the house without eating a proper breakfast. It would take less than twenty minutes to the station if I went by train. As I thought this, I experienced a strange impatience. While standing in front of a red column at the station and waiting for the train, I was very anxious.

Unfortunately, the sky was cloudy. If the sounds of train whistles ringing at factories all around made the gray steam tremble, I wondered whether it would all turn to mist and drizzle down. Under that dreary sky, a train passed over the elevated track. A horse-drawn carriage passed through to a clothing factory. The door of each shop opened. Even at the station where I was, a few people were already there, standing around. Everyone was gloomily tidying up a face that seemed to lack sleep. It was cold. The discount train arrived.

Packed inside a crowd, I was hanging onto a strap when someone tapped my shoulder from behind. Confused, I turned around.

"Good morning."

I looked to see Nose* Isō. Of course, like me, he was wearing a navy blue uniform and slung a coiled-up overcoat over his left shoulder. He wore linen gaiters. A bento package and a canteen hung from his waist.

Nose graduated from the same elementary school as I and entered the same middle school. He neither excelled nor performed poorly in any subject. Yet, his trivial skill was in popular song. If he heard a song one time, he immediately remembered the melody. On the nights we stayed in an inn during school trips, he showed off this ability. He could do anything—recite poetry, play the *biwa*, comic *rakugo* storytelling, *kōdan* storytelling, voice impersonations, and magic tricks. Also, he had a knack for making people laugh through physical movements and facial expressions.

Unsurprisingly, he was popular among the students and well thought of by the teachers. We often crossed paths but were not close.

"You're early, too."

"I'm always early," said Nose, twitching his nose.

"But, I've been late recently."

"Recently?"

"For Japanese class."

"Oh, when Baba yelled at you? That guy also makes mistakes when writing Buddhist teachings with a brush."

Nose had the habit of not referring to the teachers with respect.

"That teacher yelled at me, too."

"Were you late?"

"No, I forgot the book."

"Jintan is annoying."

Jintan was the nickname Nose gave to Instructor Baba, taken

---

* Pronounced no-say

from the name of hard candy pellets that came in a tin. While they talked, they arrived at the front of the train station.

As if we had boarded together, the packed crowd finally got off the train and entered the station. We were early, and only a few of our classmates had gathered. We greeted each other with "Good morning." We competed to be the first to the wooden bench in the waiting room to get a seat. As usual, we talked energetically. Instead of speaking politely, everyone spoke casually to each other, like the older students. Our expectations for the trip, opinions about our classmates, and the poor reputations of the teachers flowed from our mouths.

"Izumi's smart. Because that guy has the privileges of an instructor, he never prepares in advance, not once."

"Hirano is smarter. When there's a test, he writes all the historical dates on his fingernails."

"Not to mention, the teachers aren't smart. Honma asks, 'Which comes first, i or e in *receive*?' Because he doesn't even know that, he covers up for being sloppy as a teacher and isn't teaching, right?"

In the end, only smartness was mentioned; not one good rumor emerged. Then, Nose sat beside me on the bench, read a newspaper, and critiqued the shoes of what looked like a craftsman, calling them Gap-kinley. At the time, a popular shoe brand was called McKinley. The man's shoes had lost their luster, and its toe was a gaping hole.

"Gap-kinleys are nice," he said. All at once, everyone burst out laughing.

Then, we got carried away and started searching out unusual people entering and leaving the waiting room. One by one, we hurled insulting remarks befitting Tokyo middle schoolers. Not one of the well-behaved students who fell behind in this activity was in our group. Among them, Nose's descriptions were the most scathing and richest in wit.

"Nose, Nose, look at that housewife."

"She has a face like a pregnant pufferfish."

"The guy in the red hat. What does he look like? Huh, Nose?"

"That's Charles V of Spain."

Finally, Nose alone took on the role of badmouthing.

At that time, one of us discovered a strange man standing in front of the timetable, closely examining the numbers. That man wore a rusty-looking, faded black suit and passed thin legs resembling the exercise rod tipped with balls through mousey gray trousers with coarse stripes. He looked quite old after spotting the half-white hairs sticking out beneath his wide-brimmed, old-fashioned fedora.

A gaudy, black-and-white checkerboard handkerchief was twisted around his neck. A long, cold-bamboo staff, resembling a whip, was tucked under his armpit. His dress, his posture, everything about him was an illustration cut out from *Punch*. You could think he was made to stand among the crowd at this station. Like new material to be insulted had emerged, one of our group, while laughing from his shoulders, tugged Nose's hand and said, "Hey, hey, what about him?"

All of us looked at the strange man. He slightly bent his body, pulled out a large, nickel pocket watch attached to a purple braided cord from his vest pocket, and painstakingly checked the numbers on the timetable. Looking only at his profile, I immediately knew he was Nose's father.

However, not one person in our group knew him. Therefore, everyone listened for suitable words from Nose's mouth to describe this comical character. As I prepared to laugh after hearing it, I stared at Nose's amused-looking face. As a fourth-year middle school student, I didn't have the judgment to infer Nose's feelings at that time. Perilously, I was about to say, "That's Nose's father," when Nose said, "That guy is a London beggar."

Needless to say, everyone burst out laughing. Someone in the group deliberately bent his body and imitated the way Nose's father took out the pocket watch. Instinctively, I looked down. The courage only visible on Nose's face then was missing from mine.

"That's a fair assessment."

"Look, look at that hat."

"Hikage-chō?"

"Is he from Hikage-chō?"

"No, a museum."

Everyone laughed heartily again.

On the overcast day, the train station was slightly darkened like sunset. Amid this dim light, I cautiously looked at the London beggar.

Just then, a faint beam of sunlight seemed to shine. A narrow band of light from the skylight in the high ceiling shone at a blurry slant. Nose's father was encircled by that light. Every object around him was moving. Movement was in the places where the eyes could and couldn't see.

Those movements were neither voices nor sounds and covered the interior of this large building like a mist. However, only Nose's father did not move. While an elderly man unrelated to this modern age and wearing Western clothes unrelated to this modern age, who, of course, transcended modernity, wore askew a black fedora, held a pocket watch attached to a purple braided cord in the palm of his right hand, he stood as before, motionless like a pump in front of the timetable.

When casually asked about it later, Nose's father, who worked at a university pharmacy in those days, said he wanted to see his son and our group off on the school trip on his way to work. Without telling his son, he went to the train station.

Soon after Nose Isō graduated from middle school, he contracted tuberculosis and died. When his memorial service was held in the middle school's library, in front of the picture of Nose wearing his school cap, I read his eulogy and included this line.

You were a good son to your mother and father.

(March 1916)

19

THE RIVERSIDE FISH MARKET

It was a spring evening last year, but the wind was still chilly around nine in the moonlit evening. Yasukichi and three friends walked around the riverside fish market. The three friends were the poet Rosai, the Western-style painter Fūchū, and the lacquerware craftsman Jotan. Their real names were not known, but they were known as masters in their fields. Rosai was also the oldest. As a trendy poet, he quickly rose to fame.

All of them were drunk. Fūchū and Yasukichi were teetotalers, but Jotan was a classic heavy drinker. They were the same as usual. Only Rosai's footing was a bit perilous at times. With Rosai placed in the middle, they walked the streets toward Nihon-bashi, buffeted by wind gusts smelling of fish.

Rosai was an Edokko, a true-born Tokyo native. His great-grandfather was close friends with Shokusan [Ōta Nanpo], the poet and writer, and [Tani] Bunchō, the painter and poet. Every one in the area knew about his home called Marusei by the River. A long time ago, Rosai left running the family business mostly to others while he indulged in poetry, calligraphy, and seal engraving. Unlike us, Rosai had a dashing personality. Of course, he was far removed from the ostentatious Yamanote and close to the rough-and-tumble downtown. He was right at home with things like the tuna sushi found at the riverside.

Rosai continued cheerfully talking with us, sometimes flicking his jacket's sleeve like it was in the way. Jotan quietly laughed and listened attentively to the conversation. In no time, we came to the riverbank. Going out to the riverside this way was strangely unsatisfying to all of us. A Western-style restaurant stood there. A white *noren* curtain hung in the moonlight, shining on one side. Even Yasukichi had heard quite a few rumors about this establishment.

"Do you want to go in?"

"That sounds good."

While we talked this over, we had already rushed inside the narrow shop ahead of Fūchū.

Two customers were sitting inside at a long, narrow table. One customer was a young fellow from the riverside. The other one looked like a factory worker. Two of us squeezed around the same table, sitting opposite the other two. Then we started to snack on fried fan shell and sip Masamune rice wine. Of course, the teetotalers Fūchū and Yasukichi did not stack sake cups. Instead, those two were voracious and finished off the food.

This shop had unvarnished, plain wooden tables and chairs. A reed screen from the Edo period surrounded the shop. Although they ate Western food, it didn't seem much like a Western restaurant at all. When the steak Fūchū ordered came, he asked for slices. Showing great respect, Jotan cut it with a knife. Yasukichi was only thankful for the brightness of the electric lights in this place. Rosai, too, seemed a bit amazed, perhaps because he was a native son. However, the man in the flat cap became Amitābha Buddha, exchanged sake cups with Jotan, and cheerfully conversed as usual.

In the middle of this, a customer wearing a fedora suddenly passed through the noren curtain. The customer buried his chubby cheeks in the fur collar of his overcoat, but instead of looking around, he seemed to glare around the narrow shop. Without a word of greeting, his large frame squeezed into the seat between

Jotan and the young fellow. While scooping up rice curry, Yasukichi thought, What an awful guy. He also thought, This is an Izumi Kyōka novel. He's either a guy dumped by a geisha or a man with a chivalrous spirit. However, today's Nihon-bashi doesn't move at all like a Kyōka novel.

After he ordered, the customer arrogantly smoked a cigarette. The more you looked at his figure, the more he fit the mold of a villain. His fat, ruddy face did not deviate from the mold, just like his haori coat of fine Ōshima silk and his signet ring. Yasukichi had suffered enough. He forgot about this customer and began talking to Rosai beside him. Rosai only gave half-hearted replies, like "Uh-huh" or "I see." Drained, he turned away from the electric light and deliberately pulled down his flat cap.

Yasukichi was forced to chat about food with Fūchū and Jotan, but the conversation didn't flow. Since the arrival of the fat customer, slight madness in the feelings of the three of us was an unavoidable fact.

When the customer's order of fried food came, he picked up the bottle of rice wine and tried to get it into a sake cup. Someone from the side clearly said, "Kō-san." The customer couldn't hide his surprise. When his startled face seemed to find the owner of the voice, his complexion changed instantly.

"Oh, that was you, sir?"

The customer doffed his cap and bowed several times to the voice's owner. That owner was the owner of Marusei by the River.

"It's been a while."

Rosai maintained a cool expression as he brought a sake cup to his mouth. The moment the cup was empty, the newest customer poured sake from his bottle into Rosai's cup. It was so funny to the others who had inferred Rosai's mood.

Kyōka's novel is not dead. At least at the riverside fish market in Tokyo, incidents like that still happen.

Nonetheless, Yasukichi's heart sank when they left the Western restaurant. Yasukichi felt no compassion for Kō-san. According to Rosai, that customer had a bad character. Strangely, I couldn't be cheerful. On Yasukichi's writing desk was *Maximes* by Rochefoucauld. He had recently started to read these pointed observations on human nature. Yasukichi sometimes thought about them while walking in the moonlight.

(July 1922)

20

FROM YASUKICHI'S NOTEBOOK

Woof!

One winter evening, Yasukichi took a bite of greasy-smelling fried bread in a drab and dirty second-floor restaurant. In front of his table was a white wall with cracks. A long sheet of paper reading *We Have Hot Sandwiches* was pasted at a slant. A colleague misread this as *We Have Not Sandwiches* and was puzzled.

On the left was the staircase going down. Immediately to the right was a glass window. From time to time, while chewing the fried bread, he lazily gazed out the window. Outside, a secondhand clothing shop with a zinc roof facing the street hung out blue work uniforms and khaki cloaks.

From six-thirty at night school, the English conversation meeting had already started. He, who was obligated to attend the meeting, had to get there by six-thirty after school, despite the inconvenience. This was not connected to not living in this town.

I'm sure that in a song by Toki Aika—if I'm mistaken, forgive me—he sings *If I came a long way and had to chew on this leathery steak, my wife, my dear wife, I love you.* Every time he came here, he remembered this song. He had not yet received the wife he yearned for the most. However, he gazed at the secondhand shop, chewed on the greasy-smelling fried bread, and read *Hot Sandwiches*, the words *my wife, my dear wife, I love you* spontaneously rose to his lips.

Yasukichi noticed two young naval officers seated behind him and drinking beer. He recognized one of them, the paymaster from his school. Unacquainted with naval officers, he didn't know this man's name. Not only did he not know his name, he didn't know whether he was an ensign or a lieutenant junior grade. He only knew that his wages passed through this man's hands every month. The other man was a stranger. Each time the two asked for refills, they'd say "More" or "Hey." Without making a sour face, the waitress frequently went up and down the stairs while holding cups in both hands. Because of that, the cup of tea ordered was not easily brought to Yasukichi's table. This wasn't the only place that happened. It was the same no matter what cafe or restaurant he went to in this town.

While the two men drank beer, they talked in loud voices. Of course, Yasukichi had no reason to listen to their conversation. But he was suddenly surprised by the words "Say, 'Woof.'"

He didn't like dogs. He was pleased to be counted among Goethe and Strindberg as literary figures who didn't like dogs. When he heard these words, he imagined a large Western dog that people tend to raise in this place. At the same time, he felt something creepy lurking behind him.

He subtly looked back but happily didn't see anything like a dog there. While that paymaster looked outside the window, he only grinned. Yasukichi guessed that a dog was below the window. However, something felt strange. Once more, the paymaster said, "Say, 'Woof.' Say, 'Woof.'"

Yasukichi twisted his body a little to look below the window facing him. What first caught his eye was an unlit hanging lantern that also served as an advertisement for Masamane something. There was also a rolling sunshade and leather sandal straps forgotten and left to dry on a rainwater bucket made from a beer barrel. There were also puddles in the street. What else was there?

He didn't see the shadow of a dog anywhere. Instead, there were twelve or thirteen beggars. One was looking up at the second-floor window. He appeared to be standing up and cold.

"Say, 'Woof.' Will you say, 'Woof?'"

The paymaster shouted this again. These words seemed to have the power to control the heart of the beggar. Still looking up, the beggar walked several steps to get under the window. Yasukichi discovered the practical joke of the paymaster, a man of bad character.

A practical joke? Maybe it was not a practical joke? If not, it was a test. This test is related to how much a man will sacrifice his dignity to satiate his hunger.

According to Yasukichi's thoughts, this is not a problem that should be tested now. Esau threw away his birthright as the firstborn for a meal of grilled meat. Yasukichi became a teacher for bread. It is sufficient to look at the facts. A psychologist's scientific curiosity would probably not be satisfied by that test. If that's so, today I taught the students *De gustibus non est Disputandum* [people like what they like]. Some bugs love eating knotweed. If you want to experiment, it's all right to try. As Yasukichi had these thoughts, he gazed at the beggar beneath the window.

The paymaster was quiet for a time. The beggar started to look up and down the street to calm down. Although I have no particular objection to imitating a dog, the eyes of the people nearby hesitated to look. Before his eyes settled down, the paymaster shook something as he poked his red face out the window.

"Say, 'Woof.' Say 'Woof' and I'll give you this."

The beggar's face instantly seemed to brighten with desire. From time to time, Yasukichi romanticized the idea of beggars. However, he never once felt compassion or sympathy. If he felt anything, he believed it would be stupidity or deceit.

However, when that child beggar tilted his neck slightly, and he saw his eyes sparkle, it slightly warmed his heart. This "slightly" was a little genuine. More than thinking it was heartwarming, Yasukichi loved the Rembrandt-like effect in that beggar.

"Can't you say it? Hey, say, "Woof."

The beggar frowned.

"Woof."

His voice was somewhat soft.

"Louder!"

"Woof! Woof!"

The beggar barked twice. A navel orange fell outside the window. No more needs to be written. Naturally, the beggar leaped at the orange, and the paymaster laughed.

A week later, Yasukichi went to the paymaster to get his monthly wages. The paymaster seemed to be in a hurry when he opened the ledger and spread out the documents. When the paymaster looked at his face, he said, "You're here for your wages." He also answered, "Yes." The paymaster was busy and didn't easily pass out the monthly wages. In the end, with the back of his military uniform turned toward Yasukichi, the paymaster worked the abacus.

"Paymaster."

After waiting a short time, Yasukichi seemed to be pleading. The paymaster looked over his shoulder. The words "I'll be right there" clearly came from his lips. Before that, however, Yasukichi followed with polished words.

"Paymaster. Shall I say, 'Woof?' Paymaster?"

According to Yasukichi's belief, his voice when he said that was kinder than an angel's.

The Westerners

Two Westerners came to teach English conversation and composition at this school. One was Townsend, an Englishman. The other was Starlett, an American.

Mr. Townsend was a balding, friendly older man who spoke Japanese well. By nature, a Western teacher, no matter how vulgar, will chat at great length on Shakespeare and Goethe. Fortunately, however, Mr. Townsend could hardly be said to understand the *literary* part of literary arts. When Wordsworth was brought up once, he said, "I don't know anything about poems, but I may like something Wordsworth wrote."

Since Yasukichi lived in the same resort area as Mr. Townsend, they commuted to school on the same thirty-minute train ride. While the two smoked Glasgow pipes on the train, they conversed about tobacco, school, and ghosts.

Despite Mr. Townsend, a Theosophist, having no interest in Hamlet, he was interested in the ghost of Hamlet's father. However, when the discussion turned to the occult sciences, for instance, magic or alchemy, as Mr. Townsend solemnly shook his head and pipe, a habit of his, he said, "The portal to the unknown is not as hard to open as the common man thinks. It's best not to touch that."

The other man, Mr. Starlett, was a very young, fashionable man. In the winter, he wore a dark green overcoat and wrapped a red scarf around his neck. Unlike Mr. Townsend, he sometimes peeked at newly published books. He gave a lengthy lecture titled *Recent American Novels* in the school's English conversation class. According to that lecture, great contemporary American novelists were Robert Louis Stevenson and O. Henry."

Mr. Starlett did not live in the same area but lived in a town along the train route and often rode the same train. Yasukichi could barely recall their conversations. His only memory was the time he waited for the train in front of the stove in the reception room.

Yasukichi yawned and talked about the boredom of a teacher's job. The handsome Mr. Starlett, wearing rimless eyeglasses, made a slightly queer face and said, "Becoming a teacher is not an occupation. Rather, it's a true calling, a vocation. You know, Socrates and Plato are two great teachers."

It doesn't matter whether Robert Louis Stevenson is a Yankee or something else. Ever since Mr. Starlett said that Socrates and Plato were teachers, Yasukichi decided to maintain a courteous friendship with him.

A Noon Nap
A Fantasy

Yasukichi left the dining hall on the second floor. After lunch, the civilian instructors usually went to the smoking room next door.

Today, he didn't join them but went down the stairs to the garden. From below, a non-commissioned officer was climbing up like a locust, skipping every two steps. When the officer saw his face, he suddenly gave a formal salute. As soon as he did that, he leaped over Yasukichi's head in one bound. Yasukichi returned a slight bow to the empty space and calmly continued down the stairs.

Among the evergreen and kaya trees in the garden, the flowers on a magnolia tree were blooming. Why don't the specially cultivated flowers of the magnolia tree ever seem to face south where the sun hits? Although similar, the magnolia kobus always faces south. As Yasukichi lit a cigarette, he celebrated the uniqueness of the magnolia. A wagtail flew down with one wing fluttering as a rock dropped there. The wagtail was not hostile to him. The shake of its small tail was a signal to guide him.

"This way! This way! Not that way. This way! This way!"

Following the wagtail's instructions, he walked down a path spread with gravel. What was the wagtail thinking? He suddenly flew up into the sky. But now, a tall engine mechanic was walking toward him down the path.

Yasukichi felt there was something familiar in the engine mechanic's face. Of course, after the engine mechanic saluted, Yasukichi hurried past him. While smoking his cigarette, Yasukichi continued wondering who he was. Two steps, three steps, five steps, …, on the tenth step, Yasukichi figured it out. That man was Paul Gauguin.

Or he was the reincarnation of Gauguin. Surely, before long, he'll be gripping a paint brush instead of a shovel. In the end, he was shot from behind by a crazy friend with a pistol. That's unfortunate, but nothing can be done.

Yasukichi followed this path to the plaza in front of the entrance. Two captured war trophy cannons stood among the pine trees and bamboo grass. If an ear was lightly pressed on the cannon barrel, what sounded like breathing could be heard. The cannon might have yawned. He sat beneath the cannon and lit a second cigarette.

A lizard glistened on the gravel of the carriage roundabout. A human being has a leg amputated. In the end, another leg cannot be produced. However, if a lizard's tail is cut off, another tail is immediately created. Holding the cigarette in his mouth, Yasukichi believed that was more Lamarckian than Lamarck. As he watched for a few moments, the lizard was turned, at some time, into a stripe of heavy oil dripping on the gravel.

Yasukichi finally stood. While following the painted school building, he passed through the garden again and came out at the athletic field facing the sea. How many military instructors were at the red-clay tennis court in fierce competition? Something exploded continuously in the air above the court. At the same time, faint white straight lines were sprayed on the left and right sides of the net. That was not a flying ball. Unseen champagne bottles were being opened. Gods in white dress shirts were enjoying drinks of champagne. Yasukichi walked around to the garden behind the school building.

The back garden had many roses, but not one flower had bloomed. Along the way, he discovered a caterpillar on a rose branch that jutted out into the path. At that moment, another one was crawling onto the adjacent leaf. They nodded at each other. They seemed to be commenting on him. Yasukichi quietly eavesdropped.

Caterpillar 1. When will this instructor become a butterfly? From the generation of our great-great-great-grandfathers, he has been crawling around the Earth's surface.

Caterpillar 2. People may not turn into butterflies.

Caterpillar 1. No, they probably do. Look, one is flying over there now.

Caterpillar 2. Of course, he's flying. But it's rather ugly! A human appears to have no sense of beauty.

While Yasukichi covered his forehead with his hand, he looked up at an airplane flying above his head.

A demon transformed into a colleague was cheerfully walking his way. A demon who once taught alchemy long ago now teaches applied chemistry to students. Grinning, he spoke to Yasukichi.

"Hey, do you want to get together tonight?"

Yasukichi plainly sensed two lines from Faust in the demon's smile.

Gray, worthy friend, is all theory,
    And green the golden tree of life.

After he left the demon, his shoes moved inside the school building. All the classrooms were empty. He peeked in one classroom as he passed by and saw a geometry diagram left unfinished on the blackboard. When the geometry diagram realized he had looked at it, it surely thought it would be erased. While instantly stretching and contracting, it said, "I will be needed in the next hour."

Yasukichi went back up the stairs he had descended earlier and entered the faculty room for the language and mathematics instructors. No one was there besides the bald Mr. Townsend. This older instructor was bored and kept whistling and trying to dance alone. Forcing a slight smile, Yasukichi went to wash his hands at the washbasin. When he looked in the mirror, before he knew what was happening, he was shocked to see Mr. Townsend had changed into a handsome young man. Yasukichi himself changed into an old man with gray hair and was hunched over.

Shame

Before Yasukichi left for class, he always prepared by reviewing the textbook. Because he received a monthly wage, he felt an obligation to not act recklessly. By its nature, the textbook contained a lot of the school's naval terminology. If he didn't deliberately investigate them, he might commit a ridiculous misinterpretation. For example, he might assume *cat's paw* refers to the paw of a cat, when in fact, it describes a light breeze.

One time, he was teaching second-year students about short works on navigation. The prose was dreadful. Although the wind groaned at the mast or the waves poured down the hatch, those waves and winds did not take on the least bit of life from the words. While he made the students read and translate the passage, he was the first to get bored. At these times, he was not moved to engage the students in discussions over issues concerning ideology or current events.

Fundamentally, a teacher wants to teach anything other than the curriculum. Morals, hobbies, and philosophies of life, or whatever they're called, it doesn't matter. Rather than what's in the textbook or on the blackboard, the teacher wants to teach anything close to his heart. Unfortunately, students do not want to be taught any material not found in the textbook. No, it's not that they don't want to learn. They hate learning. Because Yasukichi believed this, despite being bored to death, he had no choice but to continue reading and translating.

However, even when he wasn't bored, Yasukichi was troubled by having to make meticulous corrections as he listened half-heartedly to the students' translations. After just thirty minutes had passed of the one-hour classroom time, he finally halted the reading and translating. In its place, this time, he read and translated the passage sentence by sentence.

As usual, navigation in a textbook was extremely tedious. At the same time, his manner of teaching was relentlessly and extremely boring. Like a ship crossing a windless zone, he missed verb tenses, misused relative pronouns, and plowed through dead ends.

Meanwhile, he suddenly realized that he had prepared only four or five lines. Once he finished them, he would face an unforgiving stormy sea filled with the hidden reefs of naval terminology. He glanced sideways at the clock. Twenty minutes remained until the bugle would sound for the break. As meticulously as possible, he translated the four or five lines prepared for class. However, when he started the translation, the clock hand had only moved three minutes.

Yasukichi was in a hopeless predicament. In this case, the sole way out was to answer the students' questions. If time remained, he'd declare an early finish to class.

As he picked up the textbook, he said, "Questions?" and blushed. Why did he flush red? He had no explanation. He had to think he was somehow cheating the students and blushed only at these times.

The students, clueless of course, stared with all seriousness at his face. He looked at the clock again. Then, he promptly picked up a textbook and started reading haphazardly.

After that, navigation in the textbook may have been more boring. However, Yasukichi still had confidence in his teaching method. More than a sailing ship battling a typhoon, it had reached the pinnacle of bravery.

The Brave Security Guard

It was either the end of autumn or the beginning of winter. The time was not clear but was a time when an overcoat was worn for the commute to school.

When a young military instructor sat beside Yasukichi at the table for lunch, he brought up a recent unusual incident. Late one night, a few days ago, several iron thieves landed a boat behind the school.

The night security guard who discovered this tried to catch them by himself. At the end of fierce hand-to-hand combat, they were hurled upside down into the sea. The security guard became a wet mouse but eventually crawled back onto the shore. Of course, the thieves' boat disappeared into the darkness of the open sea.

"There's this security guard called Ōura. He had a ridiculously absurd experience."

The military man stuffed his cheeks with bread and laughed painfully.

Ōura knew Yasukichi. Several men took turns standing guard at the guard station beside the gate. Whether military or civilian, each time he saw a teacher go in or out, he saluted. Yasukichi didn't like saluting or returning a salute, so he quickened his pace past the guard station to lessen their time to salute.

Only this security guard, Ōura, was not easily fooled. First, when sitting in the guard station, he focused continuously on the thirty to forty feet hemming in the gate. Therefore, when Yasukichi's shadow was visible, he assumed the posture for a proper salute before Yasukichi reached the front. This could be nothing other than fate. Yasukichi finally gave up. No, he didn't just give up. These days, as soon as he spots Ōura, like a rabbit targeted by a rattlesnake, Yasukichi doffs his hat.

Now, if asked, he'll say he was thrown into the sea because of the thieves. Yasukichi had to smile from a bit of sympathy.

After five or six days had passed, Yasukichi discovered Ōura by chance in the waiting room of the train station. Whenever Ōura saw his face, no matter where, he assumed a proper posture and always gave a formal salute. Yasukichi was worried like he could see the entrance to the guard station looming behind him.

"Recently, you——"

After a brief silence, Yasukichi continued, "Uh, you were injured when you caught those thieves——"

"It was an awful experience."

"Fortunately, it ended without any injuries——"

Ōura's bitter smile remained as he continued talking like he was mocking himself.

"If you thought capturing them was hard, one man could catch them all. But when they were caught, that was the end of the story——"

"That was the end?"

"I didn't get a bonus or anything. Nothing is explicitly written about that situation in the rules for security guards——"

"Even if you die in the line of duty?"

"Even if I die in the line of duty."

Yasukichi glanced at Ōura. According to Ōura's words, he didn't risk his life like a true hero. In addition to taking the bonus into account, he failed to catch the thieves who should have been captured. But as Yasukichi took out a cigarette, he nodded as energetically as possible.

"Of course, that was stupid. You lose by taking risks."

Ōura said "Uh-huh" or something. Yet, he seemed strangely downcast.

Yasukichi gloomily said, "But if a bonus is given——"

"But if a bonus is given, would anyone take a risk? That's a little doubtful."

This time, Ōura was quiet. Yasukichi put the cigarette in his mouth and instantly struck a match to light it. As the red, flickering flame moved to the tip of the cigarette, Yasukichi suppressed the smile that involuntarily moved his mouth.

"Thank you."

"You're welcome."

Ōura casually said these words and returned the matchbox to his pocket. However, Yasukichi believed that this brave security guard's secret had been exposed. That match fire was not only struck for Yasukichi. The match was struck for the sake of the gods who observe the samurai way of Ōura in what is unseen.

(April 1923)

21

THE BOW

Yasukichi just turned thirty. As a so-called freelance writer, he led a hectic life. Although he thought about tomorrow, he rarely thought about yesterday. However, as he walked down the streets, faced manuscript paper, and boarded trains, one past situation vividly came to mind. From his experience, associations seem to arise by stimulating the olfactory sense.

Irritants to the sense of smell are only smells labeled as stench in the melancholy life of a city dweller. For example, no one wants to smell the soot and smoke from a train. But if the scent of the memory of some young woman—the memory of a young lady seen five or six years ago—is smelled, it is revived in an instant like fireworks surging from a chimney.

He met this young woman at a station at some cool summer retreat. More precisely, it was the platform of the train station. At that time, he lived in that area. In rain or wind, he always got on the train that left Tokyo at eight in the morning and got off the 4:20 Tokyo-bound train in the afternoon.

If asked why he boarded the train every day ... well, that doesn't matter. However, if he boards the train every day, a dozen or so familiar faces emerge right away. The young woman was one of them. Until the twenty-something of March from Nanakusa in the afternoon, he has no memory of one meeting. The train boarded by the young woman in the afternoon was a train to Tokyo that had no connection to Yasukichi.

The young woman was maybe sixteen or seventeen years old. She always wore a silver-gray hat and Western clothes. She seemed short. However, she looked slender. Especially her legs ... she wore high heels over gray stockings on legs like a deer's. Her face could not be described as beautiful.

Yasukichi still did not discuss the East and the West and did not see an unconditionally beautiful heroine in a modern novel. When an author describes a woman, he mostly rejects expressions like "She's not a beautiful woman. But ..."

Considering this, the recognition of an unconditionally beautiful woman seems to be related to the appearance of modern people. Therefore, Yasukichi added the conditional *but* for this young woman. To be sure, I'll repeat it. Her face could not be called beautiful. But, she had a slightly upturned tip of her nose and a charming, round face.

The young lady stood in a daze among the boisterous crowd. She read a magazine on a bench away from the crowd. Or, she strolled to the end of the long platform.

Even at the sight of the young woman's figure, Yasukichi could not remember any heightened palpitations as described in romance novels. Of course, like seeing a familiar commander on the military base or a cat in a shop, he only thought, She's here. However, he harbored only affection for a familiar face.

At times when he did not see the young lady on the platform, he felt an emotion much like despair. He had no reason to keenly feel anything resembling despair. When the shop cat's whereabouts were unknown for a few days, Yasukichi felt an unchanging loneliness. If the military base commander were to suddenly die, the circumstances might be a little suspicious. Although not as much as a cat, only a different feeling than usual should occur.

The afternoon of twenty-something of March was warm and cloudy. Yasukichi boarded the 4:20 train to Tokyo after work that day. According to some faint memory, was it the fault of being tired of investigative work? He didn't seem to read a book as usual on the train. He recalled gazing at the mountains and fields beginning to show signs of spring. He once read a Western-style novel in which "Tratata tratata Tratata" depicted the sound of a train traveling over flat land, and "Trararach trararach" depicted the sound of a train crossing a railway bridge. Of course, when lazily listening, he could hear the droning winds. He remembered that thought.

After a listless thirty minutes, Yasukichi finally got off at the station in the summer retreat area. The train from Tokyo, arriving a little earlier, stopped at the platform. As he mixed into the crowd, he suddenly glanced at people getting off the train. Amazingly, there was the young lady. As written earlier, Yasukichi had never seen this young woman in the afternoon. Suddenly, before his eyes was a silver-gray figure, like a cloud passing sunlight or like the flowers of a pussy willow. Of course, he thought, Oh! In that instant, the young woman seemed to look at Yasukichi's face. At the same time, Yasukichi, without thinking, bowed to her.

The young woman he bowed to was surely surprised. Now, unfortunately, he couldn't remember her expression. No, at that time, he didn't have the time to assess it. He soon thought, Dammit, and immediately felt his burning ears. But that was all he remembered. The young woman also bowed slightly to him.

Finally, he was outside the station and angered by his foolishness. Why did he bow? That bow was entirely reflexive. It was just like blinking after a bright lightning flash. Doing that is not free will. Behavior without free will should be fine when no responsibility is assumed. But what were the young woman's thoughts? Of course, the young woman bowed, too. However, that may have been reflexive at a moment of surprise. At the same time, he thought, Dammit, an apology for the rudeness would have been good. He was not aware of even saying that.

Yasukichi did not return to the lodging house but walked to a deserted sandy beach. This was not amazing. He had a hard time in the world with a monthly rent of five yen and a bento lunch of fifty *sen* per meal. He always came to smoke a Glasgow pipe on the sand.

As he watched the overcast sea on this day, he moved the fire of a match to the pipe. There was nothing he could do about what happened today. However, when tomorrow comes, he will surely see the young woman's face.

What will the young woman do then? If she thinks he's a delinquent, naturally, she won't glance his way. If she doesn't think that, tomorrow, she may respond to his bow as she did today. To his bow? Will he, Horikawa Yasukichi, feel like nonchalantly bowing again to the young woman? No, he has no interest in bowing. He had bowed once, and given the chance, the young woman and he would greet each other. If they bow to each other. Out of the blue, Yasukichi recalled the beauty of her eyebrows.

Today, seven or eight years later, strangely, he vividly recalled only the silence of the sea. Before the sea, Yasukichi vacantly puffed on his now extinguished pipe. It's not that his thoughts were only about the young woman. Thoughts floated up about the novel he intended to start soon.

The protagonist of that novel is an English professor who burns with revolutionary spirit. Famous for his backbone, his head did not know how to shrink before authority. However, he only carelessly bowed to the young woman with the familiar face just once. She may be short but looked slender. Perhaps, the truth was he tended to think about the young woman, especially her legs wearing gray stockings and high heels.

Before eight-fifty the next morning, Yasukichi walked the crowded platform. His heart stretched to the expectation of seeing the young lady. He had an inkling to want to avoid seeing her. However, not seeing her was surely undesirable. In other words, his feeling was no different than the attitude of a boxer awaiting an upcoming match against a forbidding opponent.

He could not forget his strange pathological anxiety, transcending common sense, over whether he will do something stupid the moment he faces the young lady. Long ago, the poet Jean Richepin kissed the actress Sarah Bernhardt like no one else was around. Although Yasukichi, who was born Japanese, may never kiss like that, he may stick out his tongue or pull a face. He looked around at the people as if searching and not searching, while his heart grew colder.

Immediately, his eyes discovered the figure of the young woman leisurely walking toward him. As fate approached, he continued to walk in a straight line. The two rapidly approached each other. Ten steps, five steps, three steps … the young woman stood before his eyes. With his head held up, Yasukichi looked at the young woman's face. She focused her calm eyes on his face. The two faces looked at each other and passed by the other without doing anything.

At that instant, he suddenly sensed a tremor in the young woman's eyes. Simultaneously, an impulse to bow surged in his body. It's not an exaggeration to say that happened in an instant. The young woman quietly passed by the startled Yasukichi, like clouds transmitting sunlight or pussy willows adorned with flowers.

After only twenty minutes, Yasukichi mouthed the Glasgow pipe as the train swayed. The young woman was not beautiful only because of her eyebrows. Her eyes leaned toward cool black pupils.

Her nose was slightly upturned. But can this kind of thinking be called love? How did he answer that question? This does not remain in his memory. Yasukichi's only memory was a faintly glowing melancholy that occasionally attacked him.

He fixated on the pillar of smoke rising from the pipe. For a short time in this melancholy, he only thought about the young woman. Meanwhile, the train ran between the mountains bathed in the morning light.

(September 1923)

22

A ROMANCE NOVEL
OR LOVE IS SUPREME

C onference room in a women's magazine publishing company
   Editor-in-chief - A portly gentleman around forty years old
   Horikawa Yasukichi - Around thirty years old, looks thin because of the editor-in-chief's weight, can't be described in one word, but is unlikely to be called a gentleman

EDITOR-IN-CHIEF. This time, would you write a novel for one of our magazines? Readers are becoming more discerning, so a conventional romance novel is no longer satisfying. Therefore, please write a serious romance novel deeply rooted in human nature.

Yasukichi. I will write that. Lately, I've been wanting to write a certain novel for a women's magazine.

Editor-in-chief. Really? That'll be fine. If you write it, we'll publish a big ad in the newspapers saying something like *From the pen of Mr. Horikawa, a poignant, timeless romance novel.*

Yasukichi. Poignant? Timeless? But they say in my novels *love is supreme.*

Editor-in-chief. So, praise love. That would be even better. According to *A Modern Theory of Love* by Dr. Kuriyagawa, generally, the hearts of young men and women have leaned toward love for love's sake. Is that modern love?

Yasukichi. Well, I doubt that. Modern skepticism, modern robbery, and modern hair dye do exist. However, only love is believed to have changed little since the long-ago days of Japan's mythical creators, Izanagi and Izanami.

Editor-in-chief. That is only theoretical. For instance, a love triangle is one example of modern love, at least in present-day Japan.

Yasukichi. Oh, a love triangle? A love triangle will appear in my novel. Shall I sketch out the plot?

Editor-in-chief. That would be splendid if you would.

Yasukichi. The leading lady is a young married woman. Her husband is a diplomat. Of course, they live in a house in the upscale Yamanote. This leading lady has a slender build, is gentle, and her hair is always, well, what sort of hairstyle would the readers like?

Editor-in-chief. Probably a style that covers the ears.

Yasukichi. So be it. Her hair will always be styled to cover her ears. She's pale with bright eyes and some quirky habit with her lips. If turned into a motion picture, she'll be played by Kurishima Sumiko. Her diplomat husband has a modern law degree and is not unreasonable about melodramatic *Shinpa*-style dramas. During his student days, he was a baseball player and read novels for amusement. He's a good-looking fellow with a tanned complexion. The newlyweds live very happily in their Yamanote home. They attend concerts, stroll down Ginza Boulevard, and enjoy other activities together.

Editor-in-chief. Of course, this is before the earthquake.

Yasukichi. Long before the earthquake. They attended concerts, too. And stroll down Ginza Boulevard. Only silent smiles are exchanged beneath the electric lights in a Western-style room. The leading lady calls this room *Our Nest*. The walls are adorned with reproductions of Renoir's and Cezanne's paintings. The piano's ebony body gleams. The potted palm tree and leaves are withered. In other words, it's fairly stylish, but the rent is surprisingly low.

Editor-in-chief. Don't go into those sorts of explanations. At least touch on the main story of the novel.

Yasukichi. No, these are important. The monthly wage of the young diplomat is not much.

Editor-in-chief. Well, make him an aristocrat's son. If he's an aristocrat, is he a count or a viscount? Whatever he is, a duke or a marquis, doesn't often appear in novels.

Yasukichi. It doesn't matter if he's the son of a viscount. At any rate, the Western-style room is nice. This room, Ginza Boulevard, and concerts are in the first installment. However, Taeko, that's the leading lady's name, becomes close friends with a musician named Tatsuo. Later, distressful feelings gradually develop in her. The leading lady intuits that Tatsuo loves her. The distress grows stronger in her each day.

Editor-in-chief. What type of man is Tatsuo?

Yasukichi. Tatsuo is a musical genius. He could be lumped in with the character Jean-Christophe created by Romain Rolland or Daniel Nothaft created by Jakob Wassermann. Still poor, no one appreciates him, no matter what he does. I intend to model him on a musician friend of mine. Of course, my friend is handsome, but Tatsuo is not. At a glance, his face resembles a gorilla. He's a brute born in Tōhoku. Only his eyes have the spark of genius. His eyes appear to harbor continuous heat like lumps of coal.

Editor-in-chief. The genius will be well received.

Yasukichi. But Taeko has no reason to be dissatisfied with her diplomat husband. Rather, she passionately loves her husband more than before. He trusts Taeko; perhaps, there's no need to say this. Therefore, Taeko's suffering only intensifies.

Editor-in-chief. In other words, by modernity, I mean love.

Yasukichi. Every day, if the electric lights are on, Tatsuo appears at the Western-style room. If her husband is present, that's fine. Even if Taeko is home alone, he'll still show up. At those times, Taeko inevitably makes him play the piano. Even when her husband is there, Tatsuo usually sits in front of the piano.

Editor-in-chief. Is that when she falls in love?

Yasukichi. No, falling in love is not easy. But one February evening, he starts to play Schubert's *An Sylvia*. This song is filled with passion like flowing flames. Taeko leans in to listen under the leaves of a large palm. Meanwhile, her feelings of love for Tatsuo gradually begin to grow. At the same time, it begins to feel like the seduction of gold rising before her eyes. After five more minutes pass, no, in one more minute, Taeko may throw her body into Tatsuo's arms. Her happy husband returns home exactly when the piece ends.

Editor-in-chief. And then?

Yasukichi. And then … just one week later, Taeko can no longer endure the pain and decides to commit suicide. But she is pregnant and lacks the nerve to follow through. And she confesses Tatsuo's love for her to her husband. To not cause more pain to her husband, she does not confess that she loves Tatsuo.

Editor-in-chief. And then there's a duel?

Yasukichi. No, the husband simply turns Tatsuo away with cold indifference on his next visit. Tatsuo stares only at the piano while silently biting his lip. Taeko stands outside the door and holds back her silent weeping. Before two months pass, her husband receives an unexpected official order to assume a post at the consulate in Hankow, China.

Editor-in-chief. Does Taeko go with him?

Yasukichi. Of course, they go together. Before leaving, however, Taeko sends a letter to Tatsuo. In essence, it says, I sympathize with your feelings but nothing can be done. We will resign ourselves to our fates. From then until today, Taeko hasn't seen Tatsuo.

Editor-in-chief. And the novel ends.

Yasukichi. No, there's a little more. After going to Hankow, Taeko thinks about Tatsuo from time to time. Eventually, she thinks she loves Tatsuo more than her husband. Is that all right? She is surrounded by the lonely landscape of Hankow. This landscape resembles the clear waters of a river and the lush, fragrant grasses on an island described in the poem *Yellow Crane Tower* by Cui Hao. After a year, at last, Taeko writes a letter to Tatsuo with this message.

I loved you. Even now, I love you. Please, have pity on me, a soul who managed to fool herself.

Tatsuo receives the letter and ...

Editor-in-chief. And he rushes off to China, perhaps.

Yasukichi. That cannot possibly happen because Tatsuo plays the piano in a movie theater in Asakusa to support himself.

Editor-in-chief. Well, that's a little bleak.

Yasukichi. Bleak, but it's the only option. Tatsuo opens the envelope of Taeko's letter at a table in a cafe in a seedy part of town. The skies beyond the window are raining. He scrutinizes the letter like he's stunned. Somehow, he feels he can see Taeko's Western-style room between the lines. He feels he can see *Our Nest* illuminated by the electric light on the piano lid.

Editor-in-chief. That's a bit unsatisfying, but it's a future masterpiece. By all means, please write it.

Yasukichi. Actually, there's a little more.

Editor-in-chief. Oh, that's not the end?

Yasukichi. No. Tatsuo bursts out laughing. Thinking about it, he shouts a curse like "Dammit!" in frustration.

Editor-in-chief. Ha, ha, ha. He's gone mad.

Yasukichi. What? He lost his temper over the absurdity. That would make anyone lose his temper. Because, from the beginning, Tatsuo did not love Taeko, even a little.

Editor-in-chief. But that's—

Yasukichi. Tatsuo went to Taeko's home to play the piano. In other words, he only loved the piano. The impoverished Tatsuo could not afford one.

Editor-in-chief. But Horikawa—

Yasukichi. Tatsuo was happy when he played the piano at the movie theater. Meanwhile, Tatsuo trained to become a policeman after the earthquake. During the movement to protect the Constitution, he was ganged up on and beaten on behalf of the good citizens of Tokyo. Now and then while on patrol in Yamanote, he heard the sounds of a piano. He would stop outside that house and dream of fleeting happiness.

Editor-in-chief. That novel will demand great effort.

Yasukichi. Well, listen. While living in Hankow, Taeko always thinks about Tatsuo. No, not only in Hankow. Every time her diplomat husband changes posts, when they move temporarily to Shanghai, Beijing, or Tianjin, she always thinks about Tatsuo. Of course, around the time of the earthquake, she has many children. And … her family grows to four children when she gives birth to the twins, now one-year-olds. In addition, she doesn't notice as her husband becomes a heavy drinker. Taeko fattens up like a pig and thinks only Tatsuo truly loved her. Love is supreme. Otherwise, it's impossible to be happy, as it is for Taeko. At least, hating the muck and mire of life can't be avoided. Well, what do you think about this novel?

Editor-in-chief. Horikawa, are you serious?

Yasukichi. Of course, I'm serious. Please, look at the romance novels in the world. Isn't the leading lady either Mother Mary or Cleopatra? At the same time, however, a leading lady in life is never a virtuous woman; she is also never a whore. Please note, there is a man or woman among the kind-hearted readers who truly values that sort of novel. Another problem is that love ends in success. Is self-sacrifice always absurd on the day of unlikely heartbreak? If not, the more absurd spirit of vengeance is exhibited. People deeply in love delude themselves into believing that their actions are heroic. However, these negative effects tend not to propagate in my romance novel. I conclude by praising the happiness of the leading lady.

Editor-in-chief. You're joking. That will never be published in our magazine.

Yasukichi. Really? Well, who will publish it? In this wide world, there should be a women's magazine that will accept my viewpoint.

Proof of Yasukichi's correct prediction is recorded in this conversation.

(March 1924)

23

COMPOSITIONS

"**H**orikawa, will you please write a eulogy? Major Honda's funeral is on Saturday. The school principal will read it."

Captain Fujita said this to Yasukichi as he left for the dining hall. Horikichi Yasukichi taught reading and translating English to students at this school. Sometimes, he was assigned other tasks. He wrote a eulogy during spare moments in class, edited a textbook, revised the morning lecture, and translated foreign newspaper articles. Captain Fujita always assigned him these sorts of duties.

The captain was around forty years old. His gaunt face was tanned and looked high-strung. Yasukichi walked down the dim, narrow corridor one step behind the captain, who, without realizing it, exclaimed, "Oh."

"Major Honda died?"

The captain turned to look at Yasukichi's face as if he were the one who said, "Oh." Yasukichi missed the notice about Major Honda's sudden death because he skipped work for a valid reason yesterday.

"He died yesterday morning, reportedly from a cerebral hemorrhage. Please write it and bring it to me by Friday. The morning of the day after tomorrow. All right?"

"Yes, I'll write it."

The shrewd Captain Fujita immediately moved ahead of Yasukichi.

"For your reference when writing the eulogy, I'll send over his personal history."

"But what sort of man was he? I only knew Major Honda on sight."

"Well, he was a man with brotherly love. And … and always a class leader. Also, please write it in your fine calligraphy."

The two stood before the yellow-painted door of the department head's office. Captain Fujita had the role of vice principal and was called the department head. Yasukichi reluctantly abandoned his artistic conscience related to the eulogy.

"He was clever by nature and a friend to his brothers. Well, I'll figure something out."

"I'm counting on you. Thank you."

Yasukichi left the captain and returned to the empty faculty room without showing his face at the smoking room. The November sunlight shone on Yasukichi's desk to the right of the window. He sat at the desk and moved the flame to a cigarette. To this day, he had written only two eulogies.

He wrote the first eulogy for Ensign Shigeno, who succumbed to appendicitis. At the time, he had just started at the school, so his memory of the man, Ensign Shigeno, or his face was fuzzy. However, because he had some interest in his debut eulogy, he wrote a draft resembling prose by the Eight Great Writers of the Tang and Song Dynasties, such as *Serenity, a white cloud.*

The next one was written for Lieutenant Kimura, the victim of an accidental drowning. He had traveled back and forth with Lieutenant Kimura on the train from the same summer retreat area to this school every day and thus was able to express genuine sympathy.

Each time Major Honda went to the dining hall, Yasukichi glimpsed his face that resembled a vulture's but had no interest in writing the eulogy. In other words, the current Horikawa Yasukichi is a funeral business that received an order. This funeral business in a spiritual life is said to bring dragon lanterns and artificial flowers by some hour, on some month and day. Yasukichi, holding the cigarette in his mouth, slowly descended into melancholy.

"Instructor Horikawa."

Like awakening from a dream, Yasukichi looked up to see First Lieutenant Tanaka standing beside the desk. First Lieutenant Tanaka had an affable face adorned with a short mustache and a smooth, round double chin.

"This is Major Honda's personal history. The department head told me to give this to Instructor Horikawa."

First Lieutenant Tanaka placed several handwritten pages on the desk. Yasukichi only answered, "Okay," and abruptly dropped his eyes to the lined paper. Small block-style characters of only the date of his appointment were lined up. This was not a simple personal history. It was symbolic and hinted at the life of someone who was destined to become a government official of the entire country and not a civil servant or a military officer.

"I have a question about a word. It's not a naval term. It's a word from a novel."

One word in horizontal script was on a piece of paper taken out by the first lieutenant. Blue pencil marks remained. *Masochism.* Yasukichi automatically moved his eyes from the scrap of paper to the boyish face with always-ruddy cheeks of the first lieutenant.

"This one? This is ma-so-chism."

"Yes, it doesn't appear in ordinary English-Japanese dictionaries."

Keeping his head down, Yasukichi explained the meaning of masochism.

"Oh, so that's what it means?"

First Lieutenant Tanaka's always cheerful smile rose. His smile showed self-satisfaction and did not incite feelings of frustration. In particular, Yasukichi today was tempted to throw all the words of Krafft-Ebing, a psychiatrist and author of *Psychopathia Sexualis*, at the happy first lieutenant's face.

"The origin of this word was ... uh from the name Masoch. Is his novel well written?"

"Well, it's a complete failure."

"But does Masoch have an interesting personality?"

"Masoch? He's an idiot. He fervently advocates that the government spend money to protect unlicensed prostitutes."

First Lieutenant Tanaka understood Masoch's stupidity and finally left Yasukichi alone. It was unclear whether Masoch valued the protection of unlicensed prostitutes over a national defense plan. He probably paid considerable respect to the national defense plan. However, if that's not said, it's impossible to engrave the ridiculous reasons for perverse sexual desires in the head of the optimistic first lieutenant.

Alone again, Yasukichi ambled into the room while lighting another cigarette. His teaching English was mentioned earlier, but this was not his profession. At least, he didn't believe it was. He thinks creative work is his life's work. After he became a teacher, he published a short story every two months.

One was half of the story of Jean-Christophe revised in the style of the Keichō edition of *Aesop's Fables* and was published in this month's magazine. The remaining half will be published in the same magazine next month. It was already the seventh, so the deadline for next month's edition ... well, he's not writing the eulogy. Despite studying day and night, he doubted whether he could finish given the demands of his actual job. In time, Yasukichi was irritated by the eulogy.

The strike of twelve-thirty amid the silence of the large grandfather clock is identical to the apple falling at Newton's feet. Yasukichi's class had to start in thirty minutes. If he wrote the eulogy in the meantime, he thought how sad it was to fill his spare time with hard work.

Memorializing Captain Honda, intelligent by nature and a friend to his brothers, in just thirty minutes will have some problems. Like being overwhelmed by those problems, it will become boasting, as if praising the rich vocabulary beginning with Kakinomoto Hitomaro of old and extending to Mushanokōji Saneatsu of today. Yasukichi immediately faced the desk, thrust a pen into the inkwell, and started to write the eulogy on a dunce cap fashioned from an exam paper.

~

THE DAY of Major Honda's funeral was an uneventful, clear autumn day. Yasukichi wore a frock coat and a silk hat and followed after twelve or so civilian instructors and the funeral procession. When he abruptly turned, he first saw the principal Vice Admiral Sasaki, and then Captain Fujita among the officers, and Instructor Awano among the civil servants who were walking behind him.

He bowed in apology to Captain Fujita for walking ahead of him. But the captain signaled it was no problem and smiled slightly. Though speaking to the principal, Instructor Awano, sporting a short mustache, turned his attention to Yasukichi in a manner that was neither playful nor serious.

"Horikawa. You see, in naval etiquette, the higher-ranking officers are further back, so you don't have to acknowledge Fujita."

Yasukichi apologized again. Of course, when told that, the charming First Lieutenant Tanaka joined the line far in front. Yasukichi took big steps to the side of the first lieutenant. Today, too, the first lieutenant cheerfully chatted with Yasukichi like they were standing together at a wedding rather than a funeral.

"It's a nice day. Were you just added to the funeral procession?"

"No, I was way in the back."

Yasukichi relayed the whole story. The first lieutenant burst out laughing loud enough to erode the dignity of the funeral.

"Is this your first funeral?"

"No, I went to Ensign Shigeno's and Lieutenant Kimura's."

"How were they?"

"Of course, I was far behind the principal and the department head."

"Well, thank you. You've gained the rank of a general."

The procession entered a village outside of town situated near the temples. While speaking with the first lieutenant, Yasukichi didn't forget to look at the people who came to watch the funeral. The villagers have developed an unusual talent for estimating the cost of a funeral because they've watched countless funerals since childhood.

During the funeral procession for the father of the mathematics instructor, Kiriyama, on the day before summer vacation, one elderly man dressed in summer clothes stood under the eaves of a house, shading his forehead with a persimmon-varnished fan, and proclaimed, "Uh-huh, this one's fifteen yen."

Today … today, unfortunately, no one exhibits the ability seen in that time. Today, however, I recall the extraordinary sight of the Shinto priest of the Ōmoto religion carrying a pale child, probably his, on his shoulders. Yasukichi thought he'd like to write about the people of this village in a short story called *The Funeral* or something.

"This month, I wrote a short story called *A Ruined Priest*."

The amiable First Lieutenant Tanaka constantly flicked his tongue.

"That review is already out. This morning's news … let me see, it was in *The Yomiuri*. I'm going to look it over later. That's why it's in a pocket of my overcoat."

"There's no need for that."

"It seems you don't write reviews. I think I still want to write only reviews, for example, Shakespeare's *Hamlet*. That Hamlet's personality is …"

Yasukichi was instantly enlightened. In this world, the complete satisfaction of a critic was not necessarily accidental.

Finally, the procession passed through the temple gate. The temple looked down on the calm sea between the pine forest in back. It was probably always serene. Now, however, the area inside the gate was buried under the students who headed the funeral procession. Yasukichi took off his new patent leather shoes at the entrance to the temple kitchen. The sunny, long corridor led to the mourners' seats on new tatami mats.

The mourners' seats were across from the family's seats. The man seated in the seat of honor was probably Major Honda's father.

Of course, his vulture-like face was entirely pale but held more boldness and courage than his son's. A university student sat beside him. He had to be his younger brother. His younger sister, sitting in the third seat, was a very attractive young woman. In the fourth seat … well, the people in the remaining seats weren't particularly noteworthy.

On this side, the mourners' seats, the school principal took the first seat. The department head took the next seat. Yasukichi was right behind the department head. The seat of his pants settled down in the second row of the mourners' seats. Nevertheless, his knees were not aligned with the precision of the department head and the principal. He sat cross-legged so his legs wouldn't go numb.

The sutra chanting began immediately. Yasukichi loved chanting the sutras of various sects to show his love for a *Shinnai* performance. Unfortunately, the temples in Tokyo and its suburbs seem to mostly exhibit a decline in sutra chanting. Long ago, the chanting of sutras to invoke deities—beginning with the deity Zaō on Mount Kinpu, the deities in Kumano, and the deities enshrined in the Sumiyoshi shrine—drew people to gather on the grounds of the Buddhist Hōrin-ji temple where they listened to chants by senior Dōmyō Ajari monks.

However, these delicate sounds slipped away from this impure world for eternity with the arrival of American culture.

When a break in the chanting came, Vice Admiral Sasaki, the school principal, moved in front of the major's coffin. The coffin covered by white figured satin was installed at the entrance to the temple and directly faced the dais for a Buddha statue. On a desk in front of the coffin, a box of medals was displayed among glimmering artificial lotus flowers and the swaying of candle flames.

After bowing to the coffin, the school principal unfolded the eulogy, written on premium *bōsho* paper, which he held in his left hand. The eulogy is a famous literary work written by Yasukichi, of course, two or three days earlier. A famous literary work is not particularly embarrassing. His nerves felt as if they were being scraped away by an old leather strop used long ago to sharpen knives.

His being cast in the role of the eulogy's author in the comedy of this funeral and being forced to watch this reality was not particularly pleasant. Without realizing it, Yasukichi cast down his eyes to his knees at the same time the school principal cleared his throat.

The school principal began to quietly read. His voice, tinged with rust at its depth, was choked with heartbroken sorrow that transcended the written and spoken words. No one would think he was reading a eulogy written by another man. Yasukichi secretly admired the school principal's acting talent. The temple was quieter than before. No one did anything rash, not even move.

Finally, the school principal mournfully read, "You were gifted with innate intelligence and a friend to your brothers."

All of a sudden, a quiet giggle rose from the family's seats. That laughter gradually became loud. Although he was startled deep down, Yasukichi searched the people facing him over the shoulder of Captain Fujita. At the same time, he heard what he thought was laughter from someone who had forgotten where she was, but it turned out to be crying.

It was his sister. Her hair was styled in an old-fashioned, Meiji-era bun. Her pretty face was looking down and buried in a silk handkerchief. That wasn't all. His brother, a college student who looked like a country bumpkin, started sobbing.

Then, the elderly people kept taking out tissues and sorrowfully blowing their noses. The scene before him stunned Yasukichi. The author of the drama felt satisfied with the tears he wrung from the mourners. However, his last feeling was an indescribable anguish far greater than these emotions.

The wretchedness did not know or realize the spiritual depth of precious human beings and unable to apologize for stepping inside with muddy feet. Before this wretchedness, Yasukichi lowered his head in dejection for the first time in the hour-long funeral.

The relatives of Major Honda were surely unaware of the existence of this English instructor. However, *Crime and Punishment*'s Raskolnikov, dressed in a jester's costume, dug deeply into Yasukichi's heart. Now, seven or eight years later, he thought about wanting to humbly ask forgiveness from them while kneeling on a muddy road.

Sunset fell on the funeral day. After getting off the train, Yasukichi passed through the back streets of the summer resort town, connected only by a bamboo fence, to return home to the boarding house on the coast. His shoe bottoms moistened the sand on the narrow streets. Mist had been falling unnoticed by him for a short time. The sky peeked through a cluster of scattered pines within the fence. The faint aroma of resin was released. Yasukichi hung his head and ambled to the sea, indifferent to the quiet.

On the way back to the temple, he met Captain Fujita. The captain praised the success of his eulogy and observed that the words sudden death and honorable death were germane to Major Honda's death.

For Yasukichi who had seen the family's tears, that was enough to weaken him. The amiable First Lieutenant Tanaka rode the same train again. He showed the monthly review published in the *Yomiuri Shimbun* that critiqued Yasukichi's short story. Mr. N, who had gained literary fame, wrote the review. After the thorough abuse, Mr. N dealt the final blow to Yasukichi. "A hobby of the instructor at the Naval XX School is entirely unnecessary in the literary world."

The eulogy, written in less than half an hour, unexpectedly left a deep impression. The short story, heavily revised under electric lights over several nights, did not produce one-tenth of the tacitly assumed impression. Of course, he dismissed Mr. N's words with a smile. However, his current position in life cannot be easily laughed off. He found success in a eulogy and spectacular failure in a short story. When viewed from his perspective, he had doubts. When will fate drop the curtain of this sad comedy for him?

Suddenly, Yasukichi looked at the sky. The dark moon among the pine trees, branches stretching into the sky, was bronze. As he gazed at the moon, he felt the need to pee. Not one person among the passersby was happy. Unchanging, quiet lines of bamboo fences were on the left and right sides of the road. He took a long, solitary pee at the fence on the right side.

While peeing, the fence before Yasukichi's eyes was pulled backward with a creak. What he thought was the fence was probably a wooden door constructed to resemble the fence. He looked to see a man with a mustache come out of the door. Yasukichi had no choice but to keep on peeing; he could only slowly turn to the side.

"This is a problem," said the man vacantly. He sounded bewildered. When Yasukichi heard this voice, he immediately realized the sun had gone down so much that he couldn't see his pee.

(March 1924)

24

YOUTH

1 Christmas

On Christmas afternoon last year, Horikawa Yasukichi boarded the scheduled bus to Shinbashi at a corner in Suda-chō. There was only one open seat. The bus packed with passengers made it impossible to move as usual. After the earthquake, Tokyo roads were in shambles and tossed vehicles around.

Today, as always, Yasukichi took a book out of his pocket. Before arriving at Kaji-chō, he gave up reading the book. Reading a book was akin to a miracle. Miracles are not his profession. A Western saint of old with a beautiful halo of light, no, a Catholic missionary beside him carried out a miracle before his eyes.

The missionary continued to read a book with tiny, horizontal Western script as if everything had been forgotten. He was a Frenchman, probably older than fifty, wearing iron-rimmed pince-nez eyeglasses, red faced like a rooster, and short whiskers. Using his side eye, Yasukichi briefly peeked at his book *Essai sur les…* He couldn't make out the rest. However, the content looked unreadable, like trying to read tiny characters printed on yellowing newspaper.

Feeling slightly hostile toward this missionary, Yasukichi started to indulge in lazy daydreaming.

Many tiny angels maintained the serenity surrounding the missionary as he read. Of course, not one of the non-believing riders could see the angels. However, five or six of these angels stood on their hands, somersaulted, and performed other acrobatics on his wide-brimmed hat. As he thought this, five or six angels jammed into a line on the missionary's shoulders to talk and joke while looking around at the riders' faces. One small angel poked his face out of his ear hole. One on the bridge of his nose proudly crossed over the pince-nez.

The bus stopped in Ōdenma-chō. At the same time, three or four riders moved to get off. The missionary placed his book on his knee at some point and restlessly gazed out the window. The passengers quickly got off.

A girl around eleven or twelve boarded at the front of the bus. She wore a pale red Western-style outfit topped with a sky-blue hat and seemed strangely brash. She grabbed onto the brass pillar in the middle of the bus and surveyed the seats on both sides. Unfortunately, not one seat was empty.

"Young lady, please sit here."

The missionary raised his thick hips. The words he managed to speak were tinged with nasally Japanese.

"Thank you."

The girl passed by the missionary and sat beside Yasukichi. Her thank you was rich in saucy inflections. Unknowingly, Yasukichi frowned. Originally, children, especially girls, were believed to be pure like the babe born in Bethlehem two thousand years ago. From his experience, however, children aren't necessarily free of villainy. Making everything sacred is sentimentalism that has spread throughout the world.

"Young lady, how old are you?"

The missionary peeked at the girl's face with smiling eyes. The girl turned over a ball of yarn on her knees and moved the two knitting needles like an expert knitter. While her eyes carelessly followed the tips of the knitting needles, her responses were almost fawning.

"Me? I'll be twelve next year."

"Where are you going today?"

"Today? Today, I'm on my way home."

The bus ran down Ginza Boulevard during the questions and answers. More than running, it should be described as leaping. It may have been exactly like the boat carrying Christ on the Sea of Galilee as a storm approached long ago. The tall missionary, one hand gripping the brass pole and the other hand behind his back, banged his head again and again on the ceiling of the bus. The safety of his body was left to God's will. Still smiling, he continued questioning the girl.

"Do you know what today is?"

"It's December 25."

"Yes, December 25. Do you know why December 25 is special? Young lady, do you know?"

Yasukichi grimaced again. The missionary deftly moved to preaching Christianity. The proselytizing of Islam takes up the sword. At least by taking up the sword, the Koran displays mutual respect and passion for fellow men. The proselytizing of Christianity shows absolutely no respect for others. He politely teaches about God, like he's telling someone about the Western-style tailor's shop that opened next door.

Or, while feigning ignorance, he recommends selling the faith instead of tuition for a foreign language class. In particular, besides giving out picture books and toys to boys and girls, secretly kidnapping their souls for Heaven, naturally, must be called a crime. The young lady beside Yasukichi calmly replied, while her hands steadily knitted.

"Yes, I know that."

"Well, what is today? If you know, please say it."

The girl fixed her lively, deep black eyes on the missionary's face.

"Today is ... my birthday."

Without realizing it, Yasukichi stared at the girl. She was focused on the tips of the knitting needles. But how could he describe her face? It was not as saucy as he thought earlier. Instead, her face universally illuminated by the light of wisdom within her cuteness was not inferior to young Mary. At some point, Yasukichi discovered he was smiling.

"Today is your birthday!"

The missionary burst out laughing. The Frenchman's laughing expression was precisely the laughter of a kind-hearted, big man in a fairy tale. This time, the girl raised suspicious eyes to the missionary's face. She was not alone. Beginning with Yasukichi in front of her, passengers on both sides, men and women, mainly focused on the missionary. Suspicion probably was not in their eyes, but neither was curiosity. All their smiles understood the meaning of the missionary's burst of laughter.

"Young lady, you were born on a fine day. Today is an unparalleled birthday. This birthday is celebrated worldwide. Now, you … when you become an adult, you will certainly …"

The missionary struggled to find words and glanced around the bus. At the same time, his eyes met Yasukichi's. The tears of laughter in the missionary's eyes sparkled behind the pince-nez. Yasukichi felt all the beauty of Christmas in those brown eyes filled with happiness. Finally, the girl probably realized the reason for the missionary's laughter. She dangled her legs like she was sulking.

"You will probably become a wise wife and superior mother. Well, young lady, goodbye. This is my stop. Well, …"

The missionary looked around at the faces as before. The bus stopped at the corner of Owari-chō bustling with people.

"Goodbye all."

Several hours later, Yasukichi recalled this minor incident in a corner of a cafe in a shack in Owari-chō. When the electric lights began to turn on, what was the fat missionary doing? The girl who shared a birthday with Christ may be telling her mother and father about this morning's incident at the dinner table. Twenty years ago, when he did not know the pain of this world, Yasukichi possessed a small happiness, like the girl or like the missionary who had completely forgotten the pain of this world before the harmless questions and answers. In those days, grape-flavored mochi was bought on festival days at Daitoku-in Temple. In those days, motion pictures were watched in the great hall in Nishūrō.

"Honjo Fukagawa is still a mountain of ashes."

"Oh, really? What happened to Yoshiwara then?"

"What happened to Yoshiwara? They're saying princesses are turning to the sex trade in Asakusa."

At a neighboring table, two businessmen were having this conversation. That didn't matter. In the center of the cafe, the yarn-draped conifer branches of a Christmas tree held dangling toy Santas and silver stars. The flame of the gas hearth lit up the tree trunk in red.

Today is a joyous Christmas. "This birthday is celebrated world-wide." While lazily smoking a cigarette before his after-dinner tea, Yasukichi continued to dream of the happiness of twenty years ago when he became a person on the other side of a great river.

These several short works record the recollections that darted one after another through Yasukichi's mind as the cigarette turned to smoke.

2 The Mystery on the Road

Yasukichi was four years old. He passed down the street in a large trench with a maid named Tsuru. On the other side of the large trench filled with a jet-black substance was the famous bamboo grove of Otakegura, the government bamboo storehouse, that later became Ryōgoku Station.

They say the Bakabayashi dance of the tanuki, one of the Seven Wonders of Honjo, can be heard in this grove. At least, Yasukichi heard it from someone. Of course, he could hear the tanuki's Bakabayashi song and dance. The supernatural tales of Oitekibori and Kataha no Yoshi were also believed to have happened in Otake-gura. Now, the yellowing bamboo tips rustled in the crisp breeze in the sunlight like the eerie grove was driving the tanuki and other inhabitants elsewhere.

"Young Master, do you know what this is?"

While Tsūya (Yasukichi's name for the maid) looked at him, she pointed toward the road with few pedestrians. A thick stripe on the dry, dusty road ran faintly into the distance. Yasukichi felt like he had seen this line on the road before. Now like then, however, he didn't know what to say.

"What do you think? Young Master, think about it."

This was the usual practice of Tsūya. Whatever she asked, she was not meekly teaching. She always sternly repeated, "Think about it." Tsūya was stern but wasn't old like his mother. She was a teenage girl, fifteen or sixteen, with a small mole under one eye.

She likely thought saying such things enriched Yasukichi's education. He was also grateful for her kindness. But if she truly knew the meaning of these words, long ago, she probably would have avoided the folly of persistently repeating "think about it." Over the thirty years since then, Yasukichi has pondered various problems. However, I understand nothing, so little had changed since I walked along the big ditch with the clever Tsūya.

"Look, is this another one here? Hey, Young Master, think about it. What is the line for?"

Tsūya pointed to the road as before. Of course, a line of about the same thickness was placed at a distance of only three feet away, running down the dusty road. After Yasukichi thought seriously, he finally discovered the answer.

"Some kid probably made the marks. He had a cane or something?"

"But aren't the two lines lined up?"

"If two people made them, they'd make two."

Tsūya was smiling when she shook her head instead of saying, "No." Naturally, Yasukichi was dissatisfied. However, she was all-knowing. In other words, she was the Oracle of Delphi. The secret on the road surely saw far into the past. Yasukichi gradually felt marvelous emotions about the two stripes instead of dissatisfaction.

"Well, what is this stripe?"

"What could it be? Look, two stripes seem to be lined up for a long way."

Tsūya said, "When one line curves, the other line curves in the same way on the other side. The two lines seemed to pass forever down the faintly white road. Why would someone make these marks?"

While she was talking, Yasukichi thought of the great desert of Mongolia projected by a magic lantern. Two stripes continued as thin lines even in that great desert.

"Tsūya, what are you saying?"

"Well, think about it. Why are the two lined up? Why are they lined up?"

Like all oracles, Tsūya only provided an obscure hint. Finally, Yasukichi eagerly lined up two chopsticks, or mittens, or taiko drumsticks. She didn't readily show satisfaction, whatever the answer, but strangely smiled and, as usual, repeated "No."

"Come on, tell me. Tsūya. Stupid Tsūya!"

At last, Yasukichi got angry. His father rarely dared to challenge him to fight when he was mad. Tsūya, who protected him for so long, was well aware of this. Finally, she solemnly explained the mystery on the road.

"These are the tracks left by the wheels of a cart."

These are tracks left by cart wheels! The astonished Yasukichi stared at the two lines that intermittently appeared in the dust. At the same time, the vision of the great desert in Mongolia vanished like a mirage. The wheel of a cart covered in mud turned on its own in his lonely heart.

Yasukichi still relived that time, and the important lesson stayed in his mind. Thinking about it thirty years later, not having a full understanding of things may be the happiest time in life.

3 Death

This story is also from that time. While holding a Rokubei sake cup in his hand, his father faced a small dining tray with his dinner drink and, for some reason, said, "There appears to be a reason to congratulate you and the teacher of the two-string koto in Maki-chō."

Lamp light vibrantly illuminated the black-lacquered tray. There was no overflow of beautiful colors on the tray this time. Yasukichi loved the colors of foods: the dried millet roe, baked seaweed, vinegared oysters.

What he loved the most were not refined colors but only vivid colors rich in gaudy stimulation. In front of his tray that night, he scrutinized the bluefin tuna sashimi on a bed of seaweed. His slightly intoxicated father probably interpreted his artistic interest as material wants.

As soon as he lifted the ivory chopsticks, he took the sashimi that gave off the aroma of soy sauce to his nose. Of course, he ate it in one bite. To express his gratitude, he said to his father, "Before it was another teacher, this time, I'm being congratulated!"

His father, as well as his mother and aunt, laughed at the same time, but that laughter was not necessarily because they understood his witty answer. This doubt made him somewhat uneasy about his self-esteem. Making his father laugh was nothing less than a great achievement. He was extremely pleased by the cheerfulness he had created in the house. At once, Yasukichi laughed as loudly as he could with his father.

After the laughter died down, his smiling father's large hand patted the scruff of Yasukichi's neck.

"The reason for the congratulations will die."

Every answer does not cut off the root of the question like a plow. Instead of an old question, it only serves as a pruning shear to make room for a new question to bloom. Like the Yasukichi of thirty years ago, when he finally thought of an answer, he discovered a new question in another answer.

"Will die? What do you mean?"

"Listen, will die is like when you kill an ant."

His father meticulously explained death with sympathy. His father's explanation was not the least bit satisfying to the boy who clung to the logic of youth. Naturally, he was only certain an ant that he had killed no longer ran. But it didn't die; he simply killed it. More than the dead ant, it must be an ant that was not especially killed by him and did not bother to run. He doesn't remember meeting that ant under a stone lantern or at the base of a winter-green tree. For some reason, his father entirely ignores the distinction.

"The killed ant died."

"Isn't being killed just being killed?"

"Being killed is the same as dying."

"So you say the killed one was killed."

"Whatever you say, it's the same."

"No. No. Being killed and dying are not the same."

"That's stupid. You don't understand what I'm saying."

Of course, His father's scolding made Yasukichi burst into tears. Despite being scolded, there's no reason to understand what is not understood. Over the next few months, he continued to think about the problem of death like an eminent philosopher. Death is a puzzle. A killed ant is not a dead ant. Even so, it is a dead ant.

This is not an elusive problem rich in the allure of this sort of secret. Each time Yasukichi thought about death, he recalled two dogs he happened to see one day on the grounds of Ekōin Temple. Those dogs were like one dog with its faces turned in opposite directions in the light of the setting sun. Also, it was strangely solemn. Death may have aspects that somehow resemble the two dogs.

Around the time the fires were lit, Yasukichi went into the dim bathroom where his father went after returning home from the city hall. He entered the bathroom but hadn't washed his body. He fearfully stood by the bath up to his chest to make the maiden voyage of a sailboat with a raised white jib sail.

A visitor or someone else probably came. A maid older than Tsuru opened the glass sliding door and said, "Sir," followed by other words to his father. Covered in soap and holding a sponge, his father replied, "All right, I'll be right out."

Then, he looked at Yasukichi and said, "Don't get in. Your mother is next."

After his father leaves, he won't interfere with the maiden voyage of the special sailboat. Yasukichi glanced at his father and meekly replied, "Okay."

His father dried his body, slung the damp towel over his shoulder, and raised his thick waist with a grunt. Yasukichi absentmindedly adjusted the jib sail of his sailboat. He looked up at the sound of the glass door opening again and saw the naked back of his father in the steam going out to the other side of the bathroom. His hair was not yet white.

His waist was straight like a young man's. For some reason, the four-year-old Yasukichi's spirit felt stabbed by loneliness at the sight of his father's back. He forgot his sailboat for an instant and was, without thinking, about to call out "Father." However, the second sound of the glass door quietly hid his father's figure. The faint light spread and later mingled with the scent of a hot bath.

Yasukichi opened his large, dazed eyes in the quietly prepared bath. He discovered death that he previously found impossible to understand. Death is his father's figure disappearing for eternity!

4 The Sea

Yasukichi learned about the sea when he was five or six years old. The sea he learned of was not the vast ocean. He simply learned about the cramped Tokyo Bay at the Ōmori coast. At the same time, however, Yasukichi was amazed by the constricted Tokyo Bay. A poet of the Nara era sang about the love of going to the sea in

> *A great ship anchors*
> *In the sea of Katori*
> *Who's not lost in thought?*

Of course, Yasukichi knew nothing of love and things said in the poems of the *Man'yōshū*. The fact is the sea misting in the sunlight creates strange feelings of sorrowful mystery. He gazed at the sea while at the railing of a teahouse with a reed screen hanging over the water. The sea buoyed a number of ships raising brilliant white sails. A steamboat with two stacks pulling long trails of smoke through the air sailed off.

A flock of gulls with long wings flew at an angle over the surface of the sea while crying just like cats. Where did those ships and gulls come from, and where are they going? The sea was only a misty, lush green beyond layers of seaweed clumps.

However, he experienced the mystery of the sea more vividly when he went with his father or uncle to the shore of a shallow beach. For the first time, Yasukichi was scared by the ripples quietly approaching the sand.

But that was a fragment of his true emotions when he entered the sea with his father or uncle. Of course, his later self enjoyed all the fortune of the sea. The sea gazed at from the railing of the teahouse was ominous at the same time a curiosity, like an unfamiliar face.

However, the sea seen while standing on a tidal flat is the same as a large toy box. A toy box! Like a true god, he turned the world of the sea into a toy. Crabs and parasitic shellfish walked back and forth in the dazzling lagoon. The waves carried clumps of seaweed before him. Is the one that resembled a trumpet a trumpet shell? Hiding in the sand was a littleneck clam.

Yasukichi's enjoyment was splendid. However, there was no reason for loneliness within this enjoyment. He believed blue was the color of the sea. That blue was the color seen in both multicolor woodblock prints of Gekkō or Toshikata sold in Daihei in Ryōgoku and currently popular lithographs of the sea.

A scene of naval warfare, demonstrated with mechanical devices at festivals, created leaping white-capped waves; the waves so deep blue they seemed poisonous on this so-called Yellow Sea. However, the sea color before his eyes is a blue mist only off the coast. The sea close to the shore didn't have a hint of blue.

Actually, it was a muddy color, like a stagnant muddy puddle. No, it was more than a stagnant muddy puddle. It was a vibrant reddish brown. He felt the emptiness of being betrayed by the reddish-brown sea. At the same time, he also bravely recognized the brutal reality. Thinking the sea is blue is a mistake of adults looking from the shore. Anyone who has ever bathed in the sea like him knows this obvious truth. The sea is a reddish brown that resembles the rust on a bucket.

Yasukichi's attitude of thirty years ago will be the same thirty years from now. The sooner he recognized the yellowish-brown sea, the better. The change of the reddish-brown sea into a blue sea was all in vain. Moreover, he could discover the beautiful shells in the sandbars of the yellowish-brown sea. Like the coast, the sea may turn into a blue sheet. More than yearning for the future, he would live a contented life now. While Yasukichi respected a few friends rich in prophetic spirit, he thought he was always alone at the bottom of his heart.

After they returned home from the sea at Ōmori, his mother bought him the *Urashima Tarō* book from the *Old Folktales of Japan* series on the way home at some shop. Of course, he enjoyed having this tale read to him. However, he experienced another pleasure. He painted the illustrations using watercolor supplies he already had.

He quickly colored in *Urashima Tarō*. That book had just ten illustrations. He began coloring in a drawing of Urashima Tarō leaving the Palace of the Dragon King. This palace had red pillars and green roof tiles. After a little thought about Princess Otohime, he only colored her clothes red. With no need to think about it, he colored Urashima Tarō's fishermen's clothes dark indigo and a fishermen's grass skirt light yellow.

Unexpectedly, he found it difficult to color an entire thin fishing rod yellow. Also, painting only the hands of a cape-wearing turtle green was challenging work. Finally, the sea was reddish brown that resembled rust on a bucket. Yasukichi felt the satisfaction of an artist by adjusting the colors. In particular, he believed he conveyed vitality by adding pink to Otohime's and Urashima Tarō's faces.

Yasukichi hurried to show his work to his mother. She was engaged in needlework and glanced over her reading glasses to look at the colors of the illustrations. Naturally, he expected words of praise from her. However, she did not seem to be as impressed by the colors as he was.

"The color of the sea is strange. Why didn't you paint it blue?"

"But the sea is this color."

"I guess the sea is reddish brown."

"Isn't the sea at Ōmori reddish brown?"

"The sea at Ōmori is bright blue."

"Um, this is the perfect color."

His mother let slip a smile mixed with admiration of his stubbornness. No matter how much she explained ... well, after a temper tantrum and tearing up his *Urashima Tarō*, the only thing she didn't believe was the unquestionable reddish brown sea. That sums up the conversation about the sea.

Today's Yasukichi has no difficulty devising a more fitting ending for a novel. For example, before the story ends, these few lines are added. "Yasukichi made one more important discovery in the exchange of questions and answers with his mother. As for the reddish-brown sea, anyone easily overlooks the reddish-brown sea that spans human life."

This is not reality. High tide created blue waves in the sea at Ōmori. Is the sea reddish brown? Is the sea really blue? In the end, our realism is nothing other than being completely unreliable. At the same time, Yasukichi ended the story with the same artlessness as before. But what is the form of a story? Firstly, art is substance, as all of you say. Descriptions are not obstacles.

5 The Magic Lantern

"Please light the lamp like this."

The proprietor of a toy shop lit a yellow match flame in a metal lamp. Then, he opened the back door of the magic lantern and gently placed the lamp inside the instrument. Without taking a breath, the seven-year-old Yasukichi watched the proprietor's hand hesitate before the table. He watched the hand of the strangely pale proprietor, his hair parted neatly on the left. The time was around three o'clock.

The outside glass door of the toy store reflected the constant stream of pedestrians hit by the full rays of the sun. Inside the toy store, especially a corner of the store with a haphazard stack of empty toy boxes did not change under the dim light at twilight. Yasukichi was somehow spooked whenever he came here. Now, however, he forgot all his feelings about the proprietor who was showing how the magic lantern projects a picture. He even forgot about his father standing behind him.

"When you insert the lamp, the moon rises over there."

The proprietor finally stood and pointed to the white wall across the room to direct his father's rather than Yasukichi's attention. The magic lantern drew a circle of light spanning just three feet on the white wall. Naturally, the circle of soft yellow light resembled the moon. They clearly saw spider webs and dust only at that spot on the white wall.

"I'll project this picture there."

When a clicking sound was heard, the light circle instantly projected a blurry image. Yasukichi focused on the mysterious projection while his curiosity was further stimulated by the smell of heated metal. The image projected there could not be discerned as a scene or people. The little that could be distinguished were colors resembling soap bubbles. No, they were similar in ways other than color. The thing projected on the white wall was a giant soap bubble. The soap bubble was inside dimness drifting in from somewhere like something in a dream.

"Now I will focus that blur with the lens … this lens in front. As you see, it immediately becomes clear."

Once again, the proprietor hesitated. At the same time, the soap bubble changed to a landscape before their eyes. Of course, it was not a Japanese landscape. The landscape from somewhere in the West was a bird's-eye view of houses on both sides of a canal. The time was close to sunset. A crescent moon shone faint light into the sky above the houses on the right. The crescent moon, the houses, and the roses at the windows of the houses quietly cast vivid shadows on the still water. No human shadow nor lone gull came into view. The water continued in a line directly below the abutted bridge.

"This is a scene of Venice, Italy."

The Venetian charm was taught to Yasukichi thirty years later by the novels of D'Annunzio. At that time, however, Yasukichi felt the hazy loneliness of the houses and the canal. The scenes he loves are Asakusa with countless pigeons flying in front of the red-painted Kannon-dō, where a horse-drawn tram passed through Ginza beneath the tall clock tower.

Compared to these scenes, the houses and the canal seemed

steeped in sadness. It's fine not to be shown horse-drawn trams or pigeons. The thought struck him that at least a train should pass over the bridge over there. Then, the small face of a girl wearing a big ribbon suddenly appeared at one of the windows on the right. He couldn't quite remember which window it was.

He was only sure the window was beneath the crescent moon. Just as the girl showed her face, she turned her face toward them. And did a smile rise on her sweet face seen from a distance? But that incident lasted a priceless one or two seconds. When he exclaimed, "Oh," without thinking and stared, the girl's figure instantly disappeared from the window. The window, like any window, hung a solitary curtain.

"Well, you probably understand how projection works now?"

His father's words snapped him out of his daydream and back to the real world. His father held a cigarette in his mouth and stood in the back, looking bored. The street outside the toy store was an endless, unchanging stream of pedestrians. The proprietor with his tidy hair part, also beamed a smile of satisfaction near his strangely pallid cheeks like a magician who had completed a preliminary test. Yasukichi remembered how he wanted to grab this magic lantern one moment sooner and return home to his room.

That night with his father, Yasukichi projected another Venetian scene on a wax-coated cloth. The light of the water in the canal, reflecting the crescent moon in the sky; the houses on both sides; and the roses in the windows of the houses were all seen as before. For some reason, only the face of the adorable girl didn't appear this time. Even after waiting for each window, the secrets of each house were sealed behind dangling curtains. Eventually, Yasukichi could not bear the anticipation and appealed to his father over his problem with the lantern.

"Why didn't that girl appear?"

"A girl? Where is the girl?"

His father had no idea what Yasukichi was asking.

"Yeah, I can't say, but didn't her face appear at a window?"

"When?"

"When it was projected on the wall in the toy store."

"No girl appeared then."

"But I saw a face appear."

"What are you talking about?"

His father placed his palm on Yasukichi's forehead and wondered what he was thinking. Then, understanding Yasukichi's mood, he loudly said, "Well, what shall we project next?"

But Yasukichi wasn't listening but focused on the Venetian scene. The window reflected the still curtains on the dim waters in the canal. However, from a window somewhere at some time, the girl wearing a big ribbon might suddenly appear. Thinking it over, he felt an indescribable nostalgia.

At the same time, he felt both happiness and sadness that he had never known. Could the girl whose face fleetingly appeared in the magic lantern of that picture have been the manifestation before his eyes of something real or a supernatural spirit? Or, was it nothing more than a hallucination easily imagined by a boy? Of course, he had no answer. Even today, thirty years later, when exhausted by the struggles of daily life, Yasukichi recalled that Venetian girl who never came home, like remembering his first love, a woman whose face he had not seen in many years.

6 Mother

When eight or nine years old, it was some autumn or another. The army general Kawashima inspected an allied army while stopped before the stone pedestal of the Wet Buddha at Ekōin Temple. Although called an army, the allies were only Yasukichi and four others. The exception, Yasukichi, wore a school uniform with silver buttons. The others wore dark blue kimonos with a white splash pattern and plain striped, tubular sleeves.

This isn't the Ekōin that falls inside the compound, of course, in the shadow of the Kokugikan sumo arena. This is the Ekōin of twenty years ago that created a mountain of fallen ginkgo leaves near the grave of the thief Nezumi Kozō during the morning of an autumn storm. The scene at that time had strangely rustic colors.

That scene in Honjo, at the edge of Edo rather than what is properly called Edo, vanished long ago.

Only the pigeons are the same, but the pigeons may be different, too. That day, the area around the stone pedestal of the Wet Buddha was crowded with pigeons. Like today, none of the pigeons looked well-groomed.

> *In front of the gate*
> *Wild pigeons appear like friends*
> *Anise sweets for sale*

This work by a haiku poet from the Tenpō era probably didn't just chant about selling star anise candies at Ekōin. When Yasukichi saw this verse, he couldn't help but recall the pigeons always crowded around the stone pedestal of the Wet Buddha and warbling with faint sunlight trembling in their voices deep inside their throats.

After the leisurely inspection ended, Kawashima, the child of a file maker, took out a stack of playing cards along with a knife, and pachinko and rubber balls. The playing cards were for a military shōgi game sold at neighborhood candy stores.

As Kawashima passed out each playing card, he appointed his four underlings. Here, the appointments are announced. Hiramatsu, the son of a cooper, is a major general. Tamiya, the son of a policeman, is a captain. Oguri, the son of a haberdasher, is a combat engineer. Horikawa Yasukichi is a landmine explosion.

Landmine explosion is not a bad role. If he simply does not encounter the combat engineer, his role can turn the general into a prisoner. Of course, Yasukichi was a strong point. The chubby, rotund Oguri voiced his dissatisfaction with his appointment as a combat engineer.

"A combat engineer is boring. Right, Kawashima? Please make me a landmine explosion, too."

"Won't you become a prisoner at some time?" rebuked the serious-looking Kawashima.

Oguri turned red but did not hesitate to answer, "You're lying. Before, wasn't I the general who became the prisoner?"

"Really? Well, you'll be the captain the next time."

Kawashima was about to grin but immediately placated Oguri. Still, Yasukichi was surprised by the sharpness of the wicked cunning of this boy. Before he finished grade school, Kawashima died from fever. If by rare chance he hadn't died and, with luck, wasn't educated, at least by now, he should have become a promising, young city council official.

"Start the war!"

The voice raised this time was the enemy army of four or five who had taken up positions before the front gate. Today, the enemy army assigned the role of the general to Matsumoto, the son of a lawyer. Matsumoto wore a red shirt that poked through the chest of his dark blue kimono with a splash pattern. Matsumoto, who parted his hair, was waving around his school cap high to signal the start of the war.

"Start the war!"

Gripping the playing cards, Yasukichi gave Kawashima's order and shouted the battle cry far ahead of anyone. At the same time, numerous pigeons quietly flocked together and flew up by taking a large detour into the middle of the sky, accompanied by the roar of flapping wings. And then, an unprecedented fierce battle broke out.

Gunpowder smoke rapidly formed a mountain before his eyes. Enemy shells exploded around them like rain. But the allies bravely closed in on the enemy camp.

The best landmine explosion of the enemy quickly raised a fierce column of fire and turned the allies' major general into bits and pieces. However, the enemy army also lost a colonel, followed by the loss of the unique combat engineer feared by Yasukichi. Seeing this, the allies continued their attack, more ferocious than before.

Of course, this is not a fact. The fierce battle scene at Ekōin was reflected in Yasukichi's fantasy. But while he ran around inside the lonely compound brightened only by fallen leaves, he sensed the powerful smell of gunpowder smoke and flashes of gunfire leaping about. At one time, he even felt the heart of the landmine explosion waiting for a chance to explode deep underground.

After entering middle school, the lively fantasy abandoned him in a flash. Today, he doesn't see the fierce battle at the Siege of Port Arthur when playing war but only sees playing war in the Siege of Port Arthur. He had to understand the supreme pleasure of re-imagining those long-ago fantasies.

The gunpowder smoke vividly formed a mountain and exploded around them like rain. Yasukichi let fly a blade at the enemy general. He dodged and fled at top speed to his positions. Yasukichi pursued close behind but immediately tripped over a stone and fell, landing face up. In that moment, his brave fantasy vanished like a soap bubble. He was no longer the landmine explosion a moment ago that was filled with honor.

His face was smeared with blood from his nose. This boy, not even wearing a hat, opened a giant hole at the knee of his pants. When he finally stood, he bawled without thinking. The enemy boys halted the long-awaited fierce battle in this mayhem and gathered around Yasukichi. A few spoke.

"Whoa, he's hurt."

"He's flat on his back."

"Hey, that's not our fault."

Yasukichi hid his face behind his arms and kept on crying even harder out of indescribable sadness more than pain. All of a sudden, a sneering voice reached his ears. It was the general, Kawashima.

"Hey, your mother dislikes crying!"

In an instant, Kawashima's words changed the enemies' and allies' words into laughter. The loudest laughter came from Oguri, who had failed to become a landmine explosion.

"That's funny. Your mother dislikes crying!"

Although Yasukichi cried, he didn't remember saying "Mother." That slander was Kawashima being mean as usual. These thoughts increased the frustration in his sadness. He began crying and shaking. But he was spineless, and no one showed any kindness. And while they imitated Kawashima's words, they ran off and scattered somewhere.

"Hey, your mother dislikes crying!"

Yasukichi came to hate their voices receding little by little. Without looking at the numerous pigeons that descended to his feet again, he stopped the interminable sobbing.

Since then, Yasukichi only believed that "mother" was a lie invented by Kawashima. Exactly three years ago, at the same time he landed in Shanghai, he entered a hospital because of the influenza he brought from Tokyo. His fever after he entered the hospital was not easily eliminated.

He opened his hazy eyes on the white bed and gazed at the awfulness of the yellow dust carried by the Mongolian spring. One muggy afternoon, a nurse who was reading a novel suddenly left her chair, walked to his bedside, and peeked at his face. She looked puzzled.

"Oh my, are you awake?"

"What?"

"Did you just say, 'Mother'?"

As soon as Yasukichi heard this word, he remembered the Ekōin compound. Perhaps, Kawashima had not told a malicious lie.

(April 1924)

25

THE COLD

It was a snowy morning. Yasukichi gazed at the stove fire from a chair in the physics faculty room. The fire weakly flared in yellow as if it were breathed on and sinking under the black embers. This was proof of the battle with the cold drifting into the room. Yasukichi felt more sympathetic to the coals heated red while suddenly imagining the coldness of space beyond the Earth.

"Horikawa."

Yasukichi looked up at the face of Miyamoto, a bachelor of science, standing in front of the stove. With his hands shoved in his pants pockets, a pleasing smile rose on Miyamoto's lips adorned with a thin mustache. He also wore eyeglasses for nearsightedness.

"Horikawa. Do you know that women are also objects?"

"I know they are animals."

"They aren't animals. They are objects. This recently discovered truth caused me pain."

"Horikawa, you must seriously question what Miyamoto is saying."

This other person was a physics instructor with a bachelor's degree named Hasegawa. Yasukichi turned to him. Hasegawa examined the test answer sheet on the desk behind Yasukichi and grew a confused-looking weak smile on the face with a receding hairline.

"This is shameful. Shouldn't my discovery make Hasegawa very happy? Horikawa, do you know the laws of heat transfer?"

"Heat transfer? Is that the heat of electricity?"

"Literary types are a problem."

Meanwhile, Miyamoto shoveled a cup of coal through the stove door reflecting the flames.

"Two objects having different temperatures come into contact with each other. Heat moves from the high-temperature object to the low-temperature object until the temperatures of the two are equal."

"Isn't that normal?"

"That is called the law of heat transfer. Well, a woman is an object. Right? If a woman is an object, of course, a man is also an object. So love is like heat. Now, when this man and woman come into contact, like heat transfer, the transfer of love from the more obsessed man to the disinterested woman continues until the love between the two is equal. This seems true in Hasegawa's case."

"It has started."

Looking happy, Hasegawa spoke with a joking tone.

"Now, let the area passed be S and the amount of heat transferred in time T be E. Then … is this okay? H is the temperature; X, the distance measured in the direction of heat conduction; and K, the heat conductivity fixed by the material. In Hasegawa's case …"

Miyamoto began writing what looked like a formula on a small blackboard. He abruptly turned and flung away the piece of chalk, perhaps, in disappointment.

"The uninitiated Horikawa will be the subject. There will be no boasting about a precious discovery. Anyway, the woman who becomes Hasegawa's fiancée will emerge from a formula."

"If a formula existed, the world would be considerably easier to navigate."

Yasukichi stretched his legs and lazily gazed at the wintry scene beyond the window. This physics faculty room occupied a corner of the second floor. The grounds for exercise equipment, a row of pines facing the grounds, and a red brick building facing that were easily surveyed at a glance. The sea was shrouded by the hazy waves glimpsed between the buildings.

"Instead, a literary man will be presented. What do you think are the prospects for this book that was recently released?"

"As always, it won't sell at all. No heat transfer effect will develop between the author and the readers. Incidentally, Hasegawa's not married?"

"Not yet, in just a month. Various matters are involved, so I'm tired and can't study."

"You're looking forward so much you can't study."

"I'm not Miyamoto. First, it would be hard even if I had a house and didn't rent. Last Sunday, I walked around most of the city looking. But sometimes when I thought something was available, it had already been reserved."

"How about where I live? I don't mind commuting by train to school every day."

"You're a little too far away. There are rentals in that area. My wife would like that area. Hey, Horikawa, are your shoes getting scorched?"

Yasukichi's shoes appeared to be touching the stove's body. The smell of burning leather rose with water vapor.

"You, too, are experiencing heat transfer."

As Miyamoto wiped his eyeglasses, through hopeless nearsightedness, he flashed a grin at Yasukichi.

Four or five days later, the morning was frosty and cloudy. Yasukichi had to catch a train to dash as fast as possible to an out-of-town summer retreat to escape the heat. A barley field lined the right side of the road. On the left was an embankment of just twelve feet for the train tracks. The barley field was empty of people but filled with indistinct noises. It simply sounded like someone was walking between the barley, but actually sounded like an ice column crumbling under turned-over earth.

While the whistle of the 8 o'clock train to Tokyo blew for a long time, the train passed over the embankment without gaining much speed. The train leaving Tokyo to be caught by Yasukichi should arrive in thirty minutes. He took out and checked his watch. Was his watch malfunctioning? It was quarter past eight. He explained this time difference as the fault of the watch. He wasn't worried about missing the train today. The barley field next to the road slowly changed into hedges. Yasukichi lit an Asahi-brand cigarette and walked with a more relaxed gait than before.

The road spread with coal cinders came out at the train crossing at a steep hill. He inadvertently ended up there. Yasukichi discovered crowds on both sides of the crossing. He suddenly thought about being run over and killed by a train. Fortunately, on the railing side of the crossing, a familiar butcher's apprentice, carrying a bundle, had stopped his bicycle. With his hand holding the cigarette, he tapped the apprentice's shoulder from behind.

"Hey, what happened?"

"He was run over. He was hit on the way up."

The apprentice said this quickly. His face framed by rabbit earmuffs was strangely bright.

"Who was run over?"

"The crossing guard. He got run over trying to save a school student from being hit. Oh, was he the bookseller called Nagai in Hachimanmae? The girl over there was about to be run over."

"Was the child saved?"

"Yes, it looks like she's that girl crying over there."

A crowd had formed on the other side of the train crossing. Of course, a girl was being questioned by the police. From time to time, a man who looked like a junior official on that side talked to the patrolman. The crossing guard ... Yasukichi discovered the corpse covered by a straw mat in front of the crossing guard's box. The truth is he was repulsed and curious at the same time. From a distance, he could see only the shoes on his feet under the mat.

"Those people carried the corpse."

Several railroad laborers under a signal pole on this side surrounded a small bonfire. The fire of yellow flames gave off no light or smoke. It seemed bitterly cold. One laborer wearing shorts warmed his buttocks near the fire.

Yasukichi crossed the crossing. He crossed several railroad tracks because they were close to the station. Each time he crossed one, he wondered where the crossing guard had been hit. Soon, which track was obvious to his eyes. Blood still told the tragedy that had occurred two or three minutes ago on the tracks. He moved his eyes mostly to the opposite side of the crossing. But that didn't work. In an instant, the scene of the gooey red substance accumulated on the cold, shiny iron surface was vividly burned into his heart. Not only blood, but a faint water vapor rose from the tracks.

Ten minutes later, Yasukichi was still restlessly walking on the station platform. His face was still haunted by the awful scene he saw moments ago. Particularly, the water vapor rising from the blood loomed in his eyes. He remembered the heat transfer they discussed. The heat of life inhabiting blood, according to the law explained by Miyamoto, is cruelly transferred without the slightest deviation to the tracks.

Everyone's life is good but is callously transferred in the same way, whether the crossing guard who died doing his job or a hardened criminal. Of course, he understood this meaningless thought. Even a devoted child must drown in water, and the faithful wife must be consumed by fire. He repeatedly persuaded himself in his heart. However, the truths seen in his eyes left the deepest impression, not easily explained by logic.

The people on the platform were detached from his feelings and looked blissful. That irritated Yasukichi. Any discussion in raised voices, especially by commissioned naval officers, was physically unpleasant. He lit a second Asahi and walked to the front of the platform where the crossing could be seen seven hundred to one thousand feet up the line. The crowds on both sides of the crossing had mostly scattered. The bonfire of the railroad laborers under the signal pole was a speck, and the yellow flame flickered.

Yasukichi's emotions resembled that distant flame. Seeing the crossing was no different than anxiety. He turned his back and returned to the crowd. However, before he took ten steps, he realized he had dropped a red leather glove. When he lit the cigarette, he walked while carrying the glove of only his right hand. He looked back. The glove was palm up at the front of the platform. It soundlessly called to stop him.

Beneath the frosty, cloudy sky, Yasukichi felt the center of the remaining red leather glove. In a slightly chilly world, he felt the gentle rays beaming down from the warm sun.

(April 1924)

26

A TEN YEN BILL

One cloudy morning in early summer, Horikawa Yasukichi, with a heavy heart, trudged up the stone steps of the platform. That said, it was not particularly important. He had the unpleasant thought that he was broke with only sixty-something sen in his pants pocket.

In those days, Horikawa Yasukichi was constantly tormented by money problems. His salary for teaching English was a measly sixty yen a month. Although a short story he wrote in his spare time had been published in the monthly magazine *Chūōkōron*, it didn't bring him more than ninety sen. Even with a monthly room rent of only five yen and spending fifty sen per meal, he never had enough money. He loved his pride in himself rather than his style and, at least, valued its economic importance.

However, he had to read books. He had to smoke Egyptian cigarettes and attend performances at musical societies. He also had to see the faces of friends. At any rate, he had to go to Tokyo once a week to see the faces of women who weren't friends.

He chased life's luxuries, naturally, took advances on manuscript fees, and burdened his parents and siblings. Nevertheless, when he still lacked money, he entrusted a large collection of paintings to an earthen-walled warehouse that hung a lantern under the eaves of red-colored glass and where few people came and went.

Now, however, the prospect of an advance was gone, and he fought with his parents and siblings. No, that's not the current situation. Somehow, the newly tailored silk hat costing eighteen yen and fifty sen for National Foundation Day was out of reach.

While walking down the crowded platform, Yasukichi vividly remembered the beautiful, glossy silk hat. The cylindrical crown of the silk hat glimmered in the light from the warehouse window. Its crown reflected the magnolias flowering beyond the window. However, a thick finger feeling sixty-something sen at the bottom of his pants ruptured that dream.

Today makes ten days, but he had to wait around two weeks to receive a Western-style envelope addressed to Instructor Horikawa on payday, the twenty-eighth. Tomorrow, however, was Sunday, the day he goes to Tokyo for recreation. He planned to have dinner tomorrow with Hase or Ōtomo. He wanted to buy Scott's oil painting tools and canvases that were not available locally. He also wished to attend Fräulein Mellendorf's concert. But with only sixty-something sen, he had to abandon the trip to Tokyo.

"Well, goodbye to tomorrow."

Yasukichi was about to put a rolled cigarette in his mouth to dispel the gloom. Unfortunately, not even one remained in the pocket his hand searched. He felt a small smile on his face of an increasingly malicious fate and walked over to a peddler standing outside of the waiting room. He wore a green flat hat. The lightly pockmarked peddler stared, always a little bored, at the newspapers and caramels in the box slung over his neck. He was not an ordinary merchant. He was an abstraction of a negative soul that hinders our lives. Yasukichi felt a keen frustration with this peddler's attitude today, too—no, especially today.

"Asahi, please."

"Asahi?"

Avoiding eye contact, the peddler asked back as if in condemnation.

"The newspaper? The cigarette?"

Yasukichi felt tremors between his eyes.

"The beer!"

The shocked peddler focused on Yasukichi's face.

"I don't have Asahi Beer."

Feeling a sense of relief, Yasukichi stepped behind the peddler. He no longer needed a drag from the Asahi he came to buy or anything else. A kick to the despicable peddler was more pleasurable than smoking a Havana cigar. As though he forgot the sixty-something sen at the bottom of his pants pocket, he walked to the front of the platform like Napoleon after the major victory at the Battle of Wagram.

THE GRAY CLIFF, oblivious to rocks and mud, soared high into the cloudy sky. The iron shards in that cliff, devoid of grass or trees, blurred into a faded green mist. Yasukichi absentmindedly walked alone below this cliff. After being shaken on a train for thirty minutes, he experienced endless agony by then having to walk a dusty road for nearly thirty more. Agony? No, it was not agony. The law of inertia instantly stole even the sense of agony. Every day, he walked below this cliff that resembled boredom itself. Being subjected to the karmic suffering of hell is not necessarily our tragedy. Our tragedy is not sensing the karmic suffering of hell as karmic suffering. He leapt once a week outside of this tragedy. Now, however, only sixty-something sen remained at the bottom of his pants pocket.

"Good morning."

Suddenly, the voice of Awano, the head instructor, greeted him. Awano was probably over fifty. This gentleman had a dark complexion, wore glasses for nearsightedness, and stooped over slightly. An instructor at the naval school where Yasukichi worked, from the beginning, he never wore anything other than a timeless navy blue serge suit. Of course, Awano wore a new straw hat with his suit. Yasukichi politely bowed.

"Good morning."

"It's gotten rather humid."

"How is your daughter? I heard she had been ill."

"Thank you for asking. She was released from the hospital yesterday."

The Yasukichi who appeared before Awano was civil, like a different person. This was not hollow formality at all. He greatly respected the linguistic genius of Awano. Awano, who died at the age of sixty, taught about Caesar in Latin. Now, beginning with English, of course, he knew various modern languages. At one time, Yasukichi may not have known about Awano's *Asino* but was astounded by his reading an Italian book with that title. However, Yasukichi's high regard for Awano was not only for his linguistic genius. Awano possessed the generosity expected of a rich man.

When Yasukichi came across a difficult passage in an English textbook, he always sought advice from Awano. To save time when he had difficulty understanding, he sometimes didn't pull out a dictionary before he sought help. But in this case, out of respect for Awano, he expended all his energy pretending to be confused.

Awano always answered his questions with ease. However, only when the solution was too simple that Yasukichi remembered his hypocritical attitude of pretending to be in thoughtful reflection. Awano always hummed with an unlit pipe in his mouth when he faced Yasukichi's textbook. Then at the perfect moment, as if suddenly told by Heaven, he said, "This probably means ..." and explained the section in one burst. Yasukichi likely respected Awano to some degree for this play acting in his manner of teaching as a hypocrite rather than as a linguistic genius.

"Tomorrow is Sunday. Do you still go to Tokyo on Sundays?"

"Yes, well, no, I'm not going tomorrow."

"Why not?"

"The truth is ... I'm broke."

"You're joking?"

Awano let a slightly amused voice escape. He smiled with reserve, his canine teeth visible in the shadow of a reddish brown mustache.

"You have the manuscript fee in addition to a monthly wage and should possess a sizable income."

This time, his companion, Yasukichi, said, "You're joking." He intended for his words to sound far more serious than Awano's.

"As you know, my monthly wage is sixty yen, but the manuscript fee is ninety sen per page. Even if I write fifty pages in one month, that's a measly forty-five yen. Add to that the manuscript fee of a small magazine of around sixty sen …"

Yasukichi immediately launched into a fervent speech on the difficulty in making a living as a freelance writer. He wasn't only embarking on an argument. His naturally poetic passion gave rise to exaggeration in an instant. A dramatist or novelist in Japan, especially his friends, must be content with miserable poverty. Hase Masao is drinking Denki Bran cocktails instead of sake. Ōtomo Yūkichi, his wife, and children rent a three-tatami-mat room on the second floor. Matsumoto Hōjō too … Matsumoto Hōjō may be living better since marrying. Until recently, however, he went in and out of a yakitori shop.

"Appearances deceive. Don't they?"

Without joking or being serious, Awano gave a half-hearted acknowledgement.

In no time, both sides of the road changed into squalid wooden tradesmen's houses. The ornamental windows were covered in dust, and advertisements peeled from the electrical poles. Despite being called a city, the colors characteristic of a city were not seen anywhere. The streaks of black smoke and white steam stretching across the sky above the tiled roofs of large gantry cranes were frightening sights worthy of a shiver. While peering at the scene from beneath the brim of his straw hat, Yasukichi was moved by the tragedies of the freelance writers he knew and exaggerated. As if he forgot his pride in his stoicism he usually valued, he made a show of the contents of his pants with one hand thrust in a pocket.

"The truth is I want to go to Tokyo, but having only sixty-something sen settles the matter."

～

YASUKICHI BEGAN to prepare for his class by using the textbook propped on the front of the desk in the faculty room. An article about the naval battle at Jutland usually is not a pleasant read. In particular, today he lost his temper over wanting to go to Tokyo. After scanning just one page of an English naval dictionary in one hand, he started to think gloomily about the sixty-odd sen at the bottom of his pocket.

At eleven-thirty, the faculty room fell silent of human sounds when ten instructors went to their classrooms leaving Awano alone. Awano was entirely hidden on the other side of a dreary bookcase that isolated two desks. Pale blue pipe smoke hazily drifted up from time to time in a space backed by a white wall as proof of Awano's existence. Of course, the scene outside the window did not quietly change. Everything——the treetops of young leaves together in the cloudy sky, the mouse-gray school building continued after that, and the dimly lit cove beyond that——sank into humidity, melancholy, and silence.

Yasukichi remembered the cigarettes. But after the peddler suddenly gained the advantage, he discovered that he had completely forgotten to buy them. Not smoking cigarettes is tragic. Tragic? Or, it may not be tragic. Compared to the agony of poor people being chased by the costs of food and clothing, the grief over sixty-odd sen may be a luxury. However, the anguish is the same for poor people and him. No, he has more sensitive nerves than poor people and must suffer more pain.

Poor people ... it's always preferable not to say poor people. The linguistic genius Awano turned out to be extremely indifferent to *Sunflowers* by van Gogh, readings by von Wolff, and the city poems by Verhaeren. No artistry for Awano was the same as no grass for a dog. However, no artistry for Yasukichi was the same as no grass for a donkey. Sixty-odd sen produced the anguish of spiritual starvation in Horikawa Yasukichi. However, Awano Rentarō probably wouldn't be bothered in the least.

"Horikawa."

Awano, a pipe dangling from his mouth, suddenly appeared before Yasukichi. His coming was particularly mysterious. The mystery is being able to see an awkwardness close to a woman's bashfulness in his receding hairline, in his eyes seen through eyeglasses for nearsightedness, in his trimmed mustache, and, if I dare to exaggerate slightly, in the pipe shining in nicotine luster. Yasukichi was stunned. Without asking "How may I help you?" for a short time, he closely watched the elderly instructor's face momentarily resemble that of a young girl.

"Horikawa, this isn't much, but …"

As Awano chuckled to hide his embarrassment, he took out a ten-yen bill folded in quarters.

"This is very little, but please use it for the train fare to Tokyo."

Yasukichi was flustered. Borrowing money from Rockefeller is always imagined. However, he never envisioned, even in a dream, he would borrow money from Awano. He remembered the moment that morning in which he eloquently described to Awano the tragedy of writing for money. He blushed and fumbled for excuses.

"No, I do have pocket money. But if I go to Tokyo, what would I do? That's the primary reason why I'm not going."

"Well, please take it. It's better than nothing."

"The truth is I don't need it, but thank you so much."

Awano looked slightly perplexed as he removed the pipe from his mouth and dropped his eyes to the ten-yen bill folded in quarters. But he immediately raised his eyes and again displayed a nearly bashful smile inside his gold-rimmed eyeglasses.

"Is that so? Well, excuse me for interrupting your studying."

If anything, like a man refused a loan, Awano swiftly put the ten-yen bill in his pocket and rapidly retreated to the other side of the bookshelf of dictionaries and reference books. After that, he was powerless again. Only a clammy silence remained. Yasukichi took out a nickel pocket watch and gazed at his face reflected in its lid.

When he thought he lost his presence of mind, strangely, he looked at himself in the mirror, a habit of his for dozens of years. The lid of the nickel pocket watch shouldn't accurately reflect his face. His face in the small circle was blurred out. Only his nose was extremely broad. Fortunately, his spirit gradually returned to serenity. At the same time, he began to regret turning Awano's kindness into nothing. Awano certainly thought of the satisfaction of the ten-yen bill being happily received rather than it being returned. Rejecting the bill was rude. Moreover, …

Yasukichi flinched when he faced the whirlwind before this "moreover." Moreover, his rejection of the offer after he explained his dilemma was cowardly. It's acceptable to trample obligations and compassion. Courtesy is preferred even if trampled. One must only avoid becoming a coward. As for borrowing money, at least, that money will not be returned until payday on the twenty-eighth. He was fine with whatever he saved from his manuscript fee advance. But not returning the money borrowed from Awano within two weeks would be more unpleasant than becoming a beggar.

After sufficient hesitation, he returned his watch to his pocket and defiantly went to the side of Awano's desk like he was about to pick a fight. Today in the swaying pipe smoke, Awano was easily absorbed in reading a detective novel by Maurice Leblanc at his desk topped with a neat row of objects, including a cigarette tin, ashtray, attendance roster, and permanent paste. But when he noticed Yasukichi, his first thought was a textbook question. So, he closed the detective novel and slowly raised his eyes to Yasukichi's face.

"Awano, please loan me the money. I've thought it over and would like to borrow it," said Yasukichi in one breath.

He remembered Awano standing without a word but didn't notice his expression. Today, seven or eight years later, Yasukichi's dim memory of only Awano's large right hand appeared before his eyes. As if bashful, he timidly held out the one ten-yen bill folded in quarters at the fingertips of that hand; the nail of his thick second finger stained yellow, probably by nicotine.

Yasukichi was determined to return this ten-yen bill to Awano on Monday, the day after tomorrow. He repeated this to be certain. It will surely be this ten-yen bill. He had no ulterior motive. Now, when the prospect of getting a loan was gone, and he argued with his parents and siblings, he clearly could not afford to, for example, go to Tokyo. So, he had to save this ten-yen bill to return the ten yen. To save this ten yen, Yasukichi kept thinking about it and, more than this morning, became more keenly aware of the ten-yen bill mixed with the loose sixty-odd sen coins.

More keenly aware than this morning, but not more melancholy. Then, he only had unpleasant thoughts about having no money. Now, however, he was also excited morally over having to return this ten-yen bill. Moral? Unaware, Yasukichi frowned. No, it is absolutely not morality. He wanted to preserve his dignity before Awano.

The main reason he maintained his dignity was only to repay the borrowed money. If Awano also loved the arts, at least literature, the writer Horikawa Yasukichi should try to uphold his dignity by writing a masterpiece. If Awano were nothing more than a mere linguist like us, the instructor Horikawa Yasukichi should preserve his dignity through a demonstration of his linguistic proficiency.

Neither should be used in front of Awano, a linguistic genius with no interest in the arts. Whether he likes it or not, Yasukichi must maintain his dignity as a member of society. In other words, he must return the money. Even if he goes to the trouble to do this, he may force himself to maintain his dignity or may sound ridiculous. But why? More than anyone else, he wanted to preserve his dignity in the eyes of Awano, a somewhat stooped over elderly gentleman who wore gold-rimmed eyeglasses.

Meanwhile, the train started to move. Rain descending from the cloudy sky caused the battleships on the faintly blue ocean to belch smoke. Yasukichi felt some relief. Fortunately, there were only a few passengers, so he lay face up on a long cushion. He immediately remembered a magazine company in his hometown. Just a month ago, this company sent a long letter to him requesting a contribution. However, he despised and had only contempt for the magazines published by this company and ignored the request.

Selling his work to that magazine company was like having no choice but to sell a daughter into prostitution. But even now, when he looked at it, only this magazine company could provide an advance. If he could get a small advance ...

He looked up at the brightness and darkness in the car going from tunnel to tunnel and imagined how much pleasure the advance would give him. The so-called pleasure of the artist is an opportunity for self-development. Taking a chance for self-development is not a behavior one should be ashamed of in front of humans and heavenly beings. He was riding the 2:30 express train to Tokyo. To obtain a little advance, it's best to ride straight through to Tokyo.

Even if it's fifty yen or at least thirty yen, he should be able to have dinner with both Hase and Ōtomo after a long time. He should be able to attend a concert given by Fräulein Mellendorf and buy canvas and painting tools. No, there will be none of those things. He was desperate to save that ten-yen bill.

In the off chance he couldn't get the advance, he had to think about that time. Essentially, why should he care about wanting to preserve his dignity before Awano Rentarō? Of course, Awano may be a man of virtue. In Yasukichi's inner life, however, he is a strange passerby in his artistic passions after all. The loss of the chance for self-development for that strange passerby … dammit … this theory is dangerous!

Suddenly trembling, Yasukichi rose from the cushion. The train passing through a tunnel wheezed out smoke and ran through the gorge in Aosusuki, battling winds mixed with rain.

At dusk on Sunday, the next day, Yasukichi, sitting on an antique rattan chair in the lodging house, leisurely moved fire to the cigarette. His heart overflowed with the emotion of satisfaction he hadn't felt recently. The overflow was not by chance. First, he succeeded in saving the ten-yen bill. Second, a publisher's bookstore enclosed a royalty for five hundred of his writings at fifty sen per piece in the letter just received. Third, the most surprising event was the salted sweetfish added to the dinner tray by the lodging house!

The lingering light of dusk in early summer drifted over the branches of young leaves hanging in front of the house, over the sandy ground scattered with cherry fruits, and over the lone ten-yen bill placed on Yasukichi's serge-covered knee. He dropped his eyes to the ten-yen bill on the sharp crease in the evening light.

The ten-yen bill adorned with dark gray arabesque patterns and a red chrysanthemum stamp of the Imperial Seal of Japan was mysteriously beautiful paper money. Not as vulgar as he usually thought, the portrait in the ellipse had a goofy face.

The back depicted tea leaves in high-quality green and was more splendid than the front. If not so smudged by fingers, even inside the frame ... no, it wasn't just the smudges. Something was scribbled in fine ink also over the large number 10s. He gently raised the ten-yen bill to read the characters in the square.

"How about sushi?"

Yasukichi returned the ten-yen bill to his knee. A long trail of smoke from the cigarette entered the evening light in the garden. This ten-yen bill was scribbled on by a writer who wasn't sure about whether to have sushi. However, the tragedy noted on the ten-yen bill probably arises in the wider world. Yesterday afternoon, he bet his soul on this ten-yen bill. But that doesn't matter. He upheld his dignity, particularly before Awano. The royalty for the five hundred articles was sufficient spending money until his monthly payday.

"How about sushi?" muttered Yasukichi and stared sharply again at the ten-yen bill, like Napoleon looking back at the Alps traveled the day before on foot.

(August 1924)

ABOUT AKUTAGAWA

BY KAN KIKUCHI

There's so much I could write about Akutagawa's death, but each time I try, I can't write a thing.

We are unsure about the cause of his death. It's not because we don't understand, but we don't have a specific cause sufficient to persuade the public. In the end, the main reason spoken by Akutagawa himself is likely "vague anxiety."

Also, I believe this outcome resulted from the physical fatigue, nervous exhaustion, and troublesome worldly hardships he experienced over the past few years, further deepening his distressing view of life.

His illness last year took a heavy toll on his mind and body. Beginning with mental exhaustion, and then the insomnia, ravaged stomach and intestines, and chronic hemorrhoids were factors that seemed to intertwine and rob him of the ability to live. Tormented by these ailments, he probably decided to commit suicide little by little.

Over the past few years, his worldly hardships had never ended. As the most high-minded and detached among us, the worst worldly hardship dogging Akutagawa, who tried to avoid the troubles of daily life, might have been sarcasm.

One example relates to *The Modern Japanese Literary Reader* published by Kōbunsha. For this reader, Akutagawa, as the editor, poured his heart and soul into the job of compiling the works of as many authors as possible to the satisfaction of all the writers. Akutagawa's concern was not to lose the respect of anyone. Therefore, the number of included authors exceeded one hundred and twenty or thirty people. Its overly elaborate and literary nature sold few books.

Also, because the royalties were shared with several assistants, Akutagawa received only about one-tenth of the compensation for his labors.

Nonetheless, the absurd rumor emerged that "Akutagawa built a study from the profits from that book."

Even the authors grumbled, "He collected the works of poor authors like us, but only he profited."

How troubled was Akutagawa by these rumors? They must have been deeply distressing to him. Akutagawa seemed overwhelmed. He said to me, "I want to donate all the royalties from this book to The Literary Writers' Association."

I'm not bothered about things like that and talked until my mouth ached. I told him, "If you made that donation, your problems will multiply. It's best to ignore all of it. The book is not selling. You've put in a great deal of effort. Let the complainers, complain."

His inclusion of many authors was a compliment to each of them. However, it was unfortunate he became the seed of this discontent. When I opposed this idea concerning the Literary Writers' Association, he said, "In the future, the royalties will be distributed to each author."

I opposed this idea. I said, "Books like textbooks are examples of unauthorized collections. In addition to obtaining the permissions out of respect, it's another matter if extraordinary profits were obtained. However, when sales are few and far between, there is absolutely no need to do that. Isn't giving about ten yen to each of one hundred and twenty or thirty writers meaningless?"

He seemed to accept my argument. Lastly, it would be as if he gifted each author with a 10-yen stamp from Mitsukoshi. I was saddened that Akutagawa worried that much about this. However, his perfectionism forced him to do this.

This entire incident was three or four related annoying events. If it were me, I would forget about it and do as I pleased. To the end, Akutagawa seemed to worry. All worldly affairs were unbearable to Akutagawa's nerves.

In addition, various misfortunes happened one after the other, such as his brother-in-law's suicide and the illness of the younger brother of a woman he relied on.

His pessimistic view of life that progressed over the past few years became more and more practical. Together with his illnesses, they brought forward the time of his suicide.

On that point, his *Note** should be believed as written. Anything more is guesswork and an affront to the deceased. The woman involved, despite not being the lady Fumiko, was not at the level of a romantic interest but could have been, if he had pursued her. As for "talk about the woman," details about her and absurd rumors were in the suicide note addressed to me. However, I think that at some time, I will show that suicide note to people who believe those rumors.

If one reads Akutagawa's *Note*, a sensible person would understand in one reading that Akutagawa's mental state was uncluttered, restored to serenity, and not an immediate cause of his death. Akutagawa wanted to avoid shocking the public with a suicide. He probably wanted to mask it as a death from illness.

Akutagawa and I had a friendship that lasted twelve or thirteen years. In high school, he was closest to Tsunetō. During those years, the closest friendships are forged. Akutagawa's partner was Tsunetō. These two brilliant students were aloof. But my group, Kume, Sano, and Matsuoka, ran wild as the opposition. I did not associate with Akutagawa.

My association with him began after leaving high school. I believe I got closer to him around the time I returned to Tokyo from a vacation in Kyoto after graduation. Later, when I worked at the newspaper *Jiji Shinpō*, we became close. Then, after he was introduced in 1912 and became a guest writer at *Osaka Mainichi*, we gradually grew closer and visited each other. Over the last year or two, I became more involved and busy with mundane matters and only saw him once a month. Lately, his closest friend, who saw him most often, was Oana Ryūichi. Oana studied under Akutagawa and saw him every day.

---

* A Note Sent to an Old Friend - 或旧友へ送る手記

Akutagawa and I were opposites in interests and personalities. I didn't feel obligated to pretend we shared interests. Akutagawa often took no interest in my activities. However, not once in ten years were we emotionally distant. Whenever I became enraged over something, I'd immediately send an express letter. For a time, *Kikuchi's Express Mail* became known among my close friends. But I never sent an express letter to Akutagawa.

Akutagawa and I likely thought I was more of a nuisance to him than he to me. Nonetheless, he listened to my troubles most of the time. Our recent work co-editing *The Complete Works for Grade School Students* was surely awful for him, who had already decided to kill himself. I believe as a final act of friendship, he tried not to reject my proposal, not to make me feel uncomfortable, and agreed with me. The date on the suicide note addressed to me was April 16 because he had made up his mind.

Thinking about it now, I was unable to do anything for Akutagawa. Secretly, however, he seemed to be worrying about my life. Last October, when I was in Kugenuma, he worried about an incident involving me and cautioned me. He sent a telegram saying he would come to Tokyo if there was something he could do to help. However, I wasn't the least bit worried about that incident and, in my reply, told him not to worry. I was surprised but pleased that Akutagawa thought of me while struggling with nervous exhaustion. For the past few years, he seemed concerned about my lack of creative writing. Once, he said to me, "To promote *Bungei Shunjū*, isn't it important for you, as a writer, to write fine works?"

Disagreeing with Akutagawa's view, I said, "No, I don't think so. I, the writer, is different from me, the editor. As an editor, I'm still not utilizing all my powers, and if I do, I think the magazine will advance further."

Akutagawa's true motive was his concern about my not publishing even a few creative works.

My biggest regret is not having seen Akutagawa for more than a month before he died. Previously, we saw each other twice at a meeting of the *Bungei Shunjū* Roundtable. Both times, however, others were present and prevented us from having a heart-to-heart talk. I felt truly sorry for him and the trouble caused by *The Complete Reader for Grade School Students* and felt uncomfortable confronting him. After the roundtable, I had to ride with and see off some attendees.

When a roundtable was held at Hyōtei in Manseibashi, I was about to get into a car when he glanced in my direction. A strange light was in his eyes. Oh, I thought he wanted to talk with me, but the car was already driving off, and that was it. At that time, Akutagawa was not a man who bluntly spoke his wishes. His expression worried me, but as I said earlier, I felt uncomfortable meeting with him, so most matters were handled through intermediaries.

What I found out after he died is that he visited the *Bungei Shunjū* office twice in early July. I was not there either time. I heard about this later, but they said one time, Akutagawa sat listlessly for a short time in the reception room. No company employee informed me that Akutagawa had come to see me. Otherwise, the day after his visit while I was out, I would have gone to see him. However, I never knew Akutagawa had visited. Being very busy, I did not return his visit. This is my only regret over his death. Looking at this, the expression in his eyes I glimpsed in front of the restaurant Hyōtei will probably be a seed of regret for the rest of my life.

I believe his reliance on me was due to my ability to navigate this world. This was his greatest flaw, but he must have felt reassured when he befriended me. In that sense, I thought if I visited him more often and stimulated his ability to navigate life, things would be different, but it was all too late.

I'll leave the position he'll occupy in history as a writer to unbiased third parties. I can say the following. A writer with his advanced education, refined tastes, and preparation in Japanese, Chinese, and Western academic disciplines may not exist at all in the future. The embodiment of ancient Japanese and Chinese traditions and tastes, and European academic interests in one man makes him a notable writer in Japan in a transitional phase. In our next era, the classical traditions and interests of Japan and China will likely disappear from literature.

I believe he's unmatched in our age in literature. For Mainländer mentioned in the *Note*, on the way back from the crematorium, Tsunetō asked me, "Do you know about Mainländer?"

"No, I don't. Do you?"

"I don't know, either. It's someone's name, I guess."

Yamamoto Yūzō, Ikumi Seiji, and Toyoshima Yoshio didn't know either. Perhaps several people read that note and knew who Mainländer was. In a conversation several days later when Tsunetō visited, I learned he was a scholar influenced by German philosophers like Schopenhauer, embraced the philosophy of pessimism, and promoted suicide as the best path.

Akutagawa read much of Mainländer's work in various fields.

A few years ago, he extensively read Schopenhauer and became an ardent follower. More than whatever kind of socialist Schopenhauer might have been, he was impressed by his understanding of Marx. Therefore, more than being a careless professional literary man who read about topics in the social sciences, he tried to gain further insight. Based on occasional slips by Akutagawa, I think his uneasiness over social unrest somehow slipped into vague anxiety.

He stretched a fence around himself through which unpleasant people could never enter. However, he was very kind to people he trusted and who appreciated virtue. And he often looked after others. Once someone got close, even if they caused him trouble, he did not push them away.

He was sarcastic and intelligent but a moralist in practical life and a kind man. If he had been a lesser man, I believe he wouldn't have known about these trivial matters and lived a happy life.

According to an article about the women in Akutagawa's family published by *Shūkan Asahi*, shortly before he died, he lost his temper and broke a flower vase. I don't know whether that's true or false, but if he had broken a few vases, it might not have come to this. I think he had too much of the refined patience possessed by city dwellers.

I am grateful for his devoted goodwill to *Bungei Shunjū*. Because I want him to be remembered forever to repay him for his goodwill, after his death, I'd like the column *The Words of a Dwarf* to continue as long as this magazine exists. Because unpublished scraps of writing and letters exist, there's no lack of material. I think if the materials don't disappear, all writings related to him will be published. I intend to entrust the editing to Oana Ryūichi, the man closest to Akutagawa. There's a magazine called *Keigetsu* that honors the memory of Ōmachi Keigetsu. The establishment of *The Words of a Dwarf* column on one or two pages in this magazine is appropriate.

Permit me a few more words. The sentence, *I forgive everyone, and hope I am forgiven more than them*, was in a paragraph of his most recent writings. If someone among literary people or others harbors resentment toward the deceased, I think they will understand these feelings of the deceased who would appreciate their understanding on this occasion.

A NOTE SENT TO AN OLD FRIEND

BY RYUNOSUKE AKUTAGAWA

No one has written the truth about the mental state of a victim of suicide. This may be due to a lack of self-esteem in the suicide victim or a lack of interest in the victim's psychology. In this final letter I'm sending to you, I'd like to convey this state of mind. Certainly, I don't need to explain the motive for my suicide, especially to you.

Régnier wrote a short story in which a man kills himself. The protagonist did not know why he was going to kill himself. In tabloid articles in the newspapers, you find various motives for suicide, for example, life's difficulties, suffering from illness, or mental anguish. In my experience, however, those are not all of the motives. Most only indicate the path to the motive. As Régnier wrote, the person who commits suicide may not know why.

The reasons include complex motives, much like our behaviors. In my situation, at least, it was simply a vague anxiety. Somehow, this anxiety concerned my future. You are probably unable to trust my words. But my experience over the past ten years has taught me that, except for circumstances and people close to me, my words vanish as in the wind or a song. Consequently, I do not blame you.

For the past two years, I constantly thought about dying. During this period, I experienced deep emotions and read Mainländer. He adeptly described the path to death in abstract words. I think I'd like to provide the same description but in more concrete terms. Sympathy for my family does not come before this desire. You will probably use the word *inhumane*. However, there is an inhumane side to me.

No matter what, my duty is to write honestly. I also dissected my vague anxiety over my future. For the most part, I wrote about most of that in my work *A Fool's Life*.* I intentionally did not write about the social conditions surrounding me—the residue of the feudal era that cast its shadows on me. If you ask why I deliberately wrote nothing, it's because, even today, we human beings still live, more or less, in the shadow of the feudal age. I tried to write about offstage matters, such as the background, lighting, and cast of characters, but it was mostly about my behavior. It is not only the social conditions; I cannot allow myself to question whether I clearly understand my place within that social climate. My first thought was: How can I die without suffering?

Death by hanging is the method best suited to my objective. However, I imagined what I'd look like hanging there dead and was disgusted by the aesthetics, an indulgence. I remember once falling in love with a certain woman but quickly fell out of love because of her poor handwriting. I can swim and would never be able to die by drowning. If, by some rare chance, I succeeded, the suffering would be far more than by hanging. I find death by being hit by a road vehicle or a train to be even more aesthetically displeasing. Death by a gun or knife would likely fail due to trembling hands. Of course, jumping off a building would surely be hard to look at.

Given this situation, I decided to use a drug to die, although it may be more painful than death by hanging. In addition to not being more aesthetically displeasing than hanging, a benefit is the reduced danger of resuscitation. Of course, I will have trouble finding this drug. I made my mind up to kill myself and used every opportunity to obtain a drug. At the same time, I learned about toxicology.

Next, I thought about where I would kill myself. My family must inherit my estate after I die. My estate consists only of one acre of land, my house, my copyrights, and 2,000 yen in savings. I was distressed because my house would become unsellable once I committed suicide. Consequently, I envied the bourgeois who have a summer home. You may be amused by these words; I'm also tickled

---

* 或阿呆の一生 (*Aru Ahō no Isshō*)

by my words. When I had these thoughts, I felt troubled deep inside. This discomfort cannot be avoided. I think I want to kill myself so that my corpse will be seen as little as possible by people outside of my family.

But after I decided on the method, half of me still clung to life. I needed a springboard to leap into death. As the red-headed foreigners believe, I don't think committing suicide is a crime. Buddha approved of the suicide of his disciple in the *Āgama Sutras*. A follower who twists scholarship to pander to the world would probably say, "except in cases where approval is *unavoidable*." However, through the eyes of a third party, an *unavoidable* case is not an extraordinary crisis in which the death must be tragic rather than witnessed. Anyone who has committed suicide only tells himself that his case was *unavoidable*. Before that, anyone who boldly committed suicide must have been filled with courage. The most useful kind of springboard is a woman. Before his suicide, Christ often invited his friends to join him on the journey (of men). Racine tried to jump into the Seine River with Molière or Boileau.

Unfortunately, however, I do not have friends like that. Only a woman I know was willing to die with me. But after talking it over, she decided she couldn't do this for us. Meanwhile, I developed the confidence to die without a springboard. That did not happen because of despair over not dying with someone else. Rather, I gradually became sentimental and thought I'd like to be kind to my wife even if we were separated by death. At the same time, I realized that killing myself alone is easier than committing suicide with another person. Another advantage was I could freely choose when to commit suicide.

Finally, the scheme I devised was to commit suicide with enough skill that it would not be noticed by my family. After several months of preparation, I achieved some level of confidence. I am not writing about the fine points for the sake of the people who have goodwill toward me. What I'm writing about here, in legal terms, is aiding and abetting suicide.

This is not a ridiculous criminal charge. If this law were applied, the number of criminals would grow. Drug stores, gun shops, and knife and sword shops say, "We don't know," but as long as our intentions appear in our words and expressions as human beings, we must have some suspicions. Indeed, society and laws have devised the crime of aiding and abetting suicide. Finally, most of these criminals have kind hearts, but this is certainly not how they are portrayed.

I finished preparations with indifference and now simply flirt with death. My future feelings will probably approach Mainländer's words.

We human beings instinctively fear death because humans are beasts. The so-called *will to live* is nothing more than an alias for animal power. I am an animal. However, when weariness is seen among the desires for food and sex, animal power is gradually lost. I live now in a world of diseased nerves, as clear as ice. Last evening, I spoke with a prostitute about women's wages and keenly felt pity for humanity who "live in order to live."

My question is: When will I be able to boldly kill myself? Only nature is always more beautiful than I am. You love the beauty of nature and smile at my contradictions regarding suicide. Yet the beauty of nature will be reflected in the eyes on my deathbed. I saw more than others, loved, and understood. Even in the midst of accumulated suffering, I felt some degree of satisfaction.

Please, do not make this letter public for years after my death. I may kill myself in a way that resembles death from an illness.

Addendum: I read the story of Empedocles and felt how ancient the longing to be a god is. You probably remember twenty years ago when we debated Empedocles at Etna under that linden tree. At that time, I was a man who wanted to be a god.

(July 1927, Posthumous manuscript)

CREDITS

Akutagawa, Ryūnosuke. "A Day in the Life of Ōishi Kuranosuke (Aru Hi no Ōishi Kuranosuke)." In *The Collected Works of Akutagawa Ryūnosuke (Akutagawa Ryūnosuke Zenshū)*, Vol. 1, 421-439. Tokyo: Iwanami Shoten, 1928. National Diet Library Digital Collections. https://dl.ndl.go.jp/pid/1232263/1/220.

———. "Unrequited Love (Katakoi)." In *The Collected Works of Akutagawa Ryūnosuke (Akutagawa Ryūnosuke Zenshū)*, Vol. 1, 441-451. Tokyo: Iwanami Shoten, 1928. National Diet Library Digital Collections. https://dl.ndl.go.jp/pid/1232263/1/230.

Akutagawa, Ryūnosuke. "The Hell of Loneliness (Kodoku Jigoku)." In *The Collected Works of Akutagawa Ryūnosuke (Akutagawa Ryūnosuke Zenshū)*, Vol. 1, 53-56. Tokyo: Iwanami Shoten, 1954. National Diet Library Digital Collections. https://dl.ndl.go.jp/pid/1663980/1/31.

———. "Father (Chichi)." In *The Collected Works of Akutagawa Ryūnosuke (Akutagawa Ryūnosuke Zenshū)*, Vol. 1, 57-62. Tokyo: Iwanami Shoten, 1954. National Diet Library Digital Collections. https://dl.ndl.go.jp/pid/1663980/1/33.

———. "The Sake Bug (Sake Mushi)." In *The Collected Works of Akutagawa Ryūnosuke (Akutagawa Ryūnosuke Zenshū)*, Vol. 1, 70-79. Tokyo: Iwanami Shoten, 1954. National Diet Library Digital Collections. https://dl.ndl.go.jp/pid/1663980/1/40.

———. "The Monkey (Saru)." In *The Collected Works of Akutagawa Ryūnosuke (Akutagawa Ryūnosuke Zenshū)*, Vol. 1, 106-113. Tokyo: Iwanami Shoten, 1954. National Diet Library Digital Collections. https://dl.ndl.go.jp/pid/1663980/1/58.

Akutagawa Ryūnosuke. "Doubts (Giwaku)." In *The Collected Works of Akutagawa Ryūnosuke (Akutagawa Ryūnosuke Zenshū)*, Vol. 2, 249-272. Tokyo: Iwanami Shoten, 1928. National Diet Library Digital Collections. https://dl.ndl.go.jp/pid/1232280/1/132.

———. "The Foundling (Sutego)." In *The Collected Works of Akutagawa Ryūnosuke (Akutagawa Ryūnosuke Zenshū)*, Vol. 2, 569-79. Tokyo: Iwanami Shoten, 1928. National Diet Library Digital Collections. https://dl.ndl.go.jp/pid/1232280/1/292.

Akutagawa, Ryūnosuke. "The Cold (Samusa)." In *The Collected Works of Akutagawa Ryūnosuke (Akutagawa Ryūnosuke Zenshū)*, Vol. 4, 1-11. Tokyo: Iwanami Shoten, 1927. National Diet Library Digital Collections. https://dl.ndl.go.jp/pid/1232304/1/10.

———. "A Romance Novel (Aru Renai Shōsetsu)." In *The Collected Works of Akutagawa Ryūnosuke (Akutagawa Ryūnosuke Zenshū)*, Vol. 4, 13-22. Tokyo: Iwanami Shoten, 1927. National Diet Library Digital Collections. https://dl.ndl.go.jp/pid/1232304/1/16.

———. "Compositions (Bunshō)." In *The Collected Works of Akutagawa Ryūnosuke*

(*Akutagawa Ryūnosuke Zenshū*), Vol. 4, 23-40. Tokyo: Iwanami Shoten, 1927. National Diet Library Digital Collections. https://dl.ndl.go.jp/pid/1232304/1/21.

———. "Youth (Shōnen)." In *The Collected Works of Akutagawa Ryūnosuke* (*Akutagawa Ryūnosuke Zenshū*), Vol. 4, 49-81. Tokyo: Iwanami Shoten, 1927. National Diet Library Digital Collections. https://dl.ndl.go.jp/pid/1232304/1/34.

———. "A Ten Yen Bill (Jūensatsu)." In *The Collected Works of Akutagawa Ryūnosuke* (*Akutagawa Ryūnosuke Zenshū*), Vol. 4, 93-111. Tokyo: Iwanami Shoten, 1927. National Diet Library Digital Collections. https://dl.ndl.go.jp/pid/1232304/1/56.

———. "Early Spring (Sōshun)." In *The Collected Works of Akutagawa Ryūnosuke* (*Akutagawa Ryūnosuke Zenshū*), Vol. 4, 163-171. Tokyo: Iwanami Shoten, 1927. National Diet Library Digital Collections. https://dl.ndl.go.jp/pid/1232304/1/91.

———. "Asakusa Park (Asakusa Kōen)." In *The Collected Works of Akutagawa Ryūnosuke* (*Akutagawa Ryūnosuke Zenshū*), Vol. 4, 507-528. Tokyo: Iwanami Shoten, 1927. National Diet Library Digital Collections. https://dl.ndl.go.jp/pid/1232304/1/263.

———. "Taneko's Melancholy (Taneko no Yūutsu)." In *The Collected Works of Akutagawa Ryūnosuke* (*Akutagawa Ryūnosuke Zenshū*), Vol. 4, 529-539. Tokyo: Iwanami Shoten, 1927. National Diet Library Digital Collections. https://dl.ndl.go.jp/pid/1232304/1/274

Akutagawa Ryūnosuke. "Ten Needles (Juppon no Hari)." In *The Collected Works of Akutagawa Ryūnosuke* (*Akutagawa Ryūnosuke Zenshū*), Vol. 6, 829-835. Tokyo: Iwanami Shoten, 1928. National Diet Library Digital Collections. https://dl.ndl.go.jp/pid/1232370/1/428.

———. "A Note Sent to an Old Friend (Aru Kyuyu e Okuru Shuki)." In *The Collected Works of Akutagawa Ryūnosuke* (*Akutagawa Ryūnosuke Zenshū*), Vol. 6, 843-849. Tokyo: Iwanami Shoten, 1928. National Diet Library Digital Collections. https://dl.ndl.go.jp/pid/1232370/1/435.

Akutagawa Ryūnosuke. "The Riverside Fish Market (Uogashi)." In *The Collected Works of Akutagawa Ryūnosuke* (*Akutagawa Ryūnosuke Zenshū*), Vol. 6, 26-33. Tokyo: Iwanami Shoten, 1955. National Diet Library Digital Collections. https://dl.ndl.go.jp/pid/1663984/1/18.

———. "Shino (Oshino)." In *The Collected Works of Akutagawa Ryūnosuke* (*Akutagawa Ryūnosuke Zenshū*), Vol. 6, 102-108 Tokyo: Iwanami Shoten, 1955. National Diet Library Digital Collections. https://dl.ndl.go.jp/pid/1663984/1/56.

———. "From Yasukichi's Notebook (Yasukichi no Techō kara)." In *The Collected Works of Akutagawa Ryūnosuke* (*Akutagawa Ryūnosuke Zenshū*), Vol. 6, 109-121. Tokyo: Iwanami Shoten, 1955. National Diet Library Digital Collections. https://dl.ndl.go.jp/pid/1663984/1/59.

———. "The Bow (Ojigi)." In *The Collected Works of Akutagawa Ryūnosuke* (*Akutagawa Ryūnosuke Zenshū*), Vol. 6, 142-147. Tokyo: Iwanami Shoten, 1955. National Diet Library Digital Collections. https://dl.ndl.go.jp/pid/1663984/1/76.

———. "San'emon's Crime (San'emon no Tsumi)." In *The Collected Works of Akutagawa Ryūnosuke* (*Akutagawa Ryūnosuke Zenshū*), Vol. 6, 192-202. Tokyo: Iwanami

Shoten, 1955. National Diet Library Digital Collections. https://dl.ndl.go.jp/pid/1663984/1/101.

Akutagawa Ryūnosuke. "Frogs (Kaeru)." In *The Collected Works of Akutagawa Ryūnosuke (Akutagawa Ryūnosuke Zenshū)*, Vol. 7, 220-223. Tokyo: Iwanami Shoten, 1935. National Diet Library Digital Collections. https://dl.ndl.go.jp/pid/1223291.

———. "The Tiger Stories (Tora no Hanashi)." In *The Collected Works of Akutagawa Ryūnosuke (Akutagawa Ryūnosuke Zenshū)*, Vol. 7, 342-346. Tokyo: Iwanami Shoten, 1935. National Diet Library Digital Collections. https://dl.ndl.go.jp/pid/1223291/1/185.

———. "The Quality of a Hero (Eiyū no Utsuwa)." In *The Collected Works of Akutagawa Ryūnosuke (Akutagawa Ryūnosuke Zenshū)*, Vol. 7, 230-233. Tokyo: Iwanami Shoten, 1935. National Diet Library Digital Collections. https://dl.ndl.go.jp/pid/1223291/1/129.

Akutagawa, Ryūnosuke. "The Dream (Yume)." In *The Collected Works of Akutagawa Ryūnosuke (Akutagawa Ryūnosuke Zenshū)*, Vol. 8, 107-116. Tokyo: Iwanami Shoten, 1955. National Diet Library Digital Collections. https://dl.ndl.go.jp/pid/1663986.

Kikuchi, Kan. "About Akutagawa (Akutagawa no Kotodomo)," *Bungei Shunjū*, September 1927. Aozora Bunko. https://www.aozora.gr.jp/cards/000083/files/1340_19832.html.

Dostoyevsky, Fyodor. *The House of the Dead, or Prison Life in Siberia*. Translated by H. Sutherland Edwards. Edited by Ernest Rhys. New York: E.P. Dutton & Co., 1914.

Goethe, Johann Wolfgang von. *Faust: a tragedy*. Translated by Charles T. Brooks. Boston: Ticknor and Fields, 1856.

Ichiryūsai, Hiroshige. 東都名所　浅草金竜山 (Famous Places in the Eastern Capital, Asakusa Kinryuzan). Woodblock Print. National Diet Library Digital Collections. https://dl.ndl.go.jp/pid/1302540.

Around Taishō Year 10 (Akutagawa Ryūnosuke writing at desk). The Collected Works of Akutagawa Ryūnosuke (Akutagawa Ryūnosuke Zenshū), Vol. 3. Tokyo: Iwanami Shoten, 1956. Photograph. National Diet Library Digital Collections. https://dl.ndl.go.jp/pid/1663982/1/4.

Around Taishō Year 14 (Akutagawa Ryūnosuke and child). The Collected Works of Akutagawa Ryūnosuke. 1925. Photograph. National Diet Library Digital Collections. https://dl.ndl.go.jp/pid/1663983/1/4.

Tsukioka, Yoshitoshi. 本朝忠孝鑑 大石内蔵助良雄／孝子太郎作. 1881. Full-color Woodblock Print. National Diet Library Digital Collections. https://dl.ndl.go.jp/pid/1312846.

Torii, Kiyohiro. *Taka-zu* (Falcon picture). Azuma no Hana: Edo-e Burui. Shimizu, Seihū, ed. Photograph. National Diet Library Digital Collections. https://dl.ndl.go.jp/pid/2541121/1/43.

Shisei Shoin. Nakamise Arcade. *Dai-Tōkyō Shashin-chō*. 1952. Photograph. National Diet Library Digital Collections. https://dl.ndl.go.jp/pid/3025446/1/81.

Aichi Prefecture Police Department, ed. *Meiji 24 Nen Nōbi Daishinsai Shashinchō (1891 Great Nōbi Earthquake Photograph Album)*. 1925. Photographs. National Diet Library Digital Collections. https://dl.ndl.go.jp/pid/14032727/1/1.

Credits

Kikuchi_Kan,_Akutagawa_Ryūnosuke,_and_so_on.jpg. Photograph. Wiki Commons. Public domain via Wikimedia Commons. https://en.wikipedia.org/wiki/Kan_Kikuchi#/media/File:Kikuchi_Kan,_Akutagawa_Ryunosuke,_and_so_on.jpg.

Part of the suicide note (one character masked). *The Collected Works of Akutagawa Ryūnosuke (Notes, etc.)*, Vol. 15,1955. Photograph. National Diet Library Digital Collections. https://dl.ndl.go.jp/pid/1663993/1/4.